WITCH AND FAMOUS

The air was now thick with books—foreign language manuals, history books, novels, cookbooks—I choreographed their movements with the music, first into a large flower blossoming, then a moving pinwheel, then an explosion like fireworks. Rodney's soft body, vibrating with his purrs, pressed against me.

I laughed, and hundreds of books laughed around me in chortles, girlish giggles, and shrieks of joy as they danced through the air.

The gramophone began to slow. I loved these book ballets, and they were terrific exercise for my magic, but it was time to draw this one to a close. I drew another deep breath and willed the books' energy to gather as if it were a bouquet.

"Books," I instructed. "Go home."

The books spun briefly into chaos, then doubled their speed and shot back to their respective rooms. I heard the soft thunks and riffles of them settling onto their shelves just as the gramophone's needle bumped against the record's center.

I pulled myself to sitting, feeling both depleted and joyful. How amazing this magic was. A year ago, I never could have dreamed of anything like it. It was fun, and it helped me be a good librarian. A few times, magic had assisted more than that. Could it help me this time to find a murderer?

Books by Angela M. Sanders

BAIT AND WITCH

SEVEN-YEAR WITCH

WITCH AND FAMOUS

Published by Kensington Publishing Corp.

Witch
and
Famous

Angela M. Sanders

Kensington Publishing Corp.
www.kensingtonbooks.com

KENSINGTON BOOKS are published by

Kensington Publishing Corp.
119 West 40th Street
New York, NY 10018

All Kensington titles, imprints, and distributed lines are available at special quantity discounts for bulk purchases for sales promotion, premiums, fund-raising, educational, or institutional use.

Special book excerpts or customized printings can also be created to fit specific needs. For details, write or phone the office of the Kensington Sales Manager: Attn.: Sales Department. Kensington Publishing Corp., 119 West 40th Street, New York, NY 10018. Phone: 1-800-221-2647.

The K and Teapot logo is a trademark of Kensington Publishing Corp.

First Printing: August 2022
ISBN: 978-1-4967-2878-4

ISBN: 978-1-4967-2879-1 (ebook)

10 9 8 7 6 5 4 3 2 1

Printed in the United States of America

For Jacob Orr

CHAPTER ONE

I dragged two wing chairs to the front of the New Releases shelf. Wilfred's library was in a Victorian mansion, and the mahogany bookcases and fireplace made a distinguished yet homey background for Roz's upcoming television interview.

"What do you think of this?" I asked Roz, my assistant librarian. "We'll set your novel in the background, cover out, so the audience sees it."

Roz paced Circulation—once the mansion's sitting room—and batted her fan at her neck. Hot flashes again. "What does it matter? The whole thing's going to be a disaster, anyway. I'll freeze up. Worse, I bet I pass out. Or get an explosive nosebleed."

Roz's dire predictions didn't faze me. She was a confirmed pessimist, and I'd have been more shocked if she were upbeat. Besides, Roz had been over the moon when Daphne Morris's personal assistant called to say *The*

Whippoorwill Cries Love had been selected for the actress's televised book club.

When we learned Daphne Morris planned to spend a whole week in town before the interview, Wilfredians went wild. A movie star? Vacationing in tiny Wilfred? This was almost as exciting as when Mrs. Garlington's epic poem about the passing of her beagle made it into the *News-Times*.

My black cat Rodney chose this moment for an attack of the zoomies. He leapt from the desk and sped through Circulation into the atrium.

"Seriously, though, what do you think?" I asked. "Should they stage the interview here, in front of the books?"

The books whispered *yes, yes, here* in response. Practice had allowed me to keep a neutral expression. No one knew books talked to me. The skitter of Rodney's toenails on parquet resounded from Popular Fiction next door.

From the New Releases shelf came the *vroom-vroom* of engines revving. *Shoot.* It was that history of the Indy 500 again, trying to race from the stacks. Its author must have been manic with energy while writing the book. I slid discreetly in front of the shelf just in time for the book to charge smack into my hind end before I pushed it back. I was going to have to move the book somewhere safer until a few readers could absorb its enthusiasm and chill it out.

"Not bad, but too much light from the French doors," came a firm, feminine voice through the doorway. "Let's consider the atrium, instead."

Roz's head swiveled toward the voice, and her fan-wielding hand dropped. She'd clearly expected Daphne Morris. Although this woman had the same shoulder-length waves as the movie star, she was younger. Her patrician nose was more angular, and her bearing more businesslike than ingenue.

"You must be Morgan Stanhope," I said, extending a hand. "I'm Josie Way, librarian." Morgan—the actress's personal assistant—and I had traded emails about setting a date for the interview. I joined her in the center of the library's three-story atrium.

"Pleased to meet you," she said.

Accompanying her was a tall man about my age with thick glasses held together on one side with duct tape. His light brown hair was pushed behind his ears, and his smile was wide. "Hi." He extended a hand to me. "Leo Wilkington, production manager."

His handshake was warm. I felt an immediate kinship. The man was a nerd, just like some people might describe me. Bookish and curious.

Rodney skidded through the atrium at top speed and disappeared into the conservatory.

"Was that a cat I just saw?" Leo asked.

"That's Rodney," I said. If I knew him, in a few minutes he'd halt the zoomies just as fast as he'd started, and I'd find him sleeping in the banana tree pot in the conservatory.

Leo laughed. "I've never been to Oregon. The landscape here is amazing. The mountains, the trees—they're so green, even in August. Now I learn their libraries have cats that could double as cruise missiles."

"I had no idea the library was in an old mansion," Morgan said, craning her head like every newcomer did.

Rodney strolled from the conservatory as if he'd never hurried a day in his life and plopped in front of the library's main stairwell to groom a hind leg.

"Used to belong to the town's founder," I said.

"I think this will work all right. Depending on where the sun is, we could drape off these doorways." Morgan waved toward the ceiling. "The light through the stained glass on the cupola is fine. If Daphne agrees to bring in the bodyguard, we'll have him check it out, too."

"A bodyguard?" I asked.

"No need to worry about it, Josie. What do you think, Leo?"

The production manager poked his head into the kitchen to the right of the main staircase facing us, then into the conservatory to the staircase's left. "I agree. Let's stage it back here with the light of the conservatory facing Daphne. We can run power from the kitchen."

"How long will the interview take?" I asked. I planned to close the library for the day, but that didn't always stop some Wilfredians from trying to drop by for a cup of coffee. If they knew Daphne Morris was in the house, I'd have to double-bolt the doors.

"An hour for setup and makeup, another hour and a half for the interview. Not long," Leo said.

"I hope Daphne Morris likes it." I glanced from her personal assistant to her production manager. I wondered if they had any idea how big a deal her arrival was to us.

"She hardly cares these days," Morgan said. Ignoring my questioning look, she gestured toward the upper floors. "What's up there?"

"The house's old bedrooms. They hold books now."

"We can use one of the rooms for makeup," Morgan said.

We stood in the library's atrium and looked up past two floors and the polished wooden railings encircling them. The top floor was my apartment, accessible through the service staircase. Beyond the main staircase, at the atrium's rear, was the library's kitchen and my office, housed in the old pantry. A mahogany Eastlake table at my elbow held a tangle of hollyhocks and daisies. A rose-scented summer breeze drifted through the open French doors. Behind us, the life-sized oil portrait of Marilyn Wilfred, the library's founder, surveyed us with benevolence from her station over the entrance.

And all around us were books. Thousands of books, teeming with war, love, history, and tips on raising boxer puppies. Open one volume, and the sounds and smells of Tahiti enveloped you. Another book soothed with Emily Dickinson's verse. Yet another novel transported you into the galaxy, among the stars.

I took in these details with pride. This was my home, my work, and the place I loved most in the world. I looked at Morgan expectantly.

"It'll do," she said and turned for the exit, Leo behind her.

All day, the patrons who'd stopped by the library hadn't come for books, but to see if anyone had caught a glimpse of Daphne Morris yet. She'd arrived in Wilfred sometime that afternoon. Her Escalade was parked in front of the farmhouse she'd rented for the week, and people walking their dogs past the house had seen curtains open and lights go off and on. But no one had seen her. There would be a lot of tired dogs in Wilfred tonight.

At last I closed the library for the day and wandered next door to Big House. I'd come to relish my evenings with Sam on the kitchen porch. Over the months since he'd returned to his childhood home, we'd drifted into the habit of meeting for a mug of chamomile tea after dinner. Sam would lean back and rest his feet on the porch railing, while I relaxed in the Adirondack chair next to him, a chipped red side table between us. We'd talk through our days, Sam treating me like a sister, me trying to tamp down my mad crush on him.

Tonight, we faced the view down the bluff, over the Kirby River, to Wilfred. One by one, lights flickered on at the trailers at the Magnolia Rolling Estates, and the sun set to our left, over the old mill site where a crane popping above the trees signaled the new retreat center's construction. Meanwhile, Sam's son Nicky played at our feet. At ten months old, he couldn't walk yet, but he liked to bat his toys around him on an old quilt, and he was good at scooting toward Rodney, who'd learned to leap to the porch railing when the baby let out a certain assertive coo.

Tonight the air was especially soft. Days were long now, and the pink of twilight was reluctantly turning dusky. Seeing the lights still on in front of the This-N-That, we knew a small group lingered.

"They're waiting for Daphne Morris to walk by," I said. "Apparently, she hasn't left the farmhouse today. I hope she doesn't hide out all week."

That afternoon, the only place to be had been the front yard of Patty's This-N-That shop. Normally, Wilfredians would have gathered at Darla's café to talk about the movie star's arrival, but the café had been out of service since last spring's floods had eroded it into a concrete shell. Darla herself was touring Georgia. She'd long admired Southern culture—everything from gumbo to the region's famed hospitality, and it showed in her menus— but until now she had never visited.

"Still getting pestered about turning the library into the substitute café?" Sam asked.

"Duke gave me the pitch again today about keeping the library open later, and on Sundays, too." I let out an exasperated groan. "I hope Darla comes home soon and starts to rebuild. As it is, I spend half my day clearing beer out of the fridge and reminding people that some patrons actually come to the library because of the books."

For the past few months I'd battled Wilfredians who seemed determined to turn the library's kitchen into a substitute for the tavern. I was constantly clearing food wrappers and beer bottles and asking the revelers to pipe down. Mona kept bringing in animals from the shelter, and I suspected another resident of setting up a small-time gaming operation. The worst was when Mrs. Garlington decided to entertain from the music room. She pulled out all the organ's stops and once even tried to organize a square dance in the atrium. The high school debate team studying upstairs was not impressed.

Right now, the This-N-That featured kitchen appliances, a change from the usual rotating fare of small goods that varied with Patty's mood. Four vintage stoves, two refrigerators, and a pink sewing machine were lined up perpendicular to the walkway, interspersed with lawn chairs and a vinyl recliner, where Patty held court. Orange extension cords ran to one of the refrigerators and stoves, and Patty had been known to fry up the occasional plein-air grilled cheese sandwich for visitors.

Now even the string of lights zigzagging the This-N-That's front yard flickered off.

"Daphne Morris's security team contacted the sheriff's department a few weeks ago and gave us strict orders to keep her stay in Wilfred secret. I guess she gets her share of weirdos following her, and there's one stalker in particular she's worried about," Sam said.

"Her assistant mentioned something about bringing in a bodyguard." Sam had been Wilfred's sheriff for less than six months now—a real change from his former job as an FBI agent. "Having a movie star in town must feel like Los Angeles again. Do you ever get tired of small-town cases?

"Nope." He gazed over the valley, his face half-shaded by the porch roof. "The motivations for crime are the same. Greed, jealousy, anger. It's just that the stakes are lower here."

"What came up today?"

This was my favorite part of our talks. Sam ruminated over his caseload, and I helped him think through it. My magic came from my love of books, and my gift was an unusual one—I was a truth teller, a witch compelled to seek justice. Witches in my family tended to be healers and seers, but every few generations a truth teller was born. Added to that, the birthmark on my shoulder identified me as having especially strong powers, powers I was still exploring. Talking through Sam's cases satisfied my truth-telling urges.

"Here's one for you," Sam said, pulling his feet down from the railing. "Someone is stealing Ned Jolson's eggs. He said it's been going on for weeks now."

"From his box?"

Ned Jolson was a retired schoolteacher and widower who'd carried on his wife's tradition of selling eggs from the hens that clucked and scratched in his garden. The eggs were sold on the honor system. Wilfredians dropped a few dollars into a jar and filled a carton with eggs from a wooden box in his front yard.

"Yes. Sometime during the night."

"You said 'eggs.' They're not taking the money?" I asked.

"He told me he empties the jar after dinner, when the hens have gone to roost and he's restocked the box with the day's eggs."

"In other words, some omelet maniac is sneaking by after dark to rob him."

"It's up to about five dozen eggs now. Ned says his dog has barked a few of the evenings, but when he goes to the window to look for the thief, no one's there."

We pondered Ned's situation. Nicky crawled to my chair and looked up. I nudged Rodney to the side and hoisted the baby to my lap. Nicky's mother had died in the spring and although Sam wasn't his biological father, he'd embraced the baby as his own and even christened him Thurston Wilfred, as the firstborn Wilfred sons, including Sam, had been named for five generations. Of course, they'd all had nicknames, too.

"So, he's had maybe fifteen dollars' worth of eggs taken," I said.

"It's not the money. It's the idea that someone in Wilfred would actually steal from him."

"Hmm. Ned was a teacher. Could the thief be a former student who bears a grudge and wants to get under his skin?"

"Good question," Sam said. "I thought of that. He had the reputation of being a tough grader. I checked in with Roz, and she says that although he was strict, he was always fair."

"And he hasn't seen anyone at the egg box at night," I confirmed.

"Nope. No one."

I let my mind relax. Sometimes, if I was still, information slid into my brain, especially if books were present to feed me their energy. Big House had a small collection with the usual assortment of reference books, plus Sam's cookbooks and opera scores. I didn't imagine egg stealing figured in anything by Verdi. The library was across the garden—maybe twenty yards—too far for the books' energy to reach me.

Yet a book title did appear, a vintage children's book, possibly one of Sam's from when he was a boy. *Little Raccoon*, it was called. I saw its cover of a smiling raccoon holding a dandelion. I sensed it near Nicky's crib upstairs.

"I have an idea," I said. "An azalea hedge grows up against Ned's front windows, right?"

"I see where you're going with this, but I checked when I talked with him, and anyone taller than a kindergartner would show above it."

"What if the thief isn't a person at all? What if it's a raccoon? A raccoon would have no problem opening the egg chest, and he'd have no interest in money—leaving it or stealing it. Ned might simply need a raccoon-proof latch."

Sam's lip turned down—he always frowned when he was amused and smiled when he was unhappy, a habit that confounded strangers—and he laughed softly. Nicky sat up from resting against my chest and held out his arms to his father.

"I think you're right," Sam said as he took Nicky. "A raccoon. Of course." Still frowning, he shook his head. "You're good, Josie."

Warmth diffused through me, starting from my heart. Sam appreciated me. I knew that, but he never gave a hint of turning that appreciation in a romantic direction, no matter how ardently I hoped he would.

"I bet it's time to get Nicky to bed." I stood. "Wilfred might only have small-town crimes, but Daphne Morris's stay here is a big deal. Not every town, big or small, can brag that."

"True." Sam patted Nicky on his diapered hind end. "But like I said, it's all the same, no matter where you are."

CHAPTER TWO

I pushed open my bedroom window to let in the cool night air. A hint of an overture—*Aida*, maybe—drifted from Big House. Sam must have put Nicky to bed and was winding down with a beloved opera.

I looked over my apartment with satisfaction. Earlier in the summer, I'd discovered that the back attic was packed with old furniture. I'd never cared much about my surroundings before I'd come to Wilfred and found my magic, but now colors sang and textures beckoned. I'd salvaged a couple of Victorian side chairs and upholstered them in brocade from a set of heavy curtains folded in a trunk. An embroidered fringed piano shawl looked great draped over the couch. By the time I'd added dahlias to a chipped Lalique vase and hung house-plants here and there, my tiny apartment felt like a gypsy caravan perched up high.

Home was not just a refuge, it was a place I could practice magic. Tonight, I'd start my next lesson.

I slid a green wooden chest out from under my bed and unlocked it. No one knew I was a witch, and I planned to keep it that way. Rodney peered over the chest's edge, then hopped in, settling himself among dozens of sealed envelopes, all witchcraft lessons my grandmother wrote before she died, before I knew I'd inherited her gift. Before I chose a lesson, I placed a hand on Rodney's back and let myself slip into his body to feel the lessons, the murmuring of my grandmother's voice all around me. As I settled into his body for a few seconds, I vibrated with purring and felt my own palm, firm and reassuring, on my back. I drew a breath and returned to my own body.

I opened my eyes and plunged a hand into the chest, letting my fingers slide between the envelopes until they tingled. Then I grasped the nearest letter and pulled it from the pile. As with the others, this one had no label. I held it to my heart. Experience had taught me that whatever its contents were, they were something I needed to learn right now.

What would tonight's lesson be? I'd been having trouble controlling my energy lately, and when I was emotional, magic sometimes erupted in bursts powerful enough to make the lights flicker. Once, when I was frantic because Rodney had disappeared for a few hours, light bulbs shattered. I wouldn't mind a lesson with exercises for moderating my energy.

My fingers trembled as I slid a paper cutter under the envelope's flap. I slipped out the folded sheets of paper inside. At the top of the first page, in my grandmother's handwriting, were two words: *love spells*. I read it again to make sure. Yes, it was about love magic.

"Come on, Rodney." I nudged him from the chest, relocked it, and pushed it back under my bed. "This should be interesting."

Rodney and I settled in the armchair by the window, with a faraway soundtrack of Verdi and the wind through the cottonwoods along the Kirby River. I smoothed open the lesson and let my grandmother's voice read it to me. As always, the honeyed warmth of her words rippled through my heart.

Dear Josie,

I wonder how you felt when you saw the words "love spells." Were you excited? Perhaps there's someone you'd like to enchant? Or maybe you felt dread.

As I write this letter, you're playing in the garden with Grimbly, the ginger tomcat who never fails to alert me when the mugwort is ripe for harvest and the morel mushrooms have come up in the woods behind the house. You're barely six years old, and you have no inkling of the power you'll have—the magic the star-shaped mole on your shoulder promises. If you're reading this, you're a woman now.

Whatever you felt as you unfolded these pages, you were right to think that love magic isn't to be taken lightly. Love holds immense power. It's a strong, healing, nurturing power teeming with its own magic. Think about it: Can't you feel the love someone has for you simply by entering a room? Combined with reason, love can heal nations and uplift the saddest and most hopeless among us.

However, the desire for love holds an entirely different power from love itself, and when it's frustrated it can lead to depression, destruction, and even murder. The desire for love can destroy what real love is all about. It can make a thwarted lover want to bend someone else's will so that she will desire him, no matter what the object of his desire wants for herself.

A witch must be very careful when influencing the lives of others. Using magic to protect yourself or other people is one matter. Using magic to divert someone's destiny is quite another. When working with love magic, you must remember this: Love and the desire for love are not the same.

As an aside, the ability to attract romantic attention—a quality we call "glamour"—is not the same as being lovable, although it can mimic love's effects in people who fall under its spell. People who aren't too wise, that is. You don't have to be a witch to possess glamour. It's a trick of charm and unspoken promise, and it disappoints as often as it thrills people swayed by it.

That said, as a witch you have the ability to bend love's potent power. Use it with discretion and great thought, and you can accomplish good. But I can't urge you too strongly to be very, very careful.

In my grimoire, you'll find recipes for love potions I've tested. Remember Mrs. Blandstone, the pastor's wife? When Pastor Blandstone became so obsessed with the Book of Deuteronomy that he'd hardly eat, let alone look at her, I prepared her a dose of See Me. You'll recall they eventually had six children. When Jeremy Busch was on his deathbed and full of resentment over his meager life, I put a few drops of Family Bonds into his medicine, and he died grateful and full of love for his children, who truly did adore him, the old coot.

However you use this lesson, Josie, you must certainly feel my love for you now.

I sighed and refolded the lesson. Hearing my grandmother speak always left me softened and a little trembly.

I glanced toward the bed. Grandma's grimoire was at the bottom of the chest of letters. It had always felt too powerful to open. Its energy was stronger than that of any book I'd encountered so far. Simply brushing a finger against it burned. The time hadn't been right for examining it, and for the months I'd had it, I'd simply left it at the bottom of the chest.

I had to sip my lessons slowly. My dead grandmother was my only mentor.

Rodney, purring, had draped himself over the back of the chair. He now dropped like liquid into my lap.

"What do you think, baby cat?" I asked him. "What adventures are we getting into now?"

Outside, the faraway music swelled to a crescendo, and chills prickled the backs of my arms. The orchestra faded. A window closed and the music stopped.

CHAPTER THREE

The next morning I pushed back the library's curtains to August sun lifting the scent from the fir trees and a sky so blue it might have been an ocean. No one waited at the library's back door with the intention of re-creating social time at the café. My guess was that they were all wandering Wilfred's few square blocks of houses, hoping to run into Daphne Morris. I put coffee on, anyway.

The library's kitchen was built at the time when a cook and maid spread bowls and chopping boards across a long oak table so heavy that it seemed to have been built in place. The wood-burning stove had been upgraded to an electric model during the 1950s, and pendant lights replaced the old gas fixtures, but otherwise the roomy kitchen maintained the same combination of coziness and utility as it had for more than a century.

From the conservatory came the sound of Roz tapping

on her laptop. She liked to work mornings before her afternoon shift. Lyndon Forster, the library's caretaker and Roz's boyfriend, would have already lifted the ceiling's glass panels to cool the room. Roz was probably deep into a romantic world—last I'd heard, she was outlining a romance that took place in Atlantis. Its hero probably sported some version of Lyndon's name. Captain Forston Lynder, maybe.

A knock at the kitchen door startled me from my reverie. Framed by the door's glass window was Daphne Morris, the morning light casting a halo in her hair. She was here! Here in Wilfred, here in my library.

In my excitement, it took me three tries to unlatch the door. Daphne entered, and a fluffy Pomeranian the exact color of her hair—as golden as a lioness summering in Malibu—trotted next to her. Rodney jumped to the table to look on.

"Hi," she said. "I'm here to meet Eliza."

When people talked about celebrities, they usually mentioned that they were smaller than imagined. Daphne seemed larger. Not in size—she was petite—but in presence. She was also slightly older than she'd been when she played the wide-eyed ingenue roles that had earned her the title of the Golden Cutie, but she couldn't have been more than forty. An almost palpable charisma wrapped her. No matter where she was, all eyes would turn to her. This, I thought, was what my grandmother had meant about "glamour."

"Good morning," I said breathlessly and stepped aside to let her in. "Coffee?"

"No thank you. I had a turmeric latte at home."

As Daphne talked, her Pomeranian was helping herself to Rodney's food. Rodney leaped from the table and, hissing, inserted his body between his dish and the dog. The Pomeranian lifted her head abruptly and stared, dazed, at Rodney. She wagged her tail with sudden enthusiasm.

"Duchess!" Daphne said. "Bad doggie. You already had breakfast."

Chopped steak with a quail's egg, I guessed, from the dog's glossy fur and faint scent of peaches and roses. Or was that Daphne's perfume?

"Sorry about that," she said. Then she smiled. The sun had nothing on her. "I'm Daphne Morris, by the way," she said as if I didn't know.

"Josie Way," I said. "Librarian."

"Wilfred is so charming. I'm looking forward to meeting everyone. Bryce—that's my chef—is fixing up a reception tonight as a thank-you to the town for hosting us this week."

"That's kind of you." I hoped she'd stocked up on the chips and dip. Everyone in town would be at the party.

"Is Eliza in?" Noticing the blank look on my face, she added, "Eliza Chatterley Windsor. I understood she's an assistant librarian here."

"Oh, yes. Eliza's her pen name. Around here we know her as Roz. Follow me."

We exited the kitchen and rounded the corner to the conservatory, where Roz sat at a small table with her back toward us.

"Roz?" I said. "You have a visitor."

"Great," she replied without turning. "Tell them to go away. I'm in the middle of a hot scene between the Dolphin Princess and a lost scuba diver."

"Oh, Eliza—I mean, Roz—I don't want to disturb you, but I just love your work. I had to meet you."

Roz spun her chair toward us at the unmistakable sing-song voice of Daphne Morris. "Daphne! You're here."

Apparently the movie star was used to blatantly obvious greetings. "*The Whippoorwill Cries Love* really helped me through a difficult time," she said. "May I hug you?"

Eyes wide, Roz nodded. I watched as the two women—a plushly built brunette with streaks of gray and a Venus-like blonde—embraced. When they separated, Roz reached for her fan and batted at her reddening neck.

"My divorce was awful." Daphne raised her eyes first at me, then Roz. "Maybe you heard about it?"

We nodded. Everyone had heard about it. The story had drenched tabloids and entertainment shows and even spawned internet memes. I didn't remember details, but the gist was that Kevin Atchley, her ex and a chart-topping country-western singer, was caught in a compromising position with the dog trainer.

"I'm so sorry," I said.

"Your book gave me hope," Daphne said. "Hope that love is out there, if only we keep our eyes open."

"The murders didn't bother you?" Roz said. *The Whippoorwill Cries Love* featured the Mob and two deaths by electrocution. Unusual in a story set in rural Oregon, but Roz had pulled it off.

"Justice was served." Daphne's voice was at once tender and final, a tone any Supreme Court justice would have been proud to utter. She turned to me. "Does the library have any other novels as inspiring as Roz's work? I'll have time to read this week."

"I could bring some to the farmhouse this afternoon, if you'd like," I said. Even as I spoke, titles flooded my brain. Besides more Eliza Chatterley Windsor, *Leave Him and Love It* and *The Naughty Purse Pup: Training Your Dog in 10 Easy Steps* made an appearance.

"Thank you. I'd like that." She returned to Roz. "Tell me. Forest Lyndy, the hero. He was so"—she searched the air for the right word—"so real to me. Like he really existed. Lanky, quiet, and a real man. We don't get a lot of those in Hollywood. What I'd give to meet someone like him."

A dreamy look fell over Roz. "I modeled him on my boyfriend, Lyndon. He's the caretaker here. I've known him since high school, but we got together only last fall."

Roz had pined for Lyndon for more than thirty years. At first glance, Lyndon's craggy face, bony hands, and impassive expression scared kids. He'd certainly freaked me out when I first met him. In reality, he was gentle and kind—a vegan and, even more surprising, an ikebana master. He was intensely private and not much of a conversationalist, and until Roz confessed her feelings, no one would have ever guessed he'd held a long-standing love for her, too.

Daphne and Roz sighed in unison.

"Well, I'd better be getting back to the farmhouse. Folks around here sure are friendly," Daphne said.

"I bet," Roz replied.

"I'll drop some novels by for you after lunch," I said.

We followed Daphne back to the kitchen door and waved goodbye.

"She's such an angel," Roz said with uncharacteristic warmth as we watched the movie star's graceful figure cross the lawn. Duchess kept looking back, undoubtedly trying to spot Rodney. "So charming."

"She really is beautiful," I added.

"And such great taste in literature. I like her a lot more than I thought I would. I thought she'd be stuck-up. You know, snooty about the town."

Outside, Daphne stopped short as Lyndon emerged from the garden shed with the compost fork. The sun picked up strands of gold in her hair, and as she turned to the side, we saw a wide smile. She clearly recognized Lyndon as Forest Lyndy. They shook hands. With Lyndon's scarecrow frame and wrinkled work shirt, he might have been an extra from *The Grapes of Wrath*. Meanwhile, Daphne appeared lifted directly from a fairy tale. Lyndon hurriedly smoothed his hair, and he gave a smile I'd only ever seen him bestow on baby Nicky and on Roz, when he thought no one could see him. He positively glowed.

"Daphne Morris," Roz snarled. "I detest her."

Cranky Roz, Roz with a downer view—that was normal Roz. Roz fuming angry? Not normal.

"It's nothing," I told her. "She's a movie star. Of course he's mesmerized. Heck, I was mesmerized, too."

"She had a choice," Roz said. "She didn't have to smile and give him that look. I thought we shared something. I felt that sister energy."

"She probably can't help it. It's Hollywood. It's in her DNA to seduce. Don't worry about it, though. She'll only be here a week."

"A week is long enough. I mean, how long did it take the *Titanic* to sink? Or Rome to burn?"

"Oh, Roz. Be reasonable. She's here to promote your book."

"And destroy my life." With that, Roz stomped off to the conservatory.

I was about to turn away from the window, when Sam, on his way to work, came down Big House's front steps. He couldn't see me from the kitchen door's window, so I indulged myself in watching his strong figure emerge from the porch's shadow into the summer morning.

His regulation khaki uniform must have felt so different from the street clothes he wore undercover as an FBI agent, but its crisp lines suited him. He would have left Nicky with the babysitter by now. He glanced at his watch and picked up his pace.

My infatuation with Sam was going on ten months and not showing signs of letting up. I felt like an inmate who crossed days off her calendar, waiting for the time the warden would set her free. At least the view from my cell was good, I thought as Sam bent to clear something from the porch stairs.

Up to Sam strolled Daphne Morris. He stopped and frowned, meaning he was feeling good. Schedule forgotten, his arms relaxed at his side. From this angle, I couldn't see Daphne's face, but whatever she was doing, Sam liked it. After a few minutes, she walked away, clearly aware of the lure of her swaying hips. Sam watched until she disappeared on the trail to town.

The emotion in me rose and intensified until the lamp at my side fizzled and went dark, wafting ozone-scented smoke. I closed my eyes and steadied my breath. Daphne Morris, I thought with a mental snort. What's so great about her?

CHAPTER FOUR

Library open, I settled into the routine of greeting patrons, shelving returns, and occasionally checking in on the gossip fest in the kitchen, which centered on Daphne Morris: how she'd waved at one Wilfredian; how she was better looking than any of her publicity photos; and how inconceivable it was that her husband had cheated on her. Once Patty set out lawn chairs in front of the This-N-That, talk would shift to her yard, where the odds were higher of catching sight of the movie star.

When I passed the conservatory, I heard Roz's fateful mutterings and exasperated sighs, and I had a hunch it wasn't her novel-in-progress that upset her. Outside the window, Lyndon lay under the dogwood tree, hands behind his head, gazing up through its canopy. He did this when he was contemplating branches to prune, but the goofy look on his face told me he was probably thinking more about Daphne than lopping shears.

"Excuse me, Josie," a graceful woman in her fifties said. She was an ex-dancer who lived with her jazz musician husband up the highway beyond town. "Could you recommend a novel? T-Bone and I are spending a week at the beach. We're leaving tomorrow. We were going to leave tonight—"

"—but you didn't want to miss Daphne Morris's party," I finished.

She smiled and nodded.

I relaxed, and the name of a popular women's fiction novel appeared in my brain. My reading tastes tended more to vintage mystery novels, but magic let me recommend books I'd never even heard of. Somehow, I knew every bit of written material in the old mansion and where it was shelved, and I could match it to a reader whether the reader knew she wanted it or not.

"Try this." I led her to New Releases and selected a Liane Moriarty novel. "Oh, and you might enjoy *Making Oat Milk at Home*."

"Funny you mention that. I was just thinking this morning that I wouldn't mind trying my hand at oat milk or a nut milk. Thank you."

"I have one more recommendation. For your daughter." I flinched as the book title slid into my brain, but who was I to question it? "*What to Expect When You're Expecting*, upstairs in Health."

Her jaw dropped. "How did you know? We haven't told anyone yet."

Seeing the gratified looks of patrons was the best part of my job. No matchmaker could feel more satisfied about her work. A novel I handed across the circulation desk would give its reader a long afternoon of thought-provoking drama, or an absorbing dip into another world each night before bed. The books loved it, too. Volumes sighed happily in their new readers' hands.

"Hi, Lalena," I said to one of the library's regulars and my best friend in Wilfred. She often wandered up to the library to "get out of the office." She ran her business as a psychic from her trailer at the Magnolia Rolling Estates.

She waved as she wafted by in a vintage caftan festooned with large orange daisies. "I'm going upstairs to hang out in Natural History." Chances were good I'd find her napping on the couch in a few hours.

"Check under the sofa for the biography of Marie Laveau you requested."

Once I'd waved goodbye, I started collecting novels for Daphne Morris. My magical instincts led me to a few romance novels, and my cattier side was tempted to include a self-help book about women driven to seduce other women's beaux. One thing was for sure: I wouldn't send Roz to deliver these books. She needed time to cool off.

I was on the stepping stool retrieving a copy of *Pomeranians Through the Ages*, when motion at the door caught my eye. It was a woman in her thirties, a stranger. Candyfloss pink streaked her hair and a silver ring pierced one nostril. Cowboy boots and a short-sleeved Western-cut blouse with doves embroidered over a curvy torso counterbalanced her urban air. Wide-eyed, she looked around the old house's drawing room, now Popular Fiction.

"Can I help you?" I stepped down from the stool. It was unusual to see a stranger in the library. Maybe she was Mrs. Garlington's niece, the one who'd started a band in Sacramento. Mrs. Garlington had bragged about how musical talent ran in her family. Or maybe it was one of Patty's countless daughters, now scattered throughout the country.

"This is some library," the woman said.

"Thank you," I said with pride. "Are you looking for a particular book?"

"No." She traced a lotus in the rug's pattern with the toe of a cowboy boot. "Actually, could you tell me where Daphne Morris is staying? The actress? I know she's in Wilfred, but I drove up, and then, *poof*, the town was behind me. I saw the sign for the library and pulled in here."

I hesitated. Daphne Morris was supposed to be avoiding the media, and I didn't want to blow her cover. Besides, what could this woman want? Maybe Daphne had stolen her husband, and she had a bludgeon in her car's trunk.

As this thought passed through my head, I heard a vague *vroom vroom* behind me. Rodney stared at the shelf and batted a paw. It was that stupid Indy 500 history again. I silently urged it to hush up.

"Wilfred's small. I'm not surprised you barely had time to register you were here before you'd reached the edge of town." Which was about three blocks long. "What makes you think Daphne Morris is here?"

The stranger's eyes flashed from surprise to knowing. "I get it. You're covering for her. It's okay—she invited me. I know she's here for the next book club taping."

Still, I was wary. Why wouldn't she simply call Daphne or Morgan if that were the case? "You'll need to get in touch with her directly. That is, assuming she's here."

At that moment, the Indy 500 history bolted. I deftly dropped a hand to catch it as it attempted to race from the shelf and tucked the book under my arm, hoping the stranger hadn't noticed.

"All right. I get it," she repeated. "I'm sure I'll be seeing you around."

I waved goodbye to the stranger, perhaps some member of Daphne's entourage. Who was this one? Masseuse? Personal trainer? Or maybe a psychotherapist specializing in love addiction? Wilfred's grapevine would report back soon enough.

All the way down the hill, Daphne's books in a tote, I marveled at my task. Here I was, delivering hand-selected books to an internationally known celebrity—and not just a star, but the host of a popular book talk program. Rodney scampered at my feet, running ahead to scratch his claws on a tree and lagging to sniff at things I couldn't see.

The half-dozen books jostled as I walked. Most were romances, which explained the yearning sighs and occasional smooching sounds they emitted. I'd included *Who Am I Without Him?: A Guide for the Woman Who Thinks She Needs a Man.* I admit it might have been me rather than magic that had selected that one. I'd brought a book for Daphne's assistant Morgan, too. Instinct had suggested a classic by the drama coach Konstantin Stanislavsky. The book, donated by Gaston High School's drama club, was crisp and new—I didn't think anyone had checked it out before now.

Daphne Morris and her staff were lodging in an old farmhouse a few blocks behind Patty's This-N-That. Mrs. Garlington owned the farmhouse's twin a block away. Story had it the farmhouses were built long ago by sisters who'd inherited their father's cherry orchard, back when farming was second only to Wilfred's once-booming timber economy. The sisters remained spinsters, tough and wily, and over the years they'd supposedly let strings of lovers through their back doors.

The farmhouse was especially wonderful now, at summer's height. Knobby crab apple trees dotted the front yard, and hummingbirds dove for the roses twined with purple clematis that climbed its porch. White paint peeled here and there on the clapboards, but I knew the house's roomy interior was scrubbed clean. It had been Duke's— Wilfred's handyman deluxe—job to get it into shape for the actress and her entourage, including installing the espresso machine, stocking the refrigerator with freshly chopped steak for the dog, and painting the interior a custom-blended shade of peach to complement Daphne's famous complexion.

The front door was open with the screen door catching the breeze. I knocked on its wooden frame. "Hello?"

Leo, the production person I'd met earlier, opened the door. When he saw me, he pushed his glasses up the bridge of his nose, and his smile widened. "It's Josie the librarian."

I lifted my tote in response. "Here with some vacation reading."

He stepped onto the porch and set a duffel bag near the porch swing. "Does the library have a good local history section?"

"We do. What kind of information are you looking for?"

"Well, actually, folk magic," he said.

"What?" Did he say "magic"?

He glanced into the house behind him and lowered his voice. "Folk magic. I'm doing some research on superstition. You'd be surprised at the belief in magic in rural communities over the years, and I'm not just talking about the Salem witch trials."

Up the street, one of the Tohlers was walking the family's German shepherd, probably on her tenth turn around the block in hopes of spotting Daphne. Rodney rolled in the shade of the crab apple tree.

"We might have something in our collection," I told him.

"Hey, Leo, before you leave—" came a voice from inside the house. A man wearing a backward-facing baseball cap appeared at the door, wiping his hands on a dish towel.

"Josie Way, here with books for Daphne," I said.

"Oh, yes." He opened the screen door. "She said you'd be dropping by. I'm Bryce, Daphne's chef. Come in."

I followed Bryce to the open, sunny kitchen, where he'd been unpacking grocery sacks of food. A box of liquor—a full case, I noted—sat on the woodstove, cold now, near the wall. Leo left his duffel on the porch and came in with us.

"Preparing for tonight?" I asked. "The whole town's talking about the party."

Bryce spun the bill of his baseball cap to the front and lifted his eyebrows. "It's going to be a good one. The lady who owns the shop with all the appliances out front—"

"Patty," I said.

"Yep, Patty. She's letting me stage it in her front yard. I'll do a cooking demo and shake up some Golden Cuties for the crowd."

"Golden Cuties? It's a food?"

Bryce had a way of smiling that made me smile, too. He might well end up more popular than Daphne Morris, especially if his snacks were up to his patter. "Daphne's signature cocktail," he said. "Seductively sweet and superpotent."

"I'm sorry I'm going to miss it," Leo said, looking at me a second too long. "I'm headed into Portland for the night."

Through the window beyond him, a figure in the back-yard stood, arms up, like Superman aiming for the heav-ens. Chef Bryce caught my gaze.

"That's Gibbous. Working the yoga mat once again. I don't suppose he'll be partaking tonight."

The figure, tall and bald, reached down, palms flat against the ground.

"I've read about him." Thanks to his role as Daphne's stylist, Gibbous Moon had been widely featured in maga-zines. On my last visit to the dentist, I'd read an article touting his advice on the pros and cons of wearing bangs and revealing how he mixed Daphne's signature hair color. I vaguely remembered his birth name as Zachary something-or-other.

Bryce waved at him, and Gibbous bounded up the stairs through the open door with a grace that almost matched Rodney's.

"Peace," Gibbous said.

"Pleased to meet you." I set the book-filled tote on a chair. Bryce pulled a bottle of beer from the refrigerator and popped off its top. "Want one?"

"No thanks," I said. "I'm on duty."

"How about you, Leo?" Bryce asked.

"Me neither. I've got to run."

"And for the abstainer, how about a carrot juice, Gib-bous?"

In the backyard, Daphne sat in a lounge chair, tucking her long, ivory legs under a peach-tinted sundress. Her Pomeranian leaped from the lounge chair, tail wagging, to touch noses with Rodney, who'd gone around the side of the house. Rodney allowed a second of contact, then turned away from the dog in disdain.

"That's my cat," I said, keeping my eyes on him. Getting friendly with a spoiled lapdog? This couldn't end well.

"The black one?"

I passed Bryce to get to the back garden. "Rodney?"

The cat glanced at me, whipping his tail. Duchess panted nearby. He cast the dog a beckoning look and headed for the bushes.

"Rodney, you get back here," I said.

"Hi, Josie," Daphne said, now sitting up, her hair tumbling around her shoulders. "Don't worry about Duchess. She loves all creatures. She won't hurt your cat."

"It's not Rodney I'm worried about." Keeping an eye on the shrubbery, I said, "I brought some reading for you. It's in the kitchen. How do you like the farmhouse?"

Gibbous had returned to the yard and was now in cobra pose, flat on the ground, chest and chin pointed up.

"I love it. I haven't felt so relaxed in months." Her eyes half-drowsed in the warmth. "So quiet at night. Roosters to wake me in the morning."

"Did your friend find you?"

She opened an eye. "What friend?"

"I don't know, exactly. She's about this tall"—I lifted a hand to my nose—"And had a chunk of pink in her hair. Said you'd invited her and she needed to find you."

Leo had joined us in the backyard. He nodded as soon as I said "pink." "And a nose ring?"

"Uh-huh."

"You didn't tell her where Daphne was, did you?" Leo said. His gaze shot to Daphne, then to me.

"No. I didn't. Why?"

He raked back his hair and shook his head. "That was Bianca."

All at once, Gibbous dropped to a seated position.

"Bianca's here? She found us?" There was no missing the alarm in his voice.

Daphne's calm was unruffled. "Don't sweat it, Gibb. She doesn't know where we're staying."

"It's not like we're in Manhattan. This is a small town. She's not allowed to be within a thousand feet of you. If she could track us to Wilfred, she won't have any trouble finding the house."

"I said not to worry." A lazy smile spread over Daphne's face, and she shifted hips in a luxurious motion. "I'll call the sheriff, Sam. Now there's a man I wouldn't mind letting bother me. You know him well?"

Dread dropped over me like a hood. "He's very busy," I said.

"There's a lot of crime here?" Leo asked.

I could have mentioned Ned Jolson's egg situation, but thought better of it. "You know how it is," I said vaguely.

"Well, now that Bianca's in town—come to think of it, I should be more concerned," Daphne said.

Gibbous nodded vigorously. "I don't trust her one bit. Remember what she did to you."

Daphne dipped her head and drew air deep into her chest. It was a character study of *worry*. "I really had better see the sheriff."

"Let him know about Bianca," Leo urged. "Can't hurt."

Daphne's indifference from a few seconds earlier had vanished. "I didn't want to say anything, but I'm actually quite concerned."

"Say anything about what?" Leo asked.

"I knew we should have brought security," Gibbous said.

"It's not just Bianca," Daphne said. "There's the death threat."

CHAPTER FIVE

Death threat?" Bryce asked. "What death threat? Why didn't you say anything sooner?"

Daphne shrugged. "You know how it is."

"Another email?" Leo said.

"Handwritten. On the front porch. I didn't want to freak anyone out, so I didn't say anything earlier."

"You found a threatening note on the porch? What did it say?" I could imagine a Wilfredian leaving a mash note for Daphne with *I'm dying to see you* on it. Maybe it was misinterpreted.

"You know," she replied vaguely." *I'm going to kill you*, etc. The usual."

We looked at her in shock. How could she be so cavalier about a death threat?

"Someone knows you're here." Gibbous turned to me. "You're sure you didn't tell Bianca anything?"

"No," I said. "Nothing. I pointed out Wilfred proper,

and that was it. Where's the note?" Sam might want it as evidence.

Daphne looked at her hands, as if surprised it wasn't there. "The note? I ripped it to pieces and threw it away. I refuse to have that kind of negativity in the house with me."

"In the kitchen trash?" Leo pulled the garbage from under the sink. Whatever paper had been in it was now absorbed by a slurry of coffee grounds and what looked like vegetable soup. He poked at the mess with a wooden spoon, but there was no sign of paper and no hope of recovering the note now.

"Don't bother. I'll let the sheriff know about Bianca and about the threat, and that will be that," Daphne said. "He'll probably want to stay here with us—or at least check in a few times a day."

The assumption in her tone irritated me. "What about Bianca? Is she violent?" I asked.

"You know about Daphne's divorce from Kevin Atchley, right?" Chef Bryce said.

"Sure."

Everyone knew. The story was that Daphne had walked in on Atchley and the dog nanny during a dog training session. Her Pomeranian now did strange things when commanded to "lie down."

"Someone leaked it to the press," Gibbous said. "The only person who could have done it was Bianca. She was everywhere. If anything happened to Daphne, she knew about it."

Bryce picked up the thread. "Daphne and Bianca are cousins, and they used to be close. Bianca did so much for Daphne that Morgan joked about losing her job."

"She was awfully sweet to me. Before she sold me out," Daphne said.

"You're sure it was Bianca who leaked the story?" I asked. The woman I'd seen hadn't looked like she was flush with cash.

"Who else could it have been?" Leo said. "Gibbous was the one who caught on to it. Between the three of us, we convinced Daphne to put out a restraining order against her. Since then, she keeps turning up."

"I've changed my phone number I don't know how many times," Daphne said, "but somehow she gets it. We travel, she shows up outside the studio door. She's getting more insistent, too. Remember last month in Vancouver during the *Siren Sisters* shoot?"

"At least we had security then," Gibbous said.

"Maybe we should call off the party tonight," Bryce said.

Daphne stood. Sultry goddess had morphed from terrified victim to carefree movie star. Now she was benevolent VIP. "No. The party goes on. I'm sure everything will be just fine."

Duchess trotted from the bushes and sat a few feet from Gibbous, looking proud of herself. Black grease matted her golden fur, streaking up her belly to her nose.

Gibbous stood abruptly and backed toward the house. "Something smells like a dead mackerel."

"Duchess!" Daphne said. "She rolled in something. I don't get it. She's never done this before."

Rodney's head emerged from beneath a camellia bush. I knew that expression. It was pure naughty glee. He meowed silently and vanished, tail flicking behind him, into the shrubbery.

* * *

After closing the library for the night, I met up in the library's kitchen with Roz. She was gathering her purse and ever-present fan, preparing to leave.

"You coming down to the This-N-That for the party?" I asked her, sure of her "you bet." After all, everyone in Wilfred would be there for a glimpse of Daphne Morris. They'd have DVDs to sign, and they'd be clinking coupes of Golden Cuties, thanks to Chef Bryce. This party was destined for the town's history books.

"Absolutely not," Roz said.

I set down the coffeepot I was washing out. "What? Why not?"

"I'll have nothing to do with that . . . that—"

"I get it," I said. "Lyndon."

Roz looked toward her purse and the laptop bundled under her arm. "Have you seen him? He can barely walk straight. His head is full of Daphne Morris. I've tried talking to him, but he can't focus long enough to get out a few words. I don't even know him anymore, and it's all because of her."

"You're going to have to talk to her eventually. For the television interview. Besides—" I paused a moment, unsure of how to say that Daphne probably fished for lovers in more exclusive waters than Wilfred, and that Lyndon was unlikely to end up on her arm on the red carpet. "Besides, that's just how she is. I bet she can't help roping in the interest of any man she meets."

Roz lifted her red-rimmed eyes to mine. "It's not her so much as it is Lyndon. How could he do this to me? I can't even write. I spent all morning after Daphne left, just staring out the window."

"Sit down." I pointed to the table. "Can I get you a drink of something?"

Besides the box of wine left by Lalena in my apartment's refrigerator for refreshment during her weekly baths at the library, the kitchen had seen bottles come and go since Darla's café had closed and Wilfredians had co-opted the library's kitchen. I'd managed to hand most of the bottles back to their owners and push them out the door with a "coffee's fine, but that's it," but at least one half-drunk bottle of Chivas Regal and a few miniature bottles had been snuck in and left behind.

"No," she sniffed. "I'm going home. I need to be by myself for a while to think about things."

"What kinds of things?" I asked. "You're not considering breaking up with Lyndon, are you? He adores you. He's just starstruck, that's all. Come down to the party. Take the high road on this. You'll see I'm right."

She stared out the kitchen window behind me. "Maybe I'll come down, just for a minute or two. But I'll tell you this"—she lifted her chin—"My next book will not be a romance. I have a great idea for a murder scene."

"Funny you mention it." I told her about Daphne's death threat and Bianca, her stalker.

"If you see the stalker again, feel free to tell her if Daphne doesn't cool it with Lyndon, I'll take care of her work for her."

CHAPTER SIX

It was almost seven o'clock, but nightfall and cricket song were still hours away. The lowering sun cast a side-eye over the landscape, throwing halos on the cottonwood trees and shimmering in the meadow. Even the windows of the trailers at the Magnolia Rolling Estates glowed to rival the Taj Mahal.

I walked down the hill, on my way to what would surely be Wilfred's party of the century. Sure, Derwin Garlington's birthday at the café had been a big deal with its post office theme. I'd never seen a sheet cake decorated as a stamp, complete with perforated edges. The barbecue and pie-eating contest when Thom Lee retired would remain in Wilfredians' memories for a long time, too, due mostly to the subsequent run on antacids. But we'd never had a movie star as a guest of honor. I wished Sam could have been here, but he was on duty.

The front yard of Patty's This-N-That buzzed with action. Party lights zigzagged over the lawn. Wilfredians talked and laughed among the vintage kitchen appliances, and big band music sounded from the boom box Patty usually used to play her Jazzercise tapes. Mrs. Garlington stood, smiling, clasping her purse to her chest near the recliner where Patty lounged. I waved at Lalena, chatting with Daphne's assistant Morgan near a chest freezer. Whatever it was they were talking about, Morgan barely showed even polite interest. She left when Mona showed up with a baby goat, her current foster animal, and plopped it on the freezer to nurse from a bottle. Lyndon lurked near the crowd's edge. I couldn't tell if his morose expression was his usual set of face or was from missing Roz.

Probably fifty people were at the party, but no Daphne. Smart move, I reflected, given the death threat. And Roz's rancor.

"Hi, Bryce," I said to the chef, surrounded by awed Wilfredians.

"Hello, charming librarian. Care for a beer?"

Chef Bryce stood at an avocado-green stove, wielding a spatula like it was born in his hand. He wore a dented porkpie hat, and a dish towel dangled from the waistband of his jeans. The two empty beer bottles on the card table next to him explained his chattiness.

"Not at the moment, thanks."

He returned to the stove. "You don't want to touch them until you're sure the bottom is golden," he told the dozen people gathered around him. "Take a peek—just a little one." He demonstrated by edging up the corner of what looked like a dollar-sized potato pancake with his spatula, then flipping the pancake into the air, where it somersaulted like an Olympic diver and landed in the skillet, right-side up.

I wandered to the chest freezer where Lalena leaned, occasionally reaching out to run her fingers through the baby goat's fur.

"Amazing, huh?" she said. "Duke and Chef Bryce worked all afternoon to set it up. Check out the garlands." Paper garlands in pink, blue, and vivid green waved from corner to corner. "Patty's back stock from when she was into Mexican party paper."

"They're terrific. I'm going to say hi to Patty."

Patty lounged in her recliner in a baby-blue tracksuit with the sweatshirt reading *Born for Speed* across the chest.

"Your complete Jane Fonda aerobics series came in," I told her. "You have no idea how hard it was to find on VHS." Patty loved to watch—not actually exercise to—workout videos.

"Thank you. I've got to keep up my training." She sighed happily at the scene in front of her. "Isn't Chef Bryce the best?" She waved over the crowd. "There are lots of snacks on the sideboard, but he said he'd do a cooking demo for us. Good thing we had potatoes and sour cream in the refrigerator."

All summer, Wilfredians had been dropping offerings in the now-communal refrigerator. The last I'd peeked, I'd found off-brand orange soda, butter, sardines, and a supersized pack of Parker House rolls.

"Any word on Daphne?" I asked.

"Haven't seen her yet," Patty replied.

"How about Roz?"

"No Roz, either."

Duke ambled over, beer in hand. "Hello, Josie." His

brilliantined hair was especially shiny today, and the curl over his left eye carefully sculpted.

Patty's nine-year-old grandson Thor, attired in his usual cape and accompanied by his kid sister Buffy, darted into the crowd with a digital camera. Patty set down her drink. "Thor, I told you you could take photos, but don't get in the way."

"See how nice it is to have a community center, Josie?" Duke said. "This is good, but the weather won't last another two months. Like I told you, we really need to keep the library open all week. Folks got to have a place to gather."

That again. To avoid a repeat discussion again, I retreated to the crowd's edge and bumped into Morgan Stanhope, who stood, arms crossed over her chest, looking on. In the roomy purse slung over her shoulder, I heard the twang of dialogue from a Tennessee Williams play. I'd seen people having more fun in a hostage situation.

"How are you settling in?" I asked.

"All right," she said, looking not at me, but at the crowd. "Thanks for the Stanislavsky book. It's one of my favorites."

"No Daphne. Maybe she's staying home because of the death threat?"

Morgan snorted. "No doubt she's mooning over her ex. I wouldn't take the death threat seriously. She gets threatening mail all the time."

"Her stalker showed up," I said.

Morgan was unfazed. "I heard. Bianca's not a threat. I don't know why Gibbous and Leo get so worked up about her. Besides, I haven't seen Bianca around, and it's not like anyone could hide in this town."

She had a good point there. "But a death threat was left on your porch."

"You mean the note Daphne threw away before anyone saw it?"

Morgan's implication was clear, but hard to believe. "You think she faked it? She seemed worried. She was going to call the sheriff for protection."

"The sheriff is a man, right?" Morgan said. I nodded. "Well, there you go."

Everyone else at this party seemed to be having a terrific time, and here I was stuck next to the one sourpuss. I tried again. "Roz is super-excited you've chosen her novel for the show."

As if on cue, Roz arrived in what passed for her party finery, a lilac-sprigged sundress from the eighties. She stood at the crowd's edge, looking at Lyndon, who shyly returned her gaze with occasional peeks. If I wasn't mistaken, her expression had softened. Thank goodness. They needed to make up and get it over with. Having an assistant librarian who was already cranky with a grudge against the caretaker could not only make the place unpleasant, but downright dangerous. I had visions of flying staplers and a sabotaged furnace.

"Yeah, well, it wasn't me who chose that book," Morgan said.

I tore my eyes from Roz and Lyndon. "Daphne did?"

"Definitely Daphne."

"It does seem out of character compared to the other books she's featured," I had to admit. The show's last novel was about an Afghani family, a multigenerational saga that plumbed god, war, and pestilence. The book before it had been a philosophical exploration of the role of women during the Spanish-American War.

"I chose those," Morgan said. "It's one of the reasons she hired me. Truth is, Daphne's not much of a reader. Her reading tastes tend to be . . . well, she likes her TV. These days, she's hooked on the Heartbreak Haven channel. I've never actually seen her with a novel." In response to my questioning look, she added, "I give her a synopsis and questions for the author."

To me, giving up books would be like giving up sleep or dinner. "But she chose *The Whippoorwill Cries Love*. She must do some reading."

"Found it in a hotel lobby. She liked the cover. Said it reminded her of her ex. Once she started, she couldn't put it down."

The novel's cover featured a whippoorwill in full crow in the foreground with a cowboy grasping a busty brunette nearby. Come to think of it, the cowboy did bear a striking resemblance to Kevin Atchley.

In reply, I pasted on the knowing smile I reserved for literature snobs.

Morgan seemed to assume I agreed with her. "Between you and me, this is probably the last book I'll be helping Daphne with, anyway. Something—" Her gaze searched the sky for the right word. "Something interesting is in the works. My life's dream, actually."

"No kidding?"

I glanced again toward Roz and Lyndon. They were slowly edging toward each other around the party's perimeter. Roz wore a faint smile.

"I can't say anything about it yet," Morgan said. "But I'm looking forward to getting back to New York."

"Maybe this opportunity has to do with theater?" I said, remembering the drama tome the books had recommended for her.

"I'll let you know as soon as I run it by Daphne." Her voice relaxed and almost sounded happy. "Tonight, if I get the chance."

Thor, camera held high, appeared in front of us. "Smile!" Buffy said at his side.

At the stove, Chef Bryce was shaking hands and passing out napkins with potato pancakes topped with smoked salmon. Another beer bottle had joined the empties on the table. "A repeat tomorrow?" he asked the crowd. "I'll be here, if Patty invites me back."

"Definitely, definitely," Patty said from her recliner. In her lap was a sour cream–stained paper plate. "You're always welcome. I'll stock the fridge."

"Tonight, I'll make you all something special—Daphne's signature cocktail, the Golden Cutie."

Next to me, Morgan made a quiet puking sound.

"You don't like them," I said.

Morgan pursed her lips. "They're so sweet. The main ingredient is peach schnapps. Ugh."

Beyond Morgan, Roz and Lyndon were only the width of a midcentury range and a dishwasher apart. It was working—they were making up. Roz turned, her smile widening. Lyndon's taciturn features had softened, too, and he opened his mouth to speak.

Just then, a voice filled with angel song, yet with the force of a trained actress, pierced the party chatter, and it wasn't Lyndon's. "Hello, everyone," Daphne said.

She'd changed into a black cotton eyelet sundress that followed the curves of her torso, then widened to swirl around her calves as she walked—or should I say *floated*? How she made it from the farmhouse in heels that high, I had no idea. Duchess's golden fluff wagged at her feet.

"Why aren't we dancing?" she said.

For the space of a breath, Wilfredians were still. Patty sat bolt upright in her recliner, and the baby goat bleated. In our midst was the movie star we'd all seen on screens and magazine covers. Now she stood on the patchy lawn in front of the This-N-That.

Within seconds, seemingly immovable appliances were lifted aside to make room on the lawn for a dance floor. Even Patty in her recliner was transported closer to the shop's window. The boom box's volume swelled.

Duke trotted toward Daphne and extended a hand. Within seconds he was expertly swirling her across the grass. I'd heard about Duke's prowess on the dance floor, but this was the first time I'd seen how graceful he was. It was like watching a dapper buffalo at a cotillion. I wished I could have pinned a gardenia to his lapel.

Across the lawn, Roz and Lyndon's approach halted an arm's-width apart. They, like everyone else, turned to Duke and Daphne. Lyndon gawked at the actress with hearts in his eyes. Not that Lyndon was the only man who couldn't keep his eyes off her. Only Bryce, shaking cocktails, seemed immune to her charms.

From inside his rumpled suit jacket, Lyndon pulled a corsage of pink and gold roses with white clematis trailing through them on a foundation of fern leaves. It was an elaborate but tiny work of art. He stepped forward and cut in on Duke, who reluctantly relinquished Daphne, and pinned the corsage to her shoulder.

Roz's eyes narrowed.

Uh-oh.

"Ms. Way," Dylan, the library's intern, whispered at my side. I quickly took in his suit and emerald ascot, no doubt another outfit from his deceased grandfather's closet, before returning my attention to Roz and Lyndon.

"Do you think Daphne Morris would autograph my hand-kerchief?" he asked.

Dylan might have been only sixteen, but that was probably close enough to manhood for Daphne. "I wouldn't be surprised," I said.

Roz began a slow and deadly march toward Lyndon.

She was now within arm's length of Lyndon. Her earlier goodwill had vanished. Roz looked at Lyndon, and Lyndon looked at Daphne. Not good.

Roz drew back a hand.

"Picture?" Thor said to me, lifting his camera.

The smack of Roz's palm on Lyndon's face resounded across the yard. "I never want to see you again," she yelled. She turned toward the makeshift dance floor. The music continued, but the dancers stood, mouths gaping. "As for you, Daphne Morris, I'll see you again for sure. In hell."

CHAPTER SEVEN

"Roz stormed out of the party, and that was that," I told Sam later that night. "I've never seen her so angry."

"She slapped him?"

"Right across the cheek."

"I can't believe I missed it," Sam said.

We were in Big House's kitchen, and he was trimming slices from a roast beef he'd pulled from the refrigerator. He was still in uniform, and Nicky played with a stuffed donkey in a playpen near us. Sam had also set out two plates, assuming I'd want a sandwich with him. Daphne Morris might be a glamorous celebrity, but she wasn't getting this kind of attention from Sam.

"Roz thinks Lyndon's hooked. As if he could sever his ties with Roz and fall for Daphne after a two-minute interaction," I said.

"Sometimes it happens that way. Instantly. You meet someone, and that's it."

He set two stuffed roast beef sandwiches on the table, mine with mustard, as I liked it, and his with mayonnaise. His words were mild enough, but something about them rankled me.

"You believe in love at first sight?"

He frowned slightly, a sign he was amused. "Sure."

I remembered my first sight of Sam. It was my second night in the library, and I'd come downstairs to find him dozing in Children's Literature with a Hardy Boys mystery on his knee and a hole in his sock. I couldn't say my heart had exploded into chrysanthemum-petaled fireworks or that I'd heard a chorus of angelic sopranos, but something in me had deepened and unwound. *This*, it seemed to say. *This*.

He'd given no indication the feeling was mutual. Why should he have? At the time, he was married, even if in the middle of a divorce. He was also on a job.

Since then, I'd patiently waited for my feelings to fade for lack of encouragement. They hadn't. I'd be thinking I was doing all right, getting over him, when he'd do something as simple as reach for a pen and I'd think, "That forearm. What a wonderful forearm." Or his mouth, or the way he squinted when he focused. Or whatever.

Sam and I had become closer, but he'd shown me nothing more than warm fondness. Meanwhile, I was losing my mind.

"What was the scene like at Patty's?" he asked.

"Duke and Chef Bryce had strung the yard with lights and streamers. The chef did a cooking demo and mixed cocktails, and Patty played Glenn Miller CDs in her boom box. You know all that talk about Duke's ballroom dancing?"

Sam's frown deepened. "Yeah?"

"He's really good. It's like his body belongs to Humpty-Dumpty, but his feet are Fred Astaire's. You should have seen him twirling Daphne Morris."

"I dropped in on her today," Sam said, giving Nicky's black curls a pat and tucking him into a high chair. "Daphne, that is."

"Really?" I forced myself to focus on my sandwich, which had transformed in my hands from a delicious dinner to a chunk of sawdust.

"Wanted to see how she was getting on," Sam said.

"Did she tell you about her death threat?"

"She did," he said. "Too bad she hadn't kept it. We took the kitchen garbage as evidence, but it doesn't look promising."

"Morgan thinks the note's a fake. That she wrote it herself for attention." I looked at my sandwich, not Sam. "If you ask me, I wouldn't be surprised if she's right." When Sam didn't respond right away, I looked up. I couldn't read his expression.

"Someone in her crew reported a stalker she had filed a restraining order against."

"I met her. The stalker, that is. She stopped by the library," I said. Dropped in on Daphne, did he? Now he and Daphne were on a first-name basis. He could have telephoned her. What was wrong with his phone? Oh yeah, the phone didn't have the same curves. "I bet Leo reported it. You know, the tall, kind of cute guy who leads the crew? Or maybe Gibbous."

"Hmm," Sam said mildly. "You're right. I think it was the camera guy."

"Were you able to follow up on it?"

"I found the warrant. Frankly, I'm not sure we would have approved it in our county. But it's legit."

"Why wouldn't you have approved it?"

"She didn't assault or even threaten to assault Daphne, and the allegations against her—"

"That she sold the story of Daphne's divorce."

"—were never proven. Still, Daphne carries a lot of weight in LA. It shouldn't be that way, but celebrities play by different rules."

Ha. I forced myself to bite off some sandwich. Except for Nicky's cooing, Big House's kitchen was quiet. No sounds of partying drifted up from town. Lyndon had probably gone to the caretaker's cottage, tried to put through a call or two to Roz and had the phone slammed down. Now he was likely preparing for bed, dreaming of summer dahlias and blond celebrities. Duke was home washing the Brylcreem from his hair and tucking his dancing shoes into the closet next to his work boots. Daphne Morris—well, I didn't want to think about that.

"I bet she can get men to do whatever she wants," I said.

Sam set down his sandwich. "Josie, I'm surprised. This doesn't sound like you. If I didn't know you better, I'd say you were—"

The buzz from Sam's work phone interrupted him. He answered with a few words and, pushing his plate away, rose, phone still in his hand. "A body? You're sure?"

My words came the second he set down his phone. "What happened?"

"There's been a death. At Daphne Morris's farmhouse. I have to go," Sam said.

He gestured toward Nicky, assuming I'd stay to watch

him, then was out the door before I had the chance to respond. Big mistake on his part. I bundled up the baby, his bottle, and a spare diaper and hurried across the lawn to Lyndon's cottage. He loved babies and probably needed something to distract him from mooning over Daphne, anyway.

"Sam's out?" was all he said. Behind him, the cottage was dark. As far as I knew, only Roz had seen its interior since his parents had died and left him to carry on the family business of tending the old Wilfred estate, including the library.

I nodded. "I need to step away for a moment, too. I'll be back before long." Lyndon didn't need to know the details.

I nearly ran down the hill, over the river, to Wilfred's main drag. The lights were off in the front yard of Patty's This-N-That, but a few people lingered near an avocado-green range. I didn't slow to see who it was.

Soon I was pushing open the farmhouse's garden gate. Sam's government SUV was parked in front. The house's front door was locked. I went around the side of the house, the branches from a row of fuchsia bushes brushing my legs. My brain was spinning.

If Daphne were dead, Wilfred would find itself at the center of a national media storm. Television reporters and cameras would line the streets, and hotels and guesthouses would book up back to Forest Grove. Mrs. Garlington would undoubtedly compose a fitting poem. The PO Grocery would have to stock up on deli sandwiches. We'd be forever known as the place Daphne Morris met her end. Or, as the tabloids would have it, where she made the "final cut" or her "reel ran out."

Worse, each one of us would be under suspicion.

The farmhouse's back door was open, leaving only the screen between me and the fully-lit kitchen. A seemingly untouched Golden Cutie cocktail sweated condensation on a side table. I hurried through the kitchen and the living room and followed the sound of conversation upstairs to the landing.

The layout here was identical to Mrs. Garlington's sister farmhouse a block away. Upstairs was a small bedroom and bathroom along the back of the house. The largest bedroom ran across the front of the house and was undoubtedly Daphne's. Between this bedroom and the back room was another modest bedroom, likely Morgan Stanhope's, so she could be on call for Daphne.

At the top of the stairs I stopped short of Sam's khaki-clad back. He was talking to Morgan, who seemed barely able to catch her breath between sobs. Gibbous lurked in the background. Sam cast me a glance meant to send me back down the stairs, but he couldn't interrupt his talk with Morgan, and I wasn't going anywhere.

I retreated a few steps lower so I could watch without being in the way. Where was the body? The rear bedroom's door was open and the bed looked undisturbed. The middle bedroom appeared equally innocent. A glance through its partially opened door showed that the large front bedroom, although a disaster of tossed clothing and opened suitcases, didn't seem to contain a corpse. That left the bathroom, at the top of the stairs. Sam and Morgan blocked the view.

"I left the party to take care of my usual routine for Daphne," Morgan said.

"And that was?" Sam asked.

"She liked her bath ready at ten p.m. Sharp. I don't fill the tub, but I get everything else ready."

I noted her use of the past tense—she "liked" her bath. The drawn shower curtain hid anything or anyone that might be in the bathtub. Sam studiously avoided looking at me.

"What time was that?" he asked.

"About a quarter to ten."

I remembered the cocktail downstairs. Morgan had said she didn't drink Golden Cuties and Gibbous didn't drink at all. Neither person would have brought one home from the party. Who did?

"Then you went into the bathroom."

Morgan heaved a sob. This was so unlike what she'd expressed before, an emotional range from indifferent to annoyed, that I saw her in a new light. Right now she might have been the heroine of the Tennessee Williams play she'd been carrying earlier.

"Dead," she said. "I called 9-1-1 right away. I could barely see the phone, I was so upset."

For all the snide comments I was ashamed I'd tossed off earlier, I felt awful. Daphne was gone. She'd been loved by so many people, brought joy to so many movie fans. She'd been a real person with real cares and had suffered real heartache. Now she was dead.

A fluff of dog fur pushed past me, and steps sounded on the stairs. Then, to my shock, up came Daphne Morris, the gold dust shimmer of charisma wafting around her. Her expression couldn't have been more joyous. I did a double take and grasped the staircase railing as I let her pass.

"Sam," she said and although it seemed impossible, her smile brightened a few kilowatts. "So good to see you. I missed you at the party. If I'd known you were here, I would have returned sooner."

Sam was in focus mode and didn't seem to take notice of her bombshell charm. Not this very second, anyway. "I'm afraid I have some bad news for you."

I took this moment to creep behind Sam to the bathroom. His attention was on Daphne—everyone's was. Everyone's attention except mine, that is.

Keeping my gaze on Sam, I edged to the bathtub. Through the semi-opaque plastic, I saw a shape. A body. I steeled myself and lifted the shower curtain. The bathtub was full to overflowing, and a foot rested above the tap. A man's foot.

Sam gently grasped Daphne's upper arm. "I'm so sorry, but I have bad news about Chef Bryce."

CHAPTER EIGHT

"**B**ryce!" Daphne lunged toward the bathroom.
Sam grabbed her by the wrist before she reached the bathtub. "This is a crime scene. You need to wait in the hall."

"Bryce," she said. "No. You must be wrong. It can't be."

"I'm sorry," Sam said. "Morgan? Can you take Daphne?"

"What happened?" Daphne's voice was still frantic, but now mixed with befuddlement.

Morgan stepped forward, but Gibbous instead drew Daphne into his black-clad arms. "Stay here," he said. "You don't want to see it."

Behind the clawfoot tub's half-pulled shower curtain, Chef Bryce was dead. His pants, shoes, and porkpie hat were heaped on the floor, but he still wore a T-shirt and boxer shorts. His face, thankfully, was turned toward the wall.

"Are you sure he's—he's—" Daphne said.

"Yes," Sam replied.

Dangling in the bathtub was a blow-dryer. Now I realized why the hall was so dim. The fuse had blown and the hall light was off. Only moonlight illuminated the landing. I took this moment to slip back to the staircase where I could be out of the way but still listen in.

"But that was my bath," Daphne said weakly.

"I was setting out your things when I found him," Morgan said. Gibbous released the actress into Morgan's arms.

Daphne righted herself and pulled away. "I'll never bathe in that tub again."

Sam pressed his palm against the outside of the bathtub. Gauging temperature, was my guess. The crime scene technicians would figure out the rest. Sam's job would be to determine motive and, eventually, the perpetrator. Unless . . .

"Could it have been an accident?" I said. "The last I'd seen Chef Bryce, he'd been drinking." And likely hadn't stopped after I'd left.

Gibbous and Morgan turned to me, as if suddenly realizing I was there.

"That might explain why he'd want a cold bath and might even account for the fact that he's not entirely undressed," Sam said. "But it doesn't explain the blow-dryer."

"When I unpacked it, I put the blow-dryer in the cabinet," Morgan said. "Bryce must have taken it out."

Not likely, was my thought. Anyone unable to fully undress for a bath couldn't do something as fiddly as get out a blow-dryer and plug it in. Besides that, why would he?

Although Sam didn't reply, he seemed to agree. He glanced at the bathroom cupboard, slightly ajar, and back at the bathtub.

Daphne erupted into a hiccupping sob.

"Could you take her downstairs?" Sam nodded at Gibbous. "Morgan, stay here."

I remained silent, grateful I hadn't been dismissed, too.

"You say you were preparing Daphne's bath when you found the chef?" Sam closed the bathroom door behind him and stepped into the hall.

"Like I do every night," Morgan said.

"Tell me your routine." This Sam was so different from the Sam I knew whose attention seemed to drift— although he was always alert beyond the placid expression.

Morgan's eyes darted to the bathroom door, toward Daphne's bedroom, and back to Sam. She was flustered, but somehow kept her patrician cool. "Every night at ten sharp, I prepare Daphne's bath. I make sure the tub is clean—she hates grime on the porcelain—and I lay out a fresh towel, washcloth, her bath salts, and her meditation candle. I make sure she has a clean robe and slippers. I set out notes for the next day and any especially positive fan mail."

"You don't draw the bath?"

"Oh, no. I never know exactly when she'll want it, but I make sure it's ready."

"Tonight? Was there anything special about tonight?"

Morgan searched the air for a response. "Not really. I wasn't sure how long she'd be at the party, but I knew she'd want a bath once she returned. It was easiest to lay things out then go to my room."

"To do what?" Sam asked.

She shrugged. "Check my email. Read. Whatever."

"Was anyone else in the house when you arrived?"

Morgan couldn't help but look at the bathroom door.

"Besides Bryce," Sam said.

"No. Gibbous came in as I was calling you. That's all."

"You can go downstairs now, Ms. Stanhope. Thank you," Sam said.

Halfway down the stairs, Morgan glanced back at us, then continued to the living room.

From the landing, Sam turned to me. "You're not supposed to be here, you know." He didn't scold. He merely stated fact.

"I know." But I didn't move. "You don't think Chef Bryce was the intended victim, do you?"

Bryce was popular, friendly. No one would want to kill him. If they did, they surely wouldn't lead him to a bathtub and electrocute him. There'd be so many easier ways to do it.

Downstairs, a knock at the door signaled the arrival of the sheriff department's technicians.

Sam snapped out of his reverie. He kept his voice low. "I think Daphne had better watch her back."

While the technicians took over upstairs, we convened in the living room. Sam had led the way downstairs, probably figuring I'd go straight out the front door to home. Instead, I quietly perched myself on an uncomfortable side chair pushed against the wall. Daphne, Morgan, and Gibbous sat on the sectional sofa, Gibbous with his arm around Daphne.

Although I'd tried to melt into the background, Morgan wasn't having any of it.

"Why is she staying?" Morgan asked Sam, jerking a thumb at me.

Before Sam could reply, I said, "They might want to question me. After all, I was here and at the party. I saw the body. Maybe I noticed something."

Sam looked at me a long moment before deciding to let it pass. "I'm going to need to talk to each of you, one by one. In the kitchen."

"They thought it was me, didn't they?" Daphne said. "The killer thought it was me and murdered Bryce instead." She spread a throw over her knees. It was a warm evening and the breeze from the living room windows smelled of cut grass, but she shivered. "I told you someone threatened me," she said quietly. "You didn't believe me. I guess you believe me now."

Morgan looked away.

"I believed you," Gibbous said.

"Josie, I'll talk with you first."

Clever. He was going to tell me to get out of Dodge, then move on with the investigation without me. I followed him to the breakfast nook at the far side of the kitchen, overlooking the backyard. It was hard to believe that only that afternoon I'd been standing in the garden, the sun rippling on the birdbath, while Gibbous did sun salutations and Daphne perfected her tan.

I was preparing myself for a scolding, when Sam surprised me. "I need your help." He leaned close enough that I could have touched my forehead to his. I could smell the soap he used to shave. His voice was low. "Another officer is on her way. Until she arrives, watch the others. Pay attention. It will only be for a few minutes."

"I'm game."

"I thought you would be."

Smart aleck. "What do you want me to watch for?"

"Make sure no one leaves or touches anything. They probably won't talk as long as you're there, and that's good. I want them to save their talking for me."

I nodded. This was my chance to prove myself. Besides that, it was in my DNA. I might be only tangentially involved with Chef Bryce's death, but I was involved. I had to help find the person who did this.

He followed me to the living room. "Daphne? Will you come to the kitchen?"

Any elation I'd felt dissipated. I watched Daphne cross the room with a vulnerable grace. Now she'd be the one cozily ensconced in the kitchen nook with Sam. I glanced back to see Sam stand as she seated herself. He'd never done that for me.

In the living room, I took an armchair next to the sofa. From upstairs came muted voices and the creaking of floorboards as technicians moved from the bathroom to hall.

"That was quick," Morgan said.

"He told me he'd question me further later," I lied. "He wants to talk with you first so you can get back to your routines."

Morgan didn't even bother replying and I didn't blame her. What kind of routine could there be when there was a corpse upstairs?

I yearned to give Sam a lead he couldn't get on his own. People would likely say things to me they wouldn't to him. A clue toward Bryce's murder would far outshine my help solving the case of the stolen eggs. Then again,

Sam had told me to be quiet. It only took me a few seconds to decide to follow my own path.

To get conversation going, I said, "It must have been a shock to find Chef Bryce."

Morgan gave me a "no duh" look.

Gibbous said, "Peace be with him."

And that was it. Neither of them spoke further. Morgan picked up her phone, looked at it, and set it aside. From the kitchen, Daphne's melodious laugh filtered to us. Why was she laughing? Now?

"Breathe deeply," Gibbous said. "Three counts in, hold, five out." He demonstrated with three deep snorts and a drafty exhale.

Morgan ignored both of us and stared at an amateur ocean landscape that Duke had picked up at an estate sale at the Maple Grove assisted living center.

"Have you ever considered lavender eye shadow?" Gibbous asked me. "Blended with a hint of camel, of course. I could help you."

I looked at him in surprise. I wasn't sure if I had any eye shadow, actually. A swipe of powder and lipstick were my usual beauty routine—all two minutes of it.

"Shut up," Morgan said. "Bryce is freaking dead. You can talk blushers some other time."

Chagrined, I bit my lip. My efforts toward conversation weren't particularly helpful. What else could I do? I knew. Maybe there were books in the house. Maybe something here could help me. I relaxed into the armchair and let my mind go blank.

A stack of fashion magazines chattered about color and social media stars from upstairs. Daphne's room. Nothing useful there. I let my mental awareness drift to the corner bedroom, the one Gibbous, Leo, and Bryce shared. I sensed wide landscapes and—could it be?—magic. *Folk Traditions in Rural America*. Must be Leo's. He hadn't taken it with him on his trip out of town. A biography of Brillat-Savarin spoke in a suave French accent from the corner. Bryce's nightstand, I was sure. *Sorry, biography*, I told it. *You'll find readers elsewhere*. Morgan's room held a stilted discussion of acting techniques. At least three books jousted for attention, including the one I'd brought that afternoon. None of these books had a message for me that would hint at who might have killed the chef.

"What's this?" Morgan lifted the cocktail glass full of peachy liquid I'd noted earlier. She sniffed it and wrinkled her nose. "A Golden Cutie."

"Don't touch it," I said. "Leave it for Sam." Bryce's fingerprints might be on its stem—or not. Morgan's definitely were now.

"Why?" she said.

"It could be evidence."

Morgan snorted. "We already know Bryce was drunk. What's one more cocktail?"

"It's not for us to say." Sam had given me one simple task: to keep Gibbous and Morgan still and listen. "It might be important."

I was too late. Before I could reach her, she was pouring the cocktail into the potted palm next to her.

"Whoops," she said.

CHAPTER NINE

I passed a fitful night, causing Rodney to decamp for an armchair as I tossed and turned. Finally, I dragged myself from bed just as the sun was rising. The morning was still cool. I'd grown up in the east, where hot summer days meant lightning bugs, electrical storms, and steamy nights. Here, in western Oregon, no matter how warm a day was, nights were sure to be fresh. I heaved up the windows in my bedroom and let a moist breeze from the river rustle the curtains.

In the hall, I leaned on the banister to take in the deceptive quiet in the atrium. The average person would inhale the aroma of beeswax, books, and garden roses that drifted up from the two lower floors and would feel peaceful and alone. I felt peaceful, yes, but hardly alone. Not with so many books eager to tell their stories.

"Hello, books," I said.

The shushes of a thousand books' greetings lifted in

the atrium. I quickly dressed—a cotton sundress over my shoulders and my tangle of hair twisted into a topknot—and continued through the old mansion, opening windows to prepare for the coming heat. Thanks to Lyndon's ministrations, the furnace was a champ, but the library didn't have air-conditioning.

Rodney bumped his head against my calf.

"What, guy?"

He trotted in a circle and kept his gaze on my face.

"You want some magic, don't you?"

He *churrupp*ed in response and sat.

The library wasn't due to open for a few hours. Even though I generally limited my magic to night, when the odds of getting caught were lower, it was now early enough that only the farmers and I were awake. Maybe a few minutes of magic would take my mind off of Chef Bryce's murder. I could exercise my abilities.

"Okay, but just a short one," I told him.

I descended the service staircase to the kitchen and pushed open the door to my office in the former pantry, tucked under the house's main staircase. I knelt and unlatched the storage space under the staircase's narrow end and pulled out an old gramophone I'd found in the attic. When I'd discovered it earlier this summer, Duke had attacked it right away with his screwdriver, and it was now in fine working order. He never could resist a mechanical challenge. I'd unearthed a box of dusty records, too, and Mrs. Garlington had contributed some from her collection.

I set the gramophone in the atrium and selected a thick acetate Fletcher Henderson record from the 1930s and cranked. Rodney threaded between my legs and tried to leap on the gramophone.

"Down, kitten. Are you ready?" To Wilfredians kicking off the covers to the pink dawn, the library was sleeping just above the morning haze over the river. Sun barely touched Big House, to the east. But I felt energy whirling around me.

"Are you ready, books?" I said.

The books' energy rose and tightened. Rodney, feeling the buzz, meowed as if he were singing.

I lowered the needle to the spinning record. I inhaled deeply and couldn't help but smile. "Dance!"

On cue, two books soared from opposite rooms on the ground floor and rose in the atrium's center, spinning around each other in a pas de deux that would have captivated onlookers in a Jane Austen drawing room. Within seconds, other books joined the first two, swirling in a whirlwind pattern.

"Come here, Rodney," I whispered and positioned myself in the atrium's center. I lay back on the cool floor, clasped my hands over my middle, and stared straight up at the show.

I focused my thoughts like an orchestral conductor. The air was now thick with books—foreign language manuals, history books, novels, cookbooks—I choreographed their movements with the music, first into a large flower blossoming, then a moving pinwheel, then an explosion like fireworks. Rodney's soft body, vibrating with his purrs, pressed against me.

I laughed and hundreds of books laughed around me in chortles, girlish giggles, and shrieks of joy as they danced through the air. It was a Busby Berkeley production number for hardbacks.

The gramophone began to slow. I loved these book ballets, and they were terrific exercise for my magic, but it was time to draw this one to a close. I drew another deep breath and willed the books' energy to gather as if it were a bouquet.

"Books," I instructed. "Go home."

The books spun briefly into chaos, then doubled their speed and shot back to their respective rooms. I heard the soft *thunk*s and riffles of them settling onto their shelves just as the gramophone's needle bumped against the record's center.

I pulled myself to sitting, feeling both depleted and joyful. How amazing this magic was. A year ago, I never could have dreamed of anything like it. It was fun and it helped me be a good librarian. A few times, magic had assisted more than that. Could it help me this time to find a murderer?

Rodney batted at a paperback that had skittled across the atrium floor and stopped against the wall. Why hadn't it reshelved itself with the others? The book glowed with magic's halo. I walked toward it. The books had a message for me. I flipped it over. *The Whippoorwill Cries Love*.

"What's this? What do you want me to know?"

Just as the gramophone needle could turn grooves in acetate into jazz, a scene from Roz's novel engaged my brain. It washed over me in layers, like a song sung in rounds, only these verses held murder. In the scene, the killer drops a blow-dryer into a bathtub and electrocutes his victim. Just like Chef Bryce.

Of course, I thought. *The Whippoorwill Cries Love* was romantic suspense. It had two murders—both electrocutions—one uncannily like Chef Bryce's death. It seemed clear that the chef's killer had intended to kill Daphne. The whole town had heard Roz threaten her.

Sam had surely figured out the connection by now. Heck, everyone in town who'd heard about the murder would have. When Daphne Morris had selected *Whippoorwill* for her book club, I'd had to order a couple of dozen extra copies to fill requests from eager Wilfredians.

But what about the death threat Daphne had found on the farmhouse's porch? And her stalker's arrival in Wilfred?

I was thinking this over and tucking the gramophone back into its cupboard when I heard the snick of the kitchen door's bolt.

"Hi, Josie," Roz said. Her skin had a gray cast and her eyes were red. She looked like she'd had less sleep than I had, and that she'd spent the wakeful time in tears.

"Up already?" I asked.

"Couldn't sleep. I figured I might as well come in and write."

"Worried about Lyndon?" I said. I didn't know if she'd heard yet about Chef Bryce. I didn't care that his death was like the murders in *The Whippoorwill Cries Love*. The similarity was no more than a coincidence. There was no way Roz was a killer, no matter how mad she'd been or how loud her threats were.

"No comment."

"I'll start the coffee," I said.

I filled the coffeepot, then pulled a mug from the cupboard, reaching around a couple of airline bottles of booze to do so, and joined Roz at the long kitchen table. "You're not still upset with Lyndon?"

She looked at me with tired eyes. "Are you kidding?

I'm furious. Lyndon and I have known each other all of our lives, and I've loved him for decades. How could he do this to me?" She took my lack of response as encouragement to continue. "You saw him. The second Daphne arrived, I no longer existed. How long did it take to make that corsage for her? You know what flowers mean to him. That corsage was a declaration."

"Of love for Daphne?" I said incredulously.

"That he and I are through." She folded her arms over her chest. "He tried to call, but I wouldn't pick up the phone. Why should I? There was nothing he could say that could take away what he did."

I searched my mind for a helpful response. No book titles leaped to my rescue, but I did have one idea. "How about the romance you wrote a few years back, *The Prince and the Predator?*"

"What about it?" The coffeepot beeped and Roz rose to fill our mugs.

"The one featuring Prince Lyndon of Forster?" I prodded.

"Those names will be changing."

"It was the heroine's jealousy of the predator—the wicked, seductive Duchess of Pretoria—that nearly drove the prince and gardener's daughter apart. You don't want to fall into that trap."

Roz clutched her mug in her plump hands. It read, LEAVE ME ALONE, OR I'LL KILL YOU IN MY NEXT NOVEL. "So what?" She batted at her face with a hand. "Could you grab the fan in the silverware drawer?"

Roz had fans stashed everywhere at the library. I chose a pink one from the spoon compartment and handed it to her.

"You and Lyndon have something he and Daphne Morris could never have. You have history. You know and appreciate each other deeply. Of course Lyndon's going to be starstruck when there's someone like Daphne around. Why not let him enjoy it? In a week, she'll be gone."

The gruesome possibility came to mind that she'd be gone sooner than that. Gone to the morgue, that is. "And why wreck the publicity you'll get for *The Whippoorwill Cries Love*?"

"I don't know," she said, but I could tell I'd at least planted a seed of doubt. Now for my next message. I cleared my throat. "Did you hear about Chef Bryce?"

"No, why?"

"Well . . ." I began and searched for the right way to tell her before settling on the straightforward. "He died."

The words were barely out of my mouth when Roz said, "What?"

"Actually, it was worse."

"What could be worse than that?"

"He was murdered."

Her mouth hung open. "You're joking."

"It happened last night. Morgan, Daphne's assistant, found him dead in the bathtub. Sam thinks the murderer might have been trying for Daphne. Remember the death threat she found yesterday? The shower curtain was pulled, so the murderer might have mistaken Bryce for her."

"I can't—that is—what happened?"

There was not a single doubt in my mind that Roz was innocent. After pitching her fit at the party, she'd been in her trailer at the Magnolia Rolling Estates all evening, probably watching movies on the Heartbreak Haven channel, laying waste to a pint of ice cream, and cursing Daphne under her breath. I was certain. She needed to know about the link between Bryce's death and her novel.

"Roz, there's something you should know. The way the chef was killed . . . well—"

Sam came in the kitchen door in his uniform, looking sterner than I'd ever seen him.

"Coffee?" I said hopefully.

He ignored me. "Roz. I'd hoped you'd be here. I tried your trailer, but you weren't home."

"What's this about Chef Bryce being murdered? That's crazy! Right here in Wilfred," she said. "Josie just told me."

"Roz," he repeated. "I need to take you to the station for questioning."

CHAPTER TEN

You can't take Roz," I said. "She was home practically all night. Bianca—Daphne's stalker—she's the one you should be looking for."

"Yeah," Roz said, nodding. "What's this about?"

"Anyone could have read Roz's book and copied it," I added. The truth teller in me was gaining steam.

"So true," Roz said, putting two and two together. "Anyone could have electrocuted him. That's what you're getting at, isn't it?"

"You know how he died?" Sam asked.

"Just figuring it out from conversation. Am I right?" When Sam didn't reply, she shook her head vigorously. "Nope. It's a coincidence, that's all."

"It wasn't just that Bryce was electrocuted." Sam shifted his gaze from me to Roz. "You were heard threatening Daphne Morris."

"Well, of course—" Roz's face reddened.

"And we found your fan at the scene."

Her fan? Neither of us could speak.

"She has fans everywhere," I said, finally. "You know that. She had the PO Grocery order her a gross last fall. Someone must have stolen one to frame her." I leaned forward. "Maybe Roz has a hot temper, but you know she's no murderer."

Sam's voice softened. "I'm not going to lock her up, Josie. Just ask a few questions."

"Then why does she have to go to the station?"

"So we can record her, have a witness. Get her finger-prints. You know, the usual."

"I'm fine with it. Honestly," Roz said, her voice un-usually sweet. She nonchalantly slipped the pink fan under her purse. "I go, I answer a few questions, I figure out how I could have lost a fan. This way Sam can rule me out. Just one thing."

"What's that?" Sam asked.

"I need another fan. There's one in my desk." She held up both palms. "You know I'm not going to run for it."

Roz's face was reddening. Her epic hot flashes were Wilfred lore. There was no way Sam could deny her a fan.

"Fine," Sam said.

After a raised eyebrow from Roz, I followed her to the conservatory. She pulled out her desk drawer to five fans, lined up next to a box of pens.

"You've got to get me out of this," she whispered as she slipped a red fan into her hip pocket. "Someone has it in for me. Who can say what else they have lined up?"

"I know," I said, aware of Sam waiting in the kitchen.

Outside the conservatory's glass walls, Lyndon staked dahlias along the river path. He was up early, too. I hoped his head was full of Roz and not Daphne.

"Every minute counts," Roz said. "After I left, I was at home all night—honest. Except for a few minutes."

I cocked my head. "A few minutes?"

"It was nothing, really."

"Come clean, Roz."

She glanced toward the conservatory's doorway, then stepped closer to me. "I did have the thought of . . . well, making Daphne pay."

Oh no. "What did you do?"

"I changed my mind, honest. I just—well, after I left the party, I went to the farmhouse with a canister of cayenne pepper." She raised her head. "To swap out for Daphne's turmeric."

"I can't believe it. You dropped a fan, didn't you?"

"Maybe," she said. "I guess so. I didn't even go in the house, though. I cut through the backyard, then turned back. Didn't even touch the doorknob. I figured it wasn't her fault Lyndon is a no good, cheating two-timer."

"Oh, Roz. Did anyone see you?"

"I saw someone poke her head around the side of the house. I think it was a woman, but I'm not sure."

"A witness," I said. "This is not good."

"You've got to help me," she whispered.

"Did you get your fan?" Sam said from the doorway.

"Right here," Roz replied and patted her pocket. She crossed the conservatory, and before she reached the door, she turned to me. She didn't say a word, but I caught the plea in her eyes.

* * *

I needed a strategy.

First, I had to prove Roz's alibi. Timing mattered. Roz said she was at home most of the night—except for her short trip to the farmhouse. Maybe someone in the Magnolia Rolling Estates saw her in her trailer. I'd also need to establish when Bryce had left the party.

At the same time, I wanted to find out where Bianca had been. According to Leo, she was unhinged. If, as Sam had deduced, Daphne was the murderer's real intended victim, Bianca topped the list of suspects. Plus, Roz thought she'd seen a woman lurking near the farmhouse.

The problem was that I was stuck at the library. I didn't even have Roz to work in my place. Thanks to Wilfredians' need of a local hangout now that the café was closed, combined with last night's party and murder to discuss, it was sure to be busy. More than a librarian, I'd need crowd control.

Dylan, our intern, was waiting at the front door when I unlocked it.

"Good morning, Ms. Way," he said.

"Josie," I replied automatically, even though I knew he'd revert to "Ms."

As usual, he'd leaned his bicycle against the old house's porch and was unstrapping the bands that kept his trousers out of the spokes. A white rosebud was tucked into a buttonhole.

"You've been interning here a while now," I said as he followed me into Circulation and New Releases.

"Almost eighteen months," he said with pride.

"Roz is out for a few hours, and I have an important errand. How would you like to run the place? It wouldn't be for long."

He straightened. "You can depend on me, Ms. Way. I

know the Dewey decimal system inside and out. Between patrons, I'll work on my section."

I'd given Dylan his own shelf, which he used for a rotating, themed selection of materials. Right now it held movies featuring Cary Grant. I knew he was perfectly capable of helping patrons find and check out books, but he was an easygoing guy. I wasn't sure he was cut out to be a bouncer.

"Do you remember the kitchen rules?" I asked.

" 'No yelling, no booze, and feet off the table,' " he recited. " 'Animals must be on a leash and can't leave the kitchen, except Rodney.' Don't worry."

"The knitting club will be in this afternoon, but I should be back by then."

"Don't worry," he repeated. "Things will be okay."

Dylan's assurances were going to have to be good enough. "Call me if anything comes up, okay?" I told him as I left.

"I told you, everything will be just fine."

CHAPTER ELEVEN

A moment later, I was blinking into the morning sun, walking down the hill, Rodney darting along the path in front of me.

"You're going to help, are you?" I asked him.

He turned his head toward me and flicked his tail. I wouldn't send him back. He might be useful. He had been useful before.

Between the Kirby River and the washed-out shell of Darla's café, cedar trees flanked the driveway to the Magnolia Rolling Estates. The drive formed the park's central spine, with half-a-dozen trailers parked on each side. With luck, someone had seen Roz and could confirm she was home when Bryce had been killed. Better, someone might have caught a glimpse of Bianca.

Duke's home was the second trailer on the right, just behind Darla's grand double-wide with its twisted iron-work porch, undoubtedly meant to mimic a New Orleans town house. Duke had been dancing the night of Chef Bryce's death, but between foxtrots he might have noticed something.

I was in luck. Duke was in his toolshed. I crossed his lawn—mowed in sharp, crisscrossing ribbons—and cleared my throat outside the beige aluminum shed.

Duke stood up so quickly that he hit his head on the doorway. "Damn it, Josie. Why'd you sneak up on me?"

"I didn't," I said. This wasn't starting out well. "I wanted to talk to you about last night. About Daphne," I added, thinking this might spark a smile.

Instead, he scowled. "Don't say that name around me." He returned to the toolshed and packed some kind of apparatus with wires into a toolbox.

"Why not?"

"What did they expect me to do to the farmhouse? Turn it into the Ritz? I only had a little over a week to gussy it up. I certainly wasn't going to install a new electrical panel." He locked the shed behind him.

"Then you've heard."

"Saw the emergency vehicles when I was cleaning up at the This-N-That, then Sam called me over to look at the electrical situation in the basement."

By noon, everyone in Wilfred would know about Bryce's death. "Surely, Daphne doesn't blame you for it? You didn't drop a plugged-in blow-dryer into the tub." I leaned forward with a half smile. "Did you?"

His sour mood exploded into a belly laugh. "That's a good one. No. One of the investigators wanted to know why the circuit breaker hadn't tripped."

"There wasn't a circuit breaker." Duke had said the old house had a fuse box. "Wouldn't the fuse have blown?" I asked.

"Normally a fuse pops even faster than a breaker."

"You said 'normally'"

"Exactly. In this case, someone had put a penny behind the fuse."

I felt Rodney's head nudge my calf, and I crouched to scratch him between the ears. "Are you saying it was premeditated?"

Duke shook his head. "Doubt it. Every one of those fuses had a penny screwed in behind it. It's an old trick to keep the fuse from blowing if it's overly sensitive. An old and deadly trick." He inclined his head toward Rodney, who was pawing at Duke's screen door. "You keep that cat out of my trailer."

Rodney didn't want to go in. If I knew him, he was just playing with Duke's head. Rodney dropped to the ground and nosed his way behind the aluminum panels skirting the trailer's foundation.

"Someone would have had to know about the pennies to be sure the blow-dryer would electrocute Bryce, then. Or they got lucky." Another thought occurred. "In all the time you worked on the farmhouse, did you ever see Roz there?"

"Roz? Sure, I guess she came over to check out the paint job and the kitchen."

Along with everyone else, I thought. I'd been there for Duke's grand unveiling, too. He'd made quite a show of his efforts at interior decor, including a gold velveteen recliner, a macramé plant hanger he'd knotted himself, and several amateur landscape paintings. The house could have been featured in magazines as a classic example of "ironic chic."

"How about the fuse box? Did she see that?"

"Why would she? Roz wouldn't go down into that smelly basement. No way." His eyes widened. "Say, the chef died the same way Roz killed off those bad guys in her whippoorwill story, huh?"

"How do you know that?" Duke was more for reading Westerns and space operas, with the occasional DVD of a musical thrown in for variety. "Wait, you're the one who's been sneaking out romance novels and returning them on the sly, aren't you?"

"Are you calling me a thief?"

I should have felt it sooner. Three Regency romances cooed from inside his trailer with a soundtrack of galloping horses and windy sighs.

"Did you like *The Voluptuous Viscount*? How about *The Duke Who Did*?"

"I don't know what you're talking about," he said. "And keep your voice down."

"A librarian never lends and tells, Duke. You might really enjoy one of the Amish romances we just got in."

"I'm late," he said abruptly. "Got to test every one of those fuses now and make sure they work as intended, penny-free."

Rodney emerged from under the trailer, dragging a worn work glove, which he deposited in front of Duke.

Duke knelt to pick it up. "Haven't seen that glove all summer. Thanks, little guy."

"Before you go, about Roz again. Did you see her the night of the party? Maybe leaving the trailer park?"

"Didn't see a thing. My eyes were full of Daphne, that ungrateful vixen. Besides, did you try one of those Golden Cuties? Powerful. Doubt I could remember if I saw Roz even if I did. No one would."

* * *

Rodney had already trotted to my next destination: Lalena's trailer. Rodney might have taken a disliking to Duchess, but he did like dogs—certain dogs. He and Lalena's terrier mutt Sailor were buddies and played when Lalena made her weekly visit to the library for a bath in the mansion's giant second-story tub, followed by dinner with me. Rodney and Sailor chased each other through the empty library, Sailor yapping every now and again when Rodney pounced on him from some hiding spot.

Lalena's mid-century pink trailer was marked by a fluff of roses around her mailbox, and a sign lettered PALM READINGS, APPLY WITHIN hanging from its post. Sailor must have seen us, because he was already barking.

Lalena, bologna sandwich in hand and wearing a frilled pink peignoir, opened the door. Sailor bolted down the steps.

"Lunch, already?" I said.

"No," she replied between mouthfuls. "A late breakfast. What's up?"

I followed Lalena into her trailer, Rodney and Sailor on my heels. Lalena had inherited the trailer from her aunt, an accountant at the old mill with a deep love of pink. The windows were open, and the scent of roses, Duke's freshly cut lawn, and the wind off the millpond nudged me to stop and breathe deeply. Since my magic had appeared, less than a year ago, my senses were on overdrive.

Lalena relaxed into a chair at her dinette set, also where she met clients. She pushed aside a romance novel, which sighed amorously, and she clicked off the clown-shaped lamp. "I'll see you tonight for our regular Tuesday date?"

"Definitely. Nice lounging outfit," I added.

"My aunt's. It's a little short." She stood up and the ruffled hem bounced just below her knees. She sat again, polishing off the sandwich's last bite. "My psychic powers tell me you didn't come here for fashion commentary."

"Your psychic powers are right," I said. In reality, Lalena's powers leaned more toward finding out who'd drop a few dollars for her services than toward divining the future. "Did you see Roz last night?"

"At the party?" she said. "Who didn't? Wow, was she steamed about Lyndon and Daphne."

"No, I mean after that. At the trailer park."

"Sure. Why?"

"Well, since she—" I stopped short. Lalena might not have even heard about the murder. "You know about Chef Bryce, right?"

"Kind of hunky, don't you think? I gave him a palm reading. Free. Nice, strong hands that man has. I told him he could look forward to many children."

"Did you notice anything unusual about the life line?"

I told her about Bryce's death and how it pointed to Roz. I had to hand it to Lalena: She was a good audience, gasping at the right moments and shaking her head in disbelief.

When I finished, she said, "They're questioning Roz? Really? She's not a murderer. She's such a pessimist that she'd figure fate would take care of it for her."

"That's why I wanted to know if you'd seen her. If we can establish she was at home when Bryce was killed, Sam can cross her name off the list."

"I don't know," Lalena said. She drew up her legs and pulled the peignoir over her knees. "I mean, I wasn't looking for her, so it's not like I checked the clock. When I took Sailor out for a potty break, her lights were on. That doesn't mean she was in, though."

"No, but it's something," I said. "Did you see her behind the curtains, maybe? Moving around?"

"Nope. Or, if I did, I don't remember. Roz isn't that interesting to spy on."

"How long were you at the party last night? You didn't see anyone hanging around the chef, did you?"

"You mean, besides me? No. I was only there an hour or so. I had a client at eight o'clock. A new one. I didn't want to be late."

"But you did see Roz."

"Sure," Lalena said. "I went to the party, returned in time for my session, then took Sailor on his evening walkies. That had to be just shy of, oh, nine-thirty," she said before I could ask. "Roz was coming home from somewhere."

Coming home from an aborted revenge attempt on Daphne, I knew. This was good, since it reaffirmed what Roz had told me, but it was not so good in that it left plenty of time for her to have snuck out and returned to the farmhouse in time to kill Bryce.

So far, I had nothing to help Roz. As we spoke, townspeople were probably tearing up the library, while Dylan cluelessly arranged Cary Grant movies on his shelf.

I tried one last sally. "Who was the client? Maybe he or she saw something."

Lalena shrugged and popped down her knees, turning to face me on the other side of the Formica-topped table.

"A stranger in town, actually. A girl named Bianca. She had this great pink—"

I sat upright so fast that I jiggled the table. Lalena put up a hand to stop the clown lamp from toppling.

"Bianca! Why didn't you say so?"

"Why should I? You know her? I'd seen her at the PO Grocery earlier in the day, and we got to talking. I told her my biz, and we made arrangements to meet up last night. She had concerns to sort out."

"What kind of concerns?"

"Psychic-client privilege, Josie. I can't tell you the details, but I will say that she has a lot on her mind."

"Does it have to do with anger toward Daphne Morris, by chance?"

Lalena turned away and lifted her chin. "Won't say."

I put my elbows on the table and leaned forward. "You know Daphne has a restraining order against her, right? Sam says whoever killed Chef Bryce probably thought they were dropping the blow-dryer into Daphne's bath. Bianca's a suspect. Plus, the same day she arrived, a death threat appeared on the farmhouse's porch."

Lalena looked momentarily puzzled. Then determined. "She didn't say anything about killing Daphne."

I wasn't so easily convinced. "Did she say where she's staying? She can't be in town. Daphne and her crew are in the only house for rent." One thing about Wilfred, it was small enough to keep tabs on everyone.

She hesitated, then said, "She didn't tell me. I can't say anything specific, except that I don't think she'd kill Daphne. The opposite, in fact. I think you have it all wrong. But I will tell you she was eager to be somewhere and kept checking her phone for the time."

I stood just as Rodney shot from the bedroom and bounced off the half-wall dividing the kitchen from the living room. His hind end whipped around and he faced Sailor, who froze in mock terror. Rodney loved faking him out.

"The sheriff's department might not recognize the psychic's pledge of confidentiality," I said.

"Then let them come ask me." She pulled Sailor into her lap. "There was one thing, though. When I went to close the screen door after saying goodbye to Bianca, I saw someone."

"What?" I said before she'd finished her thought.

"No big deal. Daphne's assistant. What's her name?"

"Morgan," I said. "Morgan Stanhope. What was she doing?"

"Nothing, really. Probably just stretching her legs. She walked a bit up the trailer park, stopped outside my trailer, then went back toward the This-N-That. I don't think she saw me."

I drummed my fingers on the dinette table. Morgan. It wasn't much of a lead, but I'd take it.

CHAPTER TWELVE

Visiting Morgan was now next on my agenda.

Should I stop by the library first? I glanced up the bluff, over the cottonwoods sheltering the Kirby River, to the old mansion's tower and gables. It was only midday, but that didn't mean Wilfredians weren't making hay in the library's kitchen. Still looking at the sun glinting off the mansion's cupola, I called the library.

"Good afternoon," Dylan answered. "Wilfred Library. May I help you?"

His polite tone warmed my heart. "Dylan, it's me. Josie. How are things there?"

"Hi, Ms. Way. Nothing much is happening here. I'm working on my collection for Cary Grant. " His voice leaped a few notes. "Did you know he appeared in seventy-seven movies? Isn't that amazing? Do you think we could have a Cary Grant film night? We could put a screen in the atrium."

"What I'm worried about is—" *the kitchen*, I'd been planning to say, when he cut in.

"Money, right? Don't think twice about that. A couple of the best ones—*Charade* and *His Girl Friday* are in the public domain. Won't cost us a cent."

As I talked, Rodney trotted toward the main road, undoubtedly on his way to Daphne's farmhouse. I knew I'd better catch up before he got into a tussle with Duchess. At least I wasn't hearing organ music or explosions in the background during the call.

"That sounds fine," I said quickly and hung up. "Rodney, wait up."

He was already at the main road, carefully looking up and down the highway for traffic. I swept him up in my arms and he gave my cheek a lick.

"Troublemaker," I told him. "If you're coming with me, I expect you to play it cool with the Pomeranian. Understand?"

Rodney's tail switched against my waist. I put him down on the other side of the road, on the sidewalk running along Patty's This-N-That, and he set off toward the farmhouse.

Morgan was on the farmhouse's porch swing, typing at a laptop. Even with a stack of papers on the table next to her and clearly a heap of work to do, she managed to look elegantly casual, as if she'd dropped in from an East Coast lake resort and would soon be in a canoe on the lake with a Princeton undergraduate and a picnic basket.

"Josie. What can I do for you?" she asked, head still lowered, fingers on the keyboard.

Rodney leaped onto the windowsill and peered in the living room window, looking for Duchess. We hadn't passed any dead fish to roll in, so that was a plus.

"I have a question for you about last night." She hadn't invited me to take the chair next to her, so I settled on the porch rail.

She raised her head. "All I've been doing is answering questions about last night. If you want to know anything, check with the sheriff."

"Not about when you found Bryce. Earlier."

"I don't want to talk about yesterday ever again. I'm sure you understand. What's it to you, anyway?" Despite her obvious send-off, she'd set the laptop aside and looked at me full-on.

"It's about Roz." Roz was necessary to Daphne—and so to Morgan—for the book club television segment. I hoped this would be enough to secure Morgan's attention.

"And? I can't see what she has to do with anything." She lifted an eyebrow. "Unless it has to do with *The Whippoorwill Cries Love*."

"You know," I said.

"Two electrocutions." She shook her head. "Not exactly subtle. I saw it right away and told Sheriff Wilfred. Plus, they found one of her fans in the backyard."

"A total coincidence, I'm sure. I just wanted to know if you'd seen Roz earlier in the evening."

"Before she threatened to kill Daphne or after?" Morgan said.

"After." I gritted my teeth. Apparently, Duchess was nowhere to be found, because Rodney jumped to the railing next to me and butted his head on my arm. "But maybe you took a stroll at some point and saw her?"

"No." Morgan looked past me, her focus somewhere in the vicinity of Ruth Littlewood's bird-watching tower.

Mrs. Littlewood had it built during the spring and had already compiled notebooks of bird sightings destined for the library's natural history collection.

"You're sure," I said.

"No, wait. In fact, I did take a walk. I checked out the trailer court on the other side of the café. What's it called, again?"

"The Magnolia Rolling Estates," I said.

"That's right. A palm reader, too. Quaint." She smoothed her capris over her thighs. "You know, I did see someone, come to think of it. A woman. Could have been Roz."

"Where was she?"

"Walking out the back end of the trailer court, furtive-like. I just caught her back. She looked like Roz. Short-ish, and, you know." Morgan made a round shape with her hands.

Behind the trailer court was a stretch of meadow, then the millpond and old mill site. If Roz had left through the rear of the trailer court, she might have counted on circling the This-N-That without anyone seeing her. Especially with the Golden Cuties flowing. She'd miscalculated.

"What's going on out here?" Daphne pushed open the screen door, leaning against the doorframe like a calico sprigged goddess in a Great Depression drama. Duchess bounded out with her. "I'm trying to watch TV, but the power keeps going out."

"It's that handyman in the basement," Morgan said. "Checking the wiring."

Rodney twitched at my side. *Don't you dare*, I told him silently. I knew that crafty look in his eyes. He cocked his head to keep a better eye on Duchess, who panted at my feet, gazing adoringly at him.

"I was in the middle of *Love's Tortured Tune-Up*," Daphne said. "Features a mechanic and this poor girl with frazzled spark plug wires."

"I'll save you the trouble." Morgan didn't even bother to look at her. She pulled the laptop back to her lap. "They fall in love. There's a misunderstanding. They get back together. The end."

"What's with you, anyway, Morgan?" Daphne said. "You've been in the worst mood lately."

I shot a glance at Rodney. He was poised on the porch rail and his gaze was fixed on Duchess.

"Don't mind me," Morgan replied. "I'm just here doing your indispensable work. Right now it's getting the contract back from your agent. Oh, and hunting down back stock of your favorite lipstick."

I looked from one woman to the other. Something was going on here. "Daphne, did you happen to see Roz last night? I mean, after she yelled at . . . uh, Lyndon?"

She looked at me as if I'd grown another head. "No. Why should I?"

"What about Bianca?" I asked.

At that moment, Rodney leapt from the railing, landing squarely on Duchess's back and latching his nails in her collar. Duchess took off from the porch with Rodney riding her back like he was the Lone Ranger and she was Silver. The dog's nails clattered on the porch steps, then silenced as Duchess launched onto the front lawn.

"Duchess!" Daphne yelled. "I can't believe it. First Bryce, now this."

Morgan barely lifted her head from the computer.

Rodney, I willed him, *get off of her. Now.*

Duchess cut a figure eight over the lawn. Who knew those short legs could run so fast? Rodney, still holding on, looked up at me, his eyes full of terror. He couldn't let go, I realized, without flying into the bushes. Furthermore, Duchess was enjoying it. *Serves you right*, I told him silently.

Daphne, barefoot, raced down from the porch and set out after her dog, who took her mistress's yells as a sign the game was on. The animals continued their circus show, Duchess letting out a joyful yip every few seconds and Rodney hunkered down in pure panic.

Finally, Duchess veered near the crab apple tree, and Rodney leaped to its trunk and scrambled onto a branch. Duchess jumped at the trunk and wagged her squirrel-like tail.

Rodney eyed me with a *Please, help* look. No way. I rested my hands on my hips. He'd gotten himself into this mess and he could get himself out. He knew the way home.

Daphne snatched up the panting Duchess, her hair and the dog's fur shining golden in the afternoon light. She went into the house and let the screen door slam behind her. When she returned, she was alone.

"Now, what's this about Bianca?" she asked.

Morgan lifted her head. "I knew she'd be trouble."

"You haven't received any more death threats, have you?" I asked.

Daphne shook her head. "How did she find me, anyway? I thought you did things to make sure no one knew where we were."

"I honestly don't know," Morgan said. "I haven't even seen her. Josie did."

Daphne sank into the porch's other chair. "Bryce," she said simply. All of the actress's poise fell away, and I saw a woman who, in another life, might have been a small-town cocktail waitress trading on her looks and charm for tips. "I can't believe he's gone. I woke up expecting to hear him in the kitchen—"

"—making your breakfast," Morgan said wryly.

"—and then I remembered." Despite the July warmth, Daphne hugged herself, digging her fingers into her upper arms. "I'll never take a bath in that tub again."

Morgan raised an eyebrow. "Never? Your baths are so important to you. What will you do?"

I recalled the shelves upstairs of lotions and creams with fancy labels. Morgan was probably calculating the work she'd save by not being Daphne's bathing attendant. Normally, I would have sympathized, but Daphne looked truly despondent, and I didn't like Morgan's tone. Why did Daphne keep her around, anyway?

"You and Bryce, you grew up together, didn't you?" I said.

Head down, she nodded. "What a terrible idea to come to Wilfred early, thinking I could get away from everything. What was I thinking? I can never escape my fame."

"It must be difficult," I said.

"Bryce was the one who really wanted to come. He said it would be like old times out in the country. We could have picnics, go for walks. No one would know us or bother us." She sighed. "I wanted to believe him. I thought maybe, just maybe, if I had a taste of how things used to be, before the movies and the attention . . . well, maybe I'd be all right."

"I'm so sorry." Rodney had returned to the porch and nosed himself into my lap. I let a hand rest on his silky back. "We have a nice bathtub upstairs at the library, and you're welcome to use it anytime you'd like."

"Bathe in the library?" Morgan asked.

"We have a few regulars from the trailer park who like a good bath from time to time. It's a six-foot tub."

Thinking of the library, I'd been away too long. There was no telling what was happening in my absence. I stood and Rodney leaped to the porch railing, then to the lawn and stretched. Another day, another adventure.

"I'd better get back to work. Thank you for letting me drop by, and I'm sorry about my cat."

Daphne waved and vanished into the farmhouse.

Just as I turned to leave, the screen door opened and Gibbous Moon stepped out, a Japanese etching-turned-human in an angular black T-shirt and black stovepipe jeans. His feet were bare and a ring sparkled from a middle toe.

"Josie Way," he said in a clipped voice. "Just the person I wanted to see."

"Yes?"

"About last night. I've been thinking about it. Well, I want to talk to you."

CHAPTER THIRTEEN

I faced Gibbous, my breath stuck in my windpipe. He'd seen something. He had something to tell me. "Yes?"

"Who cuts your hair?" he asked.

"Why?"

"May I?"

In response to my nod, he padded across the porch as soundlessly as a cat and lifted my hair above my ears. He tipped up my chin. I had on sunscreen and a swipe of lip gloss, but that was all. Rodney watched from the front path.

"My life's mission is to create beauty," he said.

"Hmm," Morgan opined from her bench. She re-opened her laptop and resumed typing.

"Yes?" I said uncertainly.

"Do you have half an hour?" he said. "I'd like to make you over."

Crowds of people would hand over their kidneys for

the touch of Gibbous's makeup brushes. I preferred the natural look. Still, it was an opportunity to talk with him about last night without having to make excuses.

"All right, but I'm not much for makeup," I said.

"I can see that." He turned toward the house, sure I would follow.

I did. He pointed to a chair near the kitchen counter. "Have a seat. I'll be down in a moment."

Afternoon sun poured through the kitchen windows, glancing off the espresso machine's buffed chrome. From upstairs I made out the drone of a television movie with a violin-laden soundtrack. Could Gibbous be the murderer? I'd seen him briefly at the party talking to Bryce, and he'd been at the farmhouse when I arrived after Sam. As for timing—where he was and when—I knew nothing yet.

Gibbous returned with a toolbox and two spray bottles. He unfurled a towel on the counter and set the toolbox on it, popping open its lid. Again, he tipped up my chin and examined my face thoroughly. Seeming to have made a decision, he dampened a washcloth and pressed it to my forehead and chin.

"Did you have fun at the party last night?" I asked when my mouth was free, knowing he hadn't been there long—at least, not while I was around.

"I don't drink or ingest intoxicants," he said, fixed on his task. He turned to the makeup kit. "As Kapil Gupta says, 'Chasing pleasure brings pleasure. But it does not bring satisfaction.'"

Pots of color lay in meticulous rows in the toolbox, including a fungus-like green and an orange that could have been used for traffic cones. "If you could just go easy—"

"No worries," he said.

Gibbous's touch was relaxing. With the sun through the window and the acupressure of his fingertips, it would be easy to doze. Unbidden, a book title came to mind: *The New Age Guide to Filthy Lucre*.

"When you strike out on your own, you'll be a superstar," I said. "I mean, you're going to start your own business, right?"

"Lunar Looks," he said promptly. " 'For an otherworldly glow.' "

I laughed. "It's perfect."

Gibbous smiled. "It's what I was born to do. Create beauty. No—that's wrong. Each of us is already beautiful. What I do is bring it to the surface, help each person be more of themself. It's not about creating some popular look. You know, the puffy lip or smoky eye. It's about tuning in to an individual's inner beauty."

"I love that." His enthusiasm was catching. If his cosmetics line were on sale now, I'd have dropped a paycheck on them.

"You, for instance." He stepped back and appraised me again. "There's a lot you keep hidden, isn't there?" Thankfully, he didn't wait for my response before continuing. "I'll succeed if I can bring forward your sensitivity and humor—and make the most of your striking coloring."

Now I understood why Daphne kept him close. The man made me feel like a forgotten princess. "When are you going to launch Lunar Looks?"

His fingers stopped. "Not anytime soon." I thought I caught a hint of an East Coast working-class accent. Slowly, his fingers resumed their work, this time tapping lightly over my jaw. "I still need to finish my contract with Daphne."

"You can't do two things at once? Surely Daphne doesn't need you every hour of the day."

"I don't have to be doing her makeup for her to need me. She wants to know I'm on call. She gets lots of interview requests and last-minute appearances. If I'm giving seminars or traveling, I'm not available for her." His tone didn't betray his feelings one way or another.

A long time to suspend a life's dream. "No way to ease out of the contract earlier?"

"None. I have most of the investment money pulled together, but my lawyer says breaking the contract would bankrupt me."

"Daphne wouldn't let you go."

"No chance of it," he said in a matter-of-fact manner. He reached for a hand towel and patted it over my face. "But it's all good. It's all part of the universe's plan."

Or part of a motive for murder, I thought. "At some point you'll want to move on."

"Sure," he said. "I may be able to convince Daphne to renegotiate eventually. She understands what it is to know your purpose in life." He washed his hands in the kitchen sink before returning, this time to the pots of color. "I've always loved making people beautiful. When I was in middle school, I used to do my grandma's hair and makeup for church, and by the time I reached high school, her whole bridge club would come over for makeovers. It's my gift. I was born to do this. I almost feel like it's bigger than I am."

"I understand," I said and meant it. He should try being a witch. Talk about destiny. "Your fingers feel terrific. Did you train in acupressure?"

He laughed. "No. In juvenile delinquency, actually. In

high school it was more fun to pick locks than study algebra. That was a long time ago, in a land far, far away."

And a fact not emphasized in Gibbous's media coverage. "I hear a little bit of New Jersey in your voice."

"Spot-on. Trenton. We had a sweet little house a lot like this one, actually."

"Did your family give you trouble? About being a makeup artist, I mean?"

"Not a bit. You'd think I would have been bullied at school or encouraged by my parents to study engineering or work at the plant with Dad, but no. They supported me. I think they were simply glad to see me interested in something more legitimate than breaking into other students' lockers."

I noticed his use of the past tense. "Supported?"

"They died in a car wreck. After I moved to New York." His fingers dropped to the counter. I couldn't see him since he stood behind me, but I imagined him staring through the kitchen window, remembering.

"I'm so, so sorry."

He inhaled three sharp breaths and exhaled one long one. More Kundalini breathing. "I'm happy to have had them as long as I did."

"They would have been so proud to see you now—the magazine coverage, the looks you created turning up on TV and in the movies." I caught his reflection in a glass-fronted cupboard and could imagine a younger, awkward Gibbous inside the stone-faced, black-clad body. "I hope Daphne sees things your way and frees you to start your makeup line. She must understand."

"She doesn't yet, but she will. Tilt your chin toward me."

The tender Gibbous was gone. He was all business. With a clean cloth, he dabbed at my nose and forehead.

"Too bad you didn't stay longer by the party. It was a lot of fun," I said in an attempt to return to the task at hand.

"I wanted to drop by, that's all. It would have been unfriendly not to say hello. Bryce was a generous man. Making people happy was what he did best." His hand was busy spreading some sort of coconut-scented cream on my cheeks. "I'm going to miss him."

The gentle grief in his voice touched me. "You must really feel his loss."

The facial part of the makeover was finished, and I smelled faintly of orange flower and soap. Gibbous was now in his zone as a stylist. He slipped the bobby pins from my hair and fluffed its curls around my shoulders. Then he gathered up the sides and did something with them on top of my head. On the towel lay a variety of brushes and pots of color, but no hand mirror.

I had the sense he'd rather not talk, but I was determined to make something of this time. "But you weren't here last night." At his surprised glance, I added, "Morgan mentioned you'd arrived when she was calling the sheriff's office. Maybe you went for a walk?"

Deep in his work, he made a noncommittal noise and reached for a tube of concealer. I hoped he wasn't going to cake it on.

He dabbed a bit near my nose and nodded once with satisfaction.

"There's a nice trail to the old mill site," I said, hoping to encourage some sort of information.

Feathery touches swept my nose and chin. He reached for a wide-domed brush and dipped it in translucent powder. "You want to know where I was last night, is that it?"

"Well, I—"

"As I told the sheriff, I went for a walk as night was falling." His hand paused. "You can see the Milky Way from the meadow, even with half a moon."

The meadow was on the other side of the Magnolia Rolling Estates. "It's beautiful, isn't it? You didn't happen to see anyone else, did you?"

"I was alone. I meditated near the pond. Then I returned home to find the house full of police."

He'd been near the millpond, too far from the trailer court to testify that Roz was home, and too late to see the stranger she'd caught a glimpse of at the farmhouse. I took in Gibbous's shaved head and monk-like clothing. I could certainly picture him perched on a boulder near the millpond, with the frogs croaking and crickets chirping and the cool, wet smell of the river. Of course, I had only his word for where he was.

There was little to no way Bianca would be wandering the meadow at night, but it was worth a question. "I wonder where Bianca was?"

"I didn't see her, either. I told the sheriff about her. She's not well." He reached for a tube of mascara. "A pity. Her heart is warm. But she's fundamentally unstable. Dangerous, even."

"What do you mean? Has she threatened Daphne before?"

"No. Not in so many words, that is. She had an unhealthy obsession with Daphne at first. Couldn't keep her away. Then it flipped. They're cousins, you know."

"Leo mentioned that earlier."

"Same big family in Arkansas. They grew up together, along with Bryce. Daphne doesn't like to advertise it. She's clear that she doesn't want a past. She wants the public to see her as eternally what she is now." As he spoke, he did something with pots of fawn and brown powder near my eyes. "You ask a lot of questions about last night. I heard you questioning Morgan, too."

"You have to admit there are lots of questions to ask."

"And a sheriff's office to answer them." No one could call Gibbous's tone menacing, but I read a warning in it. "A word to the wise: Open that box, and you have no idea what you're walking into."

"I see," I said, aware of his cold scrutiny.

"I don't want anything to happen to you. You understand."

"Like what?" I asked.

"'Ardently do today what must be done. Who knows? Tomorrow, death comes,'" he quoted. He ignored my puzzled expression and finished his work with a tiny bit of blush and dusty rose lipstick over a liner. "This," he said, "is who you are. I've brought it to the surface and it's beautiful."

I knew that expression of satisfaction. I'd felt it myself after pairing a patron with a series of detective novels that would enrich his life for months, or when I'd helped a student find exactly the piece of research she didn't even know she needed.

Gibbous held out his hand. I took it and rose. Too bad I had no idea what I looked like.

CHAPTER FOURTEEN

With every step toward the library, my worry grew. I crossed the bridge over the Kirby River, turned right through the copse of firs at the driveway, and passed Big House. The closer I got to the library, the stronger the energy I felt from the books. Some were outright alarmed. But some, I noted, seemed to be having a good time.

Tones of "Rock Around the Clock" on the organ rang from the old dressing room window. The library was still in one piece, standing prim with its tower and bay windows, but too bad for any patrons looking for a peaceful browse in the stacks.

I burst through the front door to the organ's quavering tones and the sounds of raucous laughter and voices yelling over each other from the kitchen. Dylan lifted his head from the circulation desk, where he was drawing a portrait of Cary Grant from the cover of a biography.

"What's going on?" I said, glancing toward the kitchen.

"Hi, Ms. Way. You look pretty, like Loretta Young."

"Did you check in at the kitchen at all?" A baby goat bleated from across the atrium.

"What do you think of my drawing?" He held up the portrait. Not a bad likeness.

I sighed. I couldn't be mad at him. Dylan had a way of getting absorbed in whatever had caught his attention. I should have known better than to leave him alone when a pack of wild Wilfredians was sure to turn up. In fact, I did know better. I had only myself to blame.

I dropped my bag on a chair and proceeded to the kitchen, the racket intensifying as I crossed the atrium. As I'd expected, the kitchen was full of townspeople. At least no one was smoking, I thought absently, as I surveyed the damage. Here it was, just after noon, and the sink was already full of glasses and plates. A martini shaker sat next to a meat and cheese platter from the PO Grocery, the cheese slices already dried and curling at the edges. The unmistakable aroma of warm beer wafted through the room, despite the open windows.

Three of the town's barflies were drinking beer at the kitchen's central oak table and, surprisingly, half of the knitting club clicked their needles tipsily near them. Duke sat, feet on the table and ratchet in hand, rebuilding what looked like a carburetor. Ruth Littlewood stood at the edge, fiddling with her binoculars. My guess was she'd stopped by for particulars on the feeding habits of some local bird and ended caught up in conversation.

"I'm telling you," Orson, the tavern's former bartender, said, "'Rock Around the Clock' was the original rock and roll song. Can't beat it."

"Unless you're Chuck Berry," another man said. I'd seen him at the diner, but I didn't know his name. Neither of the men were regular library patrons.

"What about 'Rockin' Robin'?" Ruth Littlewood put in, whistling the intro's tweeting. "Of course, the actual robin's song is nothing like that."

"Give me big band music every time," said the knitting club's vice president as she dug her needles into mint-green wool. "Now that was real music."

Mona, the knitting club's youngest member, shook her head and patted the baby goat snoozing in her lap. I was happy to see she hadn't been drinking, since she wasn't of legal age. "None of you have heard of Beyoncé?"

This had to stop. "Everyone!" I said. "This is a library, not a bar. Duke, get your feet off the table."

Duke hurriedly sat up. The crowd fell silent. Finally, Orson spoke. "What happened to your face?"

In the disaster, I'd forgotten about Gibbous's makeover. "No changing the subject. You guys need to clear out."

"I like it," Mona said. "Your eyes really pop."

"Nice job with the hair," the woman with the mint-green wool added. "Can't be easy to control those curls."

"Let us stay. Come on," Duke wheedled, tossing a newspaper over his neighbor's beer. "We don't have anywhere to go now that the café's shut down. There's a murder and a movie star to discuss."

A round of agreement rose from the table.

"Did you hear anything about Roz while you were out?" Mona asked.

"No. Nothing yet." I softened my voice. "Look, everyone. You can talk without turning the library into a tavern. Besides, the This-N-That is open now," I said. "I saw Patty plugging in a stove when I came up."

"Are you sure? Last week she was shut all day while she chased down a kitchen suite."

"Harvest gold with faux-wood trim," someone added. "Looked like a station wagon from *The Brady Bunch*."

Mrs. Garlington shouldered past me and took a seat at the head of the table. She looked especially demure among the beer drinkers with her carefully set, blue-rinsed hair and tidy periwinkle vest and pants set. "What do you think, fellas? Personally, I preferred the Elvis."

"I don't know, Helen," Orson said. "'Jailhouse Rock' with a rumba beat isn't my thing."

It was clear I wouldn't be able to leave the library until Roz was back or the café reopened. Wilfredians needed a place to shoot the breeze and with Bryce's murder, there was plenty of breeze to shoot. But if they were going to meet here . . .

"Okay," I said. "You need somewhere to talk and say hello. I get that. You can use the library's kitchen as long as you keep it liquor-free and watch the language—we get kids in here, you know. We've been over this more than once."

"Josie," Mrs. Garlington said, "You look awfully pretty. Is there a party?"

"Thank you, Mrs. Garlington. Now, like I said, you can meet here, but I think we should make more of it than just a place to kill time."

"Like what?" Mona asked.

"Like finding Chef Bryce's murderer." They all turned to look at me. Orson even put down the martini shaker. "Right now, Roz is being questioned at the sheriff's office. She's not in jail, but she might be, if she's not cleared."

Mona removed a napkin from the goat's mouth. "I'm not saying Roz should win the Miss Congeniality title, but once I saw her move a worm from the sidewalk so it wouldn't get stepped on."

"Exactly," I said. "We all know Roz has been framed. The question is, who's the real murderer?" I told them what I knew, from the death threat to Roz's dropped fan and aborted attempt to ruin Daphne's turmeric lattes to the ironclad contracts Daphne held with her entourage.

Mrs. Garlington drew a powder-blue notebook and gold pen from her handbag. "Who are our suspects?"

"Top of the list is a woman named Bianca. She's stalking Daphne and she was in town yesterday. Daphne has a restraining order against her. The same day, Daphne found the death threat on the farmhouse's porch. Since then, the stalker has disappeared." I gave them the rundown on Bianca, complete with description. "As far as I can tell, she isn't staying in Wilfred, but I can't imagine she'd simply turn around and go back to Nashville. The question is, Where is she?"

"This is fascinating and all," Duke said, "but isn't the sheriff's office taking care of this?"

"Sure it is. By questioning Roz," I said.

At that moment, the kitchen door opened to Roz. The crowd around the table sat up, expecting a blow-by-blow of the morning's interview, full of the rich storytelling and sarcastic observations she was known for. Instead, Roz barely seemed to notice they were there.

"Hi Josie. Folks," she said and trudged past our table.

"Roz," Ruth said. "Are you okay? We've been worried about you."

She paused at the entrance to the atrium. "I don't want to talk about it."

"Can I make you a drink?" Orson said.

"Orson," I warned him.

"They didn't clear you?" Mrs. Garlington asked.

Roz didn't even respond. She disappeared into the library's depths.

My heart fell, and to judge by the expressions of everyone else in the kitchen, so did theirs.

Duke was the first to stand. "We need a door-to-door canvassing. See if anyone else has spotted the stalker."

"I'll put out the word in the knitting circle," Mona said. "If she goes anywhere near a yarn shop, we'll know."

"I'll have a look from my bird-watching platform," Ruth said.

Within moments, they'd dispersed to look for Bianca.

CHAPTER FIFTEEN

I found Roz in the conservatory, staring forlornly out the windows. Summer air bathed the room, rustling the leaves of the banana tree in its pot in the corner. A week ago, this would have been a glorious afternoon, full of expectation. A movie star was coming to Wilfred and Roz was going to be on television. Twenty-four hours had turned the world on its head.

"Are you all right?" I asked.

A long sigh escaped her. "I'm fine. Sam's got to know I didn't do it. They didn't find my fingerprints anywhere, and nothing looked like it had been wiped clean."

"That's good news, right? What about the fan?"

"I've left fans all over Wilfred." She turned toward me. Her eyes were puffy and rimmed with red. "You believe me. I'm pretty sure Sam believes me. But what about everyone else?"

"There was a party in the kitchen today. I'm sure you saw. Those people believe you're innocent. They're out trying to prove it this very minute." It dawned upon me. Roz didn't mean Wilfredians in general. No, there was one person in particular whose good opinion she needed. "Lyndon," I said.

She looked at her shoes. "I haven't talked to him since . . . since it happened."

"Have you tried calling?"

Lyndon adored her. Of course he did. Sure, Daphne Morris might have caught his eye, but that was to be expected. She was a Hollywood princess. Who wouldn't be infatuated with her? It wasn't like it could lead to anything serious. This thought not only brought me comfort for Roz and Lyndon, but I was beginning to feel better about Sam.

Roz looked at me with confusion. "What?"

"Just talk to him. That's all I'm saying."

"What did you do to your face?" she asked.

I touched a cheek. "Oh, I saw Gibbous this afternoon. I wanted to find out where he was when Bryce was killed, and he did this." I tried again. "Don't let this ruin things for the two of you."

She inhaled deeply and her breath caught. She let it out again. "You're right. I miss him."

"There he is now."

Lyndon, a trowel in one hand, wandered toward the compost pile. Roz wavered, and her mouth regained its firm set. "He made her a corsage from his own precious flowers. You know how he feels about the garden. He even cut an Honor rosebud."

"He brings you flowers sometimes," I pointed out.

"He didn't last night, and I don't see a bouquet in his hand right now, even though I've just been put through the wringer at the sheriff's office."

Lyndon aimlessly poked the earth with a trowel.

"He probably doesn't know, Roz."

She shook her head and turned away from the window. "That two-timing idiot. Forget it. I can get through this alone."

"You're not alone as long as I'm here, and I know others feel the same."

Keeping her head low, Roz gathered her laptop and purse. I watched her leave without stopping her.

I sent Dylan home and spent the rest of the day dumping half-drunk cans of beer down the sink and helping patrons. I recommended a travel guide to Toronto to one patron seeking a historical biography and a science fiction trilogy to a man who wanted information on Sheetrocking his basement.

I also stole a few glances at myself in the gilt-framed mirrors here and there on the library's walls. Gibbous was a genius. I'd feared he'd try to transform me into a glamour queen, but somehow he'd managed to make me look more like myself. My eyes were bluer, my skin glowed. The hairstyle he'd pulled together so quickly suited me. It was unstudied, but lovely.

Finally, the day was over. When the last patron left, I walked through the library, closing windows and locking doors. In Circulation, I paused at the open French doors to look out at Big House. Sam's SUV was parked in front. I wondered what he'd think of Gibbous's work.

The August evening was languid, humming with unsung love songs. Or was it coming from the books? Behind me, a volume of E.E. Cummings's collected sonnets whispered about unfurling roses, and Elizabeth Barrett Browning took this as a cue to murmur her own poetry. Soon, the library was full of soft voices weaving words of love.

The books' energy was getting away from me. Controlling my magic was my never-ending work, it seemed. Too often, the books' energy piggybacked on my own emotion and spiraled to the edge of my ability to contain it. I feared it was happening now and tried to gulp back the power that vibrated through me.

The light bulb in the desk lamp behind me fizzed to light and burst with tinkling glass.

"Quiet!" I said. Like a thousand swallows funneling into a chimney, the books' energy shrank and silenced.

Rodney rubbed his head against my calf. He had a knack for showing up when my magic sparked. I ran a finger down his silky fur. He rolled over and let me pet his tender belly. As I touched his star-shaped birthmark just above a rear leg, my corresponding birthmark tingled.

"All right." I stood and closed the French windows. "I'll go see him." The books began to sing love songs again, and I shut them down. "Not because of that," I said. "But he might know something more about the murder." I stopped on the way out to check myself in the mirror anyhow.

I crossed the lawn, and mounted the few steps to the kitchen porch at the back of Big House. The lowering sun seeming to illuminate each blade of grass. I knocked.

Sam should be here, warming a bottle for Nicky and laying out dinner for himself. But he didn't come to the door. Could he be upstairs?

I rose to tiptoes to peer through the screen of an open window. The kitchen was empty, lights off, but Sam's belt and holster lay over a chair. He wasn't home.

It wasn't what I saw that made my heart drop, though, or what I heard, which was nothing at all. It was what I smelled: the unmistakable peach and rose of Daphne's perfume.

CHAPTER SIXTEEN

I settled into my living room couch and tried to ignore Big House across the garden. I would not check to see if Sam was home yet. No. Absolutely not. I'd turn to something more productive: finding Bryce's killer and getting Roz off the hook.

Since uncovering my magic, I'd learned that my best thinking came when I let my mind relax and stay open to whatever insights dropped in, and reading was always relaxing. To that end, I pulled *The Lady in the Morgue*, a vintage Jonathan Latimer mystery, to my lap as a distraction. Maybe his PI Bill Crane would have insight for me on the murder. I flipped to the first chapter and the book sighed with pleasure—then let out a loud groan when my phone chimed. I fumbled for my phone on the side table. Maybe Bianca had been found. No. It was Lalena, texting from outside the library kitchen's door.

Shoot. I'd forgotten it was her weekly bath night and our evening for dinner.

I went downstairs to let her in. Sailor ran ahead, skittering into the atrium to look for Rodney. Lalena, her floral kimono dragging on the ground and a towel and basket over her arm, followed.

"I'm so sorry it slipped my mind," I said. "With Bryce's death and all the craziness surrounding Daphne Morris, my head is somewhere else."

"No matter. One of my clients brought hors d'oeuvres left over from her sister's wedding at one of the wineries. They're a little wilted, but not bad. How do you feel about snacks for dinner?" She squinted. "More importantly, since when did you start wearing makeup?"

"Oh." I raised a hand to my jaw. "I should wash this off."

"No." She pulled my hand away. "It looks good. A little mascara never hurt anyone. I bet you don't even own a tube."

"Not yet." I took the basket and peered under the gingham dish towel covering it. "I'll heat these while you take a bath. Meet me upstairs when you're finished."

An hour later, Lalena and I sat at my kitchen table, me against the window and Lalena facing the view, with her back conveniently next to the refrigerator and the box of wine she kept stored there. The scent of her lavender soap mingled with the aroma of warm puff pastry.

She poured wine into an old jelly jar and took a sip before setting it next to her plate. "Probably not as good as what they served with this food originally."

Probably not as good as served with most franks and beans, I thought, but kept it to myself. I stuck with water. "The food looks great."

Smoked salmon canapés, slices of seafood pâté, and vegetables cut into flowers filled our plates. Lalena lowered a piece of roast beef to Sailor, who snatched it and dashed away. A moment later, sounds rose of Rodney chasing him around the hall circling the second floor.

Lalena lifted a canapé toward her mouth, then returned it to her plate. "What's wrong?"

Over the ten months or so I'd been in Wilfred, Lalena had been the closest thing I'd had to a peer. Over the months, she'd told me about her relationships—often ending disastrously—and had been open about her peculiar brand of commercial magic. In turn, I'd talked with her about my adjustment to life in Wilfred after Washington, DC and about my family. I'd never told her that I was a witch.

"I'm worried about Roz. There's not enough evidence to hold her, but someone wants her jailed for attempting to kill Daphne."

"Everyone knows Roz isn't a murderer. If she did go berserk and decide to kill Daphne, she sure wouldn't accidentally knock off Bryce. She's not that subtle. No, she'd walk straight up to her and take care of business face-to-face, probably with a crowd watching."

I dabbed at my lips with a napkin, sorry I was dissolving Gibbous's expertly applied lipstick. "Sometimes I wish you were a real psychic and could tell us who the murderer was."

"Hmm," she replied, returning to her plate. "It would make a change from the usual readings, that's for sure."

"What do people ask about the most?"

"Love," she said promptly. "Money comes up a lot, too, and a surprising number of women are trying to get pregnant. But love beats them all, hands down." As she talked, she watched me, not even looking at the canapé in her fingers.

"Do people ever ask how to attract a certain person, or do they just want to know if things will work out?"

"Both. Sometimes they're looking for an excuse to leave a relationship, too."

"What do you tell them?" I already knew that the cards a client drew had scant connection to the reading Lalena delivered.

"It depends, of course. If the client hopes a relationship will survive—or start—I have a standard talk about how the best course of action is to show love and respect for themselves, and that love will follow love. Blah-blah-blah." She popped the canapé into her mouth and wiped her fingers. After she'd swallowed, she said, "This isn't personal, is it? It doesn't have to do with a certain . . . you know, sheriff?"

I didn't see any reason to deny it. Not to Lalena, anyway. "What am I supposed to do? He likes me, I know he does. But he doesn't see me as a romantic possibility. I'm getting tired of it. I just want my feelings to go away."

Sam enjoyed our nightly talks on the back porch. He joked around with me. He trusted me. In short, I may as well have been his little sister.

Lalena gave me a shrewd look. "Here's the trouble. After his wife died, he saw you as a friend. You went into the filing drawer labeled *non-romantic*, and he's never had reason to refile you."

Just as Roz had told me. "Am I stuck there?" I said the words quietly, as if the house would soak them up and broadcast them to patrons later.

"I could give you a tarot card reading about it, if you want."

I knew about her readings. They were great at revealing what her customers wanted or feared to see, but I already had those answers. "Thanks, but no thanks. I'd rather know what you think, not what the cards say. You never seem to have trouble meeting men."

"Keeping them around is another question," she said. "I'd say the new makeup is a good start. It might shake things up, make him see you in a new way."

The last I'd checked, Sam wasn't home and once I washed off Gibbous's masterpiece, it would be gone.

"Of course, you could try another age-old trick."

"What's that?"

"Jealousy. Let him see that someone else is interested in you."

I couldn't imagine Sam caring enough to feel threatened. "I don't want to play games."

"Really? Even if it worked?"

I thought of my grandmother's lesson on love potions. If Sam couldn't find his way to me naturally, then I wouldn't go there. I shook my head.

"Well, then," she said. "Maybe it's time to move on. Nothing washes away a stubborn infatuation like another infatuation. How about Daphne Morris's camera guy? I crossed paths with him at the PO Grocery. Too in-his-head for me, but he has something of the poet about him. A geeky poet. I could see you going for him."

"Are you sure you're not psychic?" I asked.

She laughed. "I'm sure. But I have razor-sharp intuition." She leaned forward. "Meanwhile, the one thing you have to worry about is competition."

"You mean, like a beautiful Hollywood actress? One with a hobby of collecting interested men?"

"Bull's-eye," Lalena said.

I tossed my napkin on the table. "I suppose men can't help falling for her. She's a freak of nature. But soon she'll be gone. At least, that's what I keep telling Roz."

"Are you sure Sam is interested in her? I mean, besides checking her out, which any man would do."

"He spends a lot of time with her," I said, remembering the scent of Daphne's perfume at Big House.

"He could be just doing his job."

A smattering of pebbles on glass behind me drew my attention. I rose and heaved up the window. A vision of white skin and peach silk stood in the darkening garden below.

"Josie?" Daphne Morris shouted. "I'm ready for that bath now."

CHAPTER SEVENTEEN

Lalena was right next to me as I opened the door for Daphne Morris. Daphne had barely crossed the kitchen's threshold before Lalena thrust out her hand.

"Lalena Dolby. Psychic and tarot card reader. I do palms, too."

This kind of situation must come up for Daphne annoyingly often, but the movie star responded with a beatific smile and automatic grace. "I'm so pleased to meet you. Wilfred has such fascinating people."

"If you ever need to contact a departed loved one or peek into the future, come see me. My schedule is busy, but I'll make time for you."

"The future?"

Daphne wore a peach sundress cut loose, yet somehow fitted enough to make the most of her legs and waist. The market basket slung over her arm held a rolled-up towel, jar of pale pink bath salts, and a scrub brush on a long handle.

"Yes. I meet with clients in my home at the Magnolia Rolling Estates," Lalena said. "Let me look at your palm."

I'd seen Lalena work this ploy many a time. I folded my arms as Daphne proffered her pink-tipped hand.

"Hmm. You've recently undergone significant struggle. I—" Lalena stopped cold. This was not part of her regular schtick.

"What?" Daphne said.

"I—I'd rather not say." She pushed Daphne's hand away. "Palm reading isn't always accurate."

No duh, I thought. Still, Lalena had seen something alarming in Daphne's palm, or she'd really taken her pitch in a new direction.

"What?" Daphne said. "What did you see?"

Lalena took a gulp from her jelly jar of wine. "I can fit you in on Thursday. Do you have time then?"

She nodded. "I'm on vacation. Call Morgan and get on my schedule."

"We'll have lots to talk about, I'm sure," Lalena said in the smooth patter I was more used to.

"Lalena was just on her way out." I gave her elbow a little push.

"See you on Thursday at the pink trailer. My sign is on the mailbox," Lalena said as she left, Sailor at her feet. "Enjoy your bath."

I led Daphne to the old mansion's second-floor bathroom.

"It's huge," she said. "Almost as big as my bathroom back home."

The dining room of my one-bedroom apartment in suburban DC could have fit inside the library's second-floor bath. When I'd arrived in Wilfred last fall to take on the position of librarian, two of the bathroom's walls had been lined with shelves of cookbooks. To prevent water damage, I'd cleared them out and moved in a cabinet to store bath items. Now it was home to a low boudoir chair I'd hauled from the attic and a cabinet with baskets holding soap and towels for each of the regular bathers from the trailer park.

"It gets a fair amount of traffic," I said.

"The important thing is that no one's died in it," Daphne said, her voice softening.

Whatever she felt, grief had not muddied her looks. The slight shadows under her eyes could easily be lightened by Gibbous, but even without a pat of powder they gave her the air of a fifteenth-century Flemish Madonna.

"Enjoy your bath," I said.

"Will you—" She touched the back of my arm. "Will you stay? I mean, in the hall, of course. I don't want to bathe alone. Not after last night. Is that okay?"

I couldn't resist her plea, although part of me noted it was too bad I didn't have an in with an internet fan site. "Morgan couldn't make it tonight?"

Daphne unpacked her basket onto the boudoir chair next to the clawfoot tub that Lalena usually balanced her books and herbal tea on. "I didn't ask her to come. I'm afraid she's not too happy with me right now."

"No?" I remembered my conversation with Morgan at the party and her testiness this morning.

Daphne bit. "Someone called from New York to offer her a role, and I said no."

"Oh." How to say this delicately? "She—"

Daphne replied before I could even craft a response. "I need her. It's selfish of her to audition for things without telling me. Here I am, prepping for an interview—"

With a week of vacation, I added silently. And not too arduously.

"—and she decides to go off, just like that, to act?" She shook her head. "I don't know what she was thinking."

"The play was scheduled to start right away?" I moved to the hall to give Daphne privacy.

"This winter, but that's not the point."

What was the point, then? That Morgan couldn't have her own career? I began to understand why she might be angry.

"Just because it was some fancy intellectual playwright. It's not like it was Hollywood or anything." I heard the swish of her dress dropping to the tile floor. "She was angry with me."

As Daphne drew her bath, I stood in the hall and pondered. My money was still on Bianca as Bryce's killer, but Morgan certainly had a motive for a crime of passion. The thing was, except for a stroll through the trailer park, she had been at the party all night. However, she'd also called in the death. Could she have killed Bryce just before she'd called? Surely she would have first made sure it was Daphne.

"I might be a while. Why don't you take the chair?" Daphne called from the bathtub.

The opaque cotton shower curtain was pulled around the tub, and Daphne had pushed open the casement window to let in the warm night air and the chirping of crickets. I set Daphne's basket on the cabinet and pulled the boudoir chair into the hall. Listening to movie stars in bathtubs? This was not a skill they taught in library school.

"Comfortable?" I said from outside the door.

"What can you tell me about Sam?" she replied, ignoring my question.

Now we were getting down to the real reason she

wanted me there. Thankfully, she couldn't see my grimace. "What do you want to know?"

"Doesn't look like he's married. Does he have a girlfriend?" Splashing water and the warm scent of jasmine—a rare switch from her usual roses and peaches—accompanied her remarks.

I hesitated. I couldn't lie. Before I could respond, she added, "Sorry. I hadn't realized. Maybe you're interested in him."

"We're not romantic." That was all I could say.

"I hope you don't mind me confiding in you. I feel like you're my little sister, especially since you're wearing my makeup. Did Gibbous do that?"

I'd forgotten about the makeover and was grateful Daphne couldn't see me blush. "He offered. I hope you don't mind."

"Not at all. Gibbous can't help himself when he sees a face he can improve." Now that I was in my place, she returned to her favorite topic. "What Sam needs is a real woman. Someone with experience."

Hmm. I wondered who she meant?

"I always did like a country man. Like Kevin, my ex. What's with the kid?"

"Nicky," I said, fighting to keep my voice neutral. "His name is Nicky. Sam's wife died earlier this year."

Water sloshed as she turned in the tub. "He's a widower. Hmm." More sloshing. "I find a slightly receding hairline sexy, don't you?"

"Sure," I said quietly.

"What?"

"Nothing. I was just agreeing with you," I said more loudly. A book title came to mind: *Snake in the Grass*.

"And that quiet way he has, how he squints and

frowns. I bet you didn't know that he frowns when he's happy," she said.

The titles kept coming: *Frenemies 101. History of the Home-wrecker*. "No kidding?" Of course I knew it. And she'd better watch out if he smiles. "Well, I'll leave you to finish your bath."

"No! Stay."

Her tone of voice made it clear I was to do what she commanded. If it weren't for smoothing relations between Roz and her, I would have left. Instead, I sympathized with Morgan and returned to the chair.

Rodney butted the bathroom door and slinked in. I willed him to return, but he ignored me.

Well, if I had to stay, I planned on changing the topic. "Have you seen Bianca around at all?"

"I imagine she's far away by now. Who knows? Maybe she thinks she killed me. With Sam to protect me, I'm not worried."

Rodney emerged from the bathroom with a lacy bra clasped in his mouth. He deposited it at my feet and jumped into my lap. I tossed the bra back through the door and made a mental note to upgrade my lingerie.

"But it had to be someone who's in Wilfred. You found the note right on your porch. What exactly did it say, anyway?" I asked.

"You know. The usual. I don't remember exactly."

She took the situation so lightly. If it weren't for Bryce's death, I'd have been tempted to believe Morgan's suggestion that Daphne had written the note herself. Or that there'd never been a note. "There's no one else who wants you dead?" I asked. "Roz was taken in for questioning, you know."

"I heard. Why would she kill me? Especially before

her interview? I'm promoting her book. She's not that stupid."

"There was some suggestion," I said carefully, "that her boyfriend might have shown some interest in you."

She snorted. "Josie, I'm a celebrity, and I didn't get this way because I'm hard to look at. Every man and more women than you'd guess show interest in me. If that's all it took, I'd have been dead long ago. I'm sure Sam has ruled out Roz by now."

That was something, at least. Daphne didn't suspect Roz, and as far as she was concerned the interview was still on. "I hope so." Rodney head-butted my chin. "Who could it be, then?"

"Who knows? Maybe it was an accident. Bianca is long gone, I'm sure, and I'm safe. Let's drop that subject and talk about something more interesting."

I screwed my eyes shut as I anticipated her next word.

"Sam," she said. "If I asked him over for dinner, do you think you could take care of Ricky? I was thinking I could order something in. Maybe suggest Morgan and Gibbous get out of the house and catch a movie in town."

"Nicky," I corrected. "I don't know. I get busy in the evening with meetings at the library—"

"You can't be busy every night. There's no one here now, for instance. You'd be doing me a big favor." Her voice turned soft and pleading. "Please? Morgan's no good with babies and Gibbous would probably set him somewhere to meditate." Water splashed as she sat up. "I know, I could send over Leo and you could babysit together. I noticed that you two seemed to have hit it off. He's supposed to be back tomorrow morning."

I opened my mouth to deliver another excuse when I heard banging on the kitchen door downstairs. Again.

"I've got to get that," I said and followed Rodney down the main staircase, letting my hands surf the satiny banister.

Duke's face was pressed against the kitchen window, and the figures of others crowded behind him. It was the afternoon crew from the kitchen, back with their findings.

"Open up," he said. "Now! We have big news."

I unlocked the door. Duke pushed it open and people filed into the kitchen around me.

"It's Bianca," he said. "We found her."

"Where?" I asked.

"Camping in the woods west of town."

I fumbled for my phone. "We've got to tell Sam. He'll want to talk to her."

"He won't have to find her. She's here," Duke said.

He stepped aside and Bianca, bewildered, appeared. Her face was scrubbed of makeup, and the pink streak in her hair looked jarring next to her pale lips and wide eyes.

"Bryce is dead?" she said. "I can't believe it." She looked around the library's kitchen as if she weren't sure where she was or what was happening.

I'd expected to be angry when I saw her. She may have framed Roz, not to mention murdered a man. At that moment, Bianca looked more the victim than the perpetrator. I couldn't help putting an arm around her shoulders and led her to the kitchen table, where she slumped into a chair. Tears dampened her cheeks. This kitchen had sure seen a lot of drama today.

"She loved Bryce so much. They had such a long history. Childhood friends, you know." Bianca looked at me, her eyes rimmed in scarlet. She didn't need to specify who *she* was.

Bianca and Daphne were cousins, I remembered. Bianca must have grown up with him, as well. No wonder she grieved. Either that, or she was in shock that her attempt to kill Daphne had failed so spectacularly.

"Bianca Morris?" It was Sam, Duke behind him. Duke must have run over to Big House to fetch him.

Bianca stared at the tabletop. Sam took the chair next to hers.

"We've been looking for you," he said firmly, yet gently.

The group of Wilfredians at the door watched nearly without breathing, like this was the kick for the final point at a championship football game.

"How did it happen?" Bianca asked.

"Last night, Morgan found him electrocuted in the bathtub."

She gasped. "Electrocuted?"

Sam nodded, watching her closely.

"Morgan found him," Bianca repeated. If she was the murderer, she was a better actress than Daphne.

"They think the murderer might have mistaken him for Daphne," Duke said.

Bianca sucked in a sharp breath. "No," she whispered on the exhale. Then, "I need to see Daphne."

"Do you think that's a good idea?" I told her.

For the first time, Sam turned toward me. He opened his mouth to talk, seemed to think better of what he was going to say. He stared at me for two full seconds and frowned faintly before I remembered Gibbous's work, which I complemented with a natural blush.

He rose and turned to the crowd around us. "You all go home. Bianca, I need to talk with you."

She still looked stunned. "Okay."

"You'll want an attorney present," he said. "We can wait until morning. But we'll have to hold you tonight."

Reluctantly, people filed out of the kitchen, tossing glances back toward Bianca and Sam. Finally, they were gone.

Moments later, shafts of red light pulsed through the trees. Sam motioned to two uniformed officers to join him outside the kitchen door. They talked for a moment, and one deputy pointed to something on a sheet of paper. Sam folded the paper and slipped it into his chest pocket before returning to the kitchen, the deputy behind him. The deputy looked at Bianca, then Sam, and Sam nodded.

"Sam," I said, "you've found out something new."

He tapped his chest pocket and lowered his voice. "It turns out that Bryce not only had a high blood alcohol level, he also had elevated levels of benzodiazepine in his blood. We think someone had added it to his cocktail."

"Xanax," the fat manual of drug classification in Reference stated drily. I pretended not to hear. "Librium, alprazolam, lorazepam, Klonopin."

This fact changed everything. Bryce's murder wasn't a crime of opportunity, a mistaken attempt on Daphne's life. It was premeditated. Then why the death threat against Daphne?

Sam joined Bianca at the other end of the kitchen table. "Bianca, Deputy Caruso will take you into town." Then, to the deputy, "There's no need to cuff her."

Bianca rose slowly and the deputy grasped her by the elbow.

At this moment, Daphne Morris rounded the corner. She dropped her basket and threw a palm to her chest. "No! Get her out of here." With wet hair slicked over her scalp and no makeup, Daphne should have looked washed-out. I would have. Instead, she seemed to glow in ivory and rose petal pink, like a porcelain figurine lit from within.

"Daphne." Bianca pulled away from the deputy's grasp. "I have to talk to you."

"No!" Daphne shouted.

The deputy pulled Bianca back but couldn't help stealing a few glances at Daphne before leading Bianca outside to the SUV waiting in the drive. Meanwhile, Daphne rushed to Sam's side, laying her head on his chest. His arm looped around her automatically. I turned away.

"Poor Bryce," Daphne murmured, her voice absorbed by Sam's chest. "Is she gone?"

Earlier, Daphne hadn't seemed worried about Bianca at all. "Is that all?" I said, maybe a bit too curtly.

"I don't see your car," Sam said to Daphne.

"I walked up." She drew back a little but kept a hand on his forearm.

"I'll take you home. Are you going to be cold?"

Good question. I wondered if Daphne had planned to spend the rest of the evening here, maybe insisting I blow-dry her hair.

"I'll be okay," she said, gazing at Sam.

Without a second look at me, Sam and Daphne walked into the moonlight, Daphne clinging to his arm, her basket swinging from her other elbow. Rodney leaped onto the table next to me and let out a mournful yowl.

I shut the kitchen door and bolted it.

CHAPTER EIGHTEEN

I leaned against the kitchen door. My emotions—and so my magic—surged like a flash flood. Throughout the library, lamps responded by flickering and, strangely, the blender whirred in fits and starts. I hadn't known we had a blender. Orson had probably brought it in to make piña coladas.

I closed my eyes and drew a deep breath. *Calm.* The energy tensed and then relaxed until it hummed just above normal.

I went up to my apartment's tiny bathroom and wet a cool washcloth. Why should Sam be so caught up with Daphne? It's not like it could go anywhere. She was leaving town soon. I scrubbed at Gibbous's handiwork, leaving brown and pink marks on the washcloth. Even if they wanted to try a relationship, they were so poorly suited for each other.

Daphne couldn't even remember Nicky's name, for

goodness' sake. She'd never understand how Sam needed long silences and hours of chopping herbs and cooking to think. She wouldn't like his opera. She wouldn't give him the space to open up and be himself. Instead, she'd babble about herself and play the victim.

A thought surfaced in my brain like a diver coming up for air. *They're wrong for each other. You're right for him, Josie. Fix it.*

I rinsed the washcloth as I considered this. I could fix it, in fact. I wasn't your average woman with recourse to nothing but self-help books and high heels. I didn't need to rely on chance to draw love. I had magic.

I dried my face and went to my bedroom. On my bed, Rodney purred like a boat engine. Next to him rested my grandmother's grimoire. I stopped at the doorway and stared. Books I needed had a way of turning up on my nightstand, and the witchcraft lesson right for me in my grandmother's trunk reliably found its way to my fingers. But the grimoire had always stayed at the bottom of the trunk, as if warning me away from it.

Now here it was. I approached it slowly. From looking at the book, a stranger wouldn't have suspected the power it held. It was a scarred leather binder stuffed with yellowed pages. Bits of leaves and the pale purple and yellow of old flower petals poked from its pages. Only if you looked closely could you see my grandmother's initials etched in small letters in the corner of the cover. The old book shimmered in pink and orange.

The grimoire tingled beneath my fingers, but instead of being too hot to touch, as it had been in the past, it was merely warm with the summer night. I remembered the fat grimoire from when I was a girl. It was always on a high shelf in Grandma's kitchen, and it always seemed to drop flower petals and rosemary needles. Once, in the kitchen alone, I had heard women's voices quietly singing a cappella but had seen no one. Now I knew: It was the grimoire.

I took it to the living room and settled into my reading chair facing the empty fireplace. Normally, Rodney liked to nap in the kindling box, but tonight, still purring, he squeezed onto the chair, filling the space between me and the chair's arm. He gave me a slow blink.

The grimoire smelled of dried sage and winter savory. I opened its front cover and the book sighed luxuriously. It had been cramped, unread, in the trunk for decades, and now a dozen quiet voices rose from it, yawning and letting whispers of song escape. My fingers trembled. In all the thousands upon thousands of books I'd handled—even going back to my days in the Library of Congress's American Folklife Center—I'd never felt this kind of energy. It was an engrossing tapestry of voices I couldn't absorb in one glance, as I could with other books.

Above the energy, above the smells and the songs, my grandmother's voice rose high and strong. "Josie. Use this grimoire with care. What it contains can enrich your life—or end it."

I inhaled sharply as the vellum pages flipped themselves a third of the way in, then slowed to peel back a few pages and lay open on my lap. Rodney sat up, alert. When the book rested again, so did he, his purring amping up.

Love Spells and Potions, it read in blue ink at the top of the page. I'd expected some sort of baroque cursive, but the writing was my grandmother's in loose ballpoint pen. Its y's and g's dipped into the lines below. My birthmark tingled as I read.

Never-Fail Love Potion. Use with caution. The person who consumes this potion will develop a deep passion for the first person he or she looks in the eyes. The effect will last a week, ample time to cement bonds. The dose is one teaspoon per hundred pounds.

Because its potency comes from energy, Never-Fail doesn't require hard-to-find ingredients. As such, it is important to tap your richest energy source when creating the potion. For instance, I mix it in my garden, as plants feed my magic. Find your magic place.

The library was my magic place. That much was easy, I thought.

The potion is simple. Under the light of the moon, gather a quantity of red and pink rose petals the size of a human heart. Place them in a fireproof vessel. Add something you truly love. You will lose this object forever, but you must have invested a lot of affection in it for the spell to be effective. Pour over this mixture a cup of sweet wine.

Now for the most important step, without which the potion will not work. Cup the vessel in your hands and infuse it with your greatest energy. Wait and continue to build magic within it. You will know when the potion is ready.

A week was plenty of time. In four days, Daphne would be gone. If Sam could love me just for a week . . . Chills raced up my arms and my breath caught in my throat. I imagined him waiting for me at the end of the day at Big House, not with his usual take-it-or-leave-it affection, but with longing. Beyond the day's challenges, he'd share his deepest fears and hope with me, and I with him. The potion would smooth out any hiccups my magic might cause in a relationship. I could even tell him I was a witch, and he'd love my magic because it was part of who I was. The thought was heady enough that I set down the grimoire and held a hand to my chest to absorb the warmth that seemed to radiate from me.

And at the end of the week? There was that. When the potion's effects faded, would he look at me curiously, wondering what had got into him? Would he begin to think of Daphne again and wonder what he'd lost? Maybe he'd even be ashamed of his feelings for me.

Could I cheat him of his future?

Say he did love me beyond the week. How much of it would be from duty, because he'd unaccountably started something with me. Wilfred was a small town and Sam was a decent man.

I closed the grimoire. Yes, I could make Sam love me. But I wouldn't.

CHAPTER NINETEEN

I opened my bedroom curtains to streaming sun. Mother Nature was stubbornly oblivious to murder. And heartache. Whatever pain lingered in the minds of Wilfredians—money trouble, the disappointments of family, persistent bunions—the summer morning doused it in birdsong and warm, pink light.

In my quest to run down information that might elude Sam, I'd questioned nearly everyone who could have killed Chef Bryce. Everyone except Leo. I'd felt a kinship with him. He was curious, interested in the world, and so was I. Besides, he hadn't even been in town when Bryce was murdered. I felt sure Leo was innocent, but he still might know something that would help find the murderer and clear Roz. His information might complement whatever Sam had learned from Bianca.

I dressed and took my coffee to the hall overlooking the atrium. The library was dark, illuminated only by morning sun through the stained-glass windows in the cupola. I sensed rather than saw Marilyn Wilfred's "good morning" from her portrait shrouded in shadow. Neither Lyndon nor Roz would be in for at least an hour, and the library didn't open for two hours.

I closed my eyes and let the books' energy rise in my body. When my birthmark tingled, it was time.

"Books," I said. "Tell me about local folk magic." For dramatic effect, I added, "Abracadabra!" and waved my arms.

Before I'd even finished speaking, books and papers sailed in from the old mansion's corners, making their way to Old Man Thurston's desk in the former office of the town's founder. Their energy played in me like an orchestra and I couldn't help smiling. It didn't look like a large collection, and I was surprised to see one old tome swirl in from the cookbook collection and a few DVDs zip across the atrium behind it. Behind me, low, sacred voices hummed from what could only have been my grandmother's grimoire. *I found some books that might interest you*, I tapped into my phone to Leo. *The library opens at ten.*

Leo was on the front porch when I unlocked the library's heavy front door. He stood awkwardly a moment, then a grin spread over his face.

"Hi," he said.

"Good morning," I said. "How was your time in Portland? "

"Good, thank you. I saw an old friend, spent some time at the historical society. Then, when I came home . . ."

"I'm so sorry. Someone told you about Bryce while you were away?"

"Morgan texted me." He shook his head. "It's unimaginable."

"Maybe this will be a distraction. I remembered your interest in folk magic and found a few things you might be interested in. Oh, leave the door open. It's going to be hot today."

No matter how bright the day was, thanks to floor-to-ceiling oak paneling that had darkened with age, Old Man Thurston's office was dim, even with the heavy brocade curtains pulled open. I clicked on the gooseneck lamp craned over the wide desk.

Stacked neatly—by me, not by the books, who'd tossed themselves into a frenzied pile—were the materials I'd summoned.

"This should get you started," I said.

He set his satchel on the desk. "Thank you. This is great. What's this? A cookbook?"

"Sure." I hadn't had a chance to examine in detail everything the library had collected for me, and I didn't know exactly how the cookbook pertained to Leo's research. I flipped it open to its title page. "Women in the valley submitted their recipes to it in the 1920s." I let my brain relax, and the book spoke. "Check out page ninety-two."

Leo settled into the oak swivel chair. "It's a recipe for a witch bottle." He rummaged through his satchel for a pen and notebook. "I've heard about them in oral histories and seen a few old ones dug up at construction sites, but I've never seen actual instructions."

I came around the desk and peered over his shoulder. It

was a nice shoulder, strong and covered in a blue T-shirt. He'd changed the tape on his glasses from gray duct tape to white medical adhesive. "What's a witch bottle?"

"A bottle or jar filled with odd things—herbs, dirt, water, fingernail clippings—then buried or hidden in a house. It was meant to protect against evil. Archeologists have found them dating back as far as the sixteenth century." His voice picked up excitement. *"Fir needles and a scrub jay's feather,"* he read.

I felt the tug of my grandmother's grimoire upstairs. In there I'd find something about witch bottles, I knew.

"Do you believe in them? Witches, I mean?" I asked.

"Of course," he said, absorbed by the old cookbook.

"Really?"

This time he looked at me. "Of course," he repeated. "That doesn't mean I think witches fly around on brooms and turn people into frogs. But there are definitely witches out there. More of them than we know, and I don't mean hippie chicks who hang out in New Age stores, either."

I pulled up a side chair. "Then who are they?"

"Pagan religions have been around for centuries. When Christianity swept through Europe, pagan families went underground, but some of their rituals survived. Like witch bottles," he said, tapping the cookbook.

My mother's grandparents had come from rural Scotland and, somewhere there, stemmed my own witchy roots. All the women in my family showed some magical ability, but it was minor enough that in the normal world it wouldn't stand out. My mother's occasional visions were "intuition" and "coincidence." My sisters Toni and Jean's healing abilities were because they were so "nurturing." But my own magic, like that of my grandmother, was impossible to deny.

"What about magic? Do you believe in magic?"

I prepared for the kind of response Lalena had given me in the past. About how magic was little more than cognitive bias, how people believe what they need to believe, yet how those beliefs could be healing. After all, everyone needed hope. Instead, Leo surprised me.

"I do," he said. "Do you?"

I couldn't do more than nod.

"I mean," he continued, "How else do you explain love at first sight?"

Not this again. This conversation had taken a wrong turn. I pulled my chair back a few inches. "By the desire for love, maybe? I bet there's a lot of so-called love at first sight that is quickly relabeled something else, like 'what the heck was I thinking?' "

Leo laughed. "I can't argue with that. Just because people may be witches doesn't mean they have magical powers. To me, witches and magic are separate."

"Why do witches fascinate you so much? I mean, why all the research?"

"Well." He leaned forward and lowered his voice. "I make documentary films and I want to do something on folk magic. Filming Daphne's book club is a great job, but it's not my life's work. Traveling with her gives me the chance to see the world, learn things."

I nodded. I was beginning to understand. "You have a contract with her?"

"Exactly. I'm not actively filming the project, but even my research is a gray area, contract-wise. Daphne wouldn't hesitate to sue. I'd appreciate it if you didn't tell her about this."

As with Gibbous's contract. And Morgan's. "I won't advertise it."

"Thank you." He leaned back again and smiled, but his smile dimmed within seconds. "Bryce. I still can't believe it. I keep thinking I hear him in the kitchen. Or I read something I want to tell him, then I remember he's not here anymore."

"He seemed like such a good guy." The birdsong outside was jarringly chipper.

"You wouldn't know it to look at him, but Bryce was really into classical French cuisine. Daphne needs a special diet—you know, micro greens, tonics, whatever— but when she was out of town, he'd made these elaborate dishes with crazy sauces."

I smiled at the thought of him unmolding aspics and ladling turtle soup.

"We used to joke about doing a cooking show together," Leo said. "We even filmed a segment for social media, but Daphne put the kibosh on that."

"Your contracts," I said.

He nodded. "Bryce was a good friend." He pushed away the materials I'd collected. Even the cookbook couldn't keep his interest now. "The sheriff questioned me about where I was the night I left town—the night of the party."

"Don't take it personally," I said. "It's his job. He checked in on everyone."

"The idea is that someone was after Daphne and got Bryce by mistake, right?"

"Yes. Remember the death threat. Plus, Bryce was found in the bathtub"—I looked up to see if Leo knew the details, and he nodded—"and the shower curtain had been pulled. Whoever dropped in the blow-dryer probably thought Bryce was Daphne." I let that hang in the air a second. "There's one other detail. Apparently, Bryce was drugged. The working theory is that someone spiked his cocktail. Could someone have put something in Daphne's Golden Cutie, and Bryce drank it by mistake?"

"She doesn't actually drink them," Leo said. "Just turmeric lattes."

"I don't get it. Who would want to kill Daphne, anyway?"

"I can think of half-a-dozen people right off the top of my head."

"Morning, Ms. Way." Dylan, nattily dressed in blue-and-white–striped seersucker, paused at the office entrance. He looked curiously from me to Leo. I realized we were sitting kind of close.

"Good morning." I didn't even bother to correct the "Ms. Way." I turned back to Leo, eager to continue our conversation, but Dylan lingered.

"I've got the plans for movie night all written out," he said.

Movie night? I didn't remember—oh, right. Cary Grant. Dylan and I would talk. Later. "That's fine." Dylan ambled across the atrium toward Circulation. Then, to Leo I said, "Who? Who could possibly want to see Daphne dead?"

"Her ex, for sure. Daphne has dragged his name through the mud."

As far as I knew, Kevin Atchley was on tour nowhere near Wilfred. "We can safely cross him off the list."

"Then there's Bianca. I heard she's in for questioning."

"They picked her up last night," I said. "She seemed genuinely shocked about Bryce's death. Are you sure she'd try to kill Daphne?"

"No. Not sure, actually."

"What other suspects are there?"

Leo folded his arms over his chest. "Well, Daphne's been a real pain to Gibbous. He can't seem to do anything right when Daphne's in a mood."

"No wonder he meditates so much."

"Let's not forget Morgan," Leo said. "She and Daphne have a complicated relationship."

"I've noticed," I admitted. "How well do you know her?"

He looked away and sun through the oak trees outside glinted off his glasses. "As well as anyone, I guess."

"Daphne pays her rent. Why would she want Daphne dead?" I wanted to see if Leo knew about Morgan's squelched acting job.

"Morgan has her own ambitions as an actor, but Daphne refuses to see her as anything more than a personal assistant. Morgan says it's jealousy. She's a serious actor. Theater quality. I wouldn't peg her as a murderer, though."

Something in the way Leo spoke nudged my brain. It wasn't magic, but sheer women's intuition. "Have you and Morgan worked together a long time?"

"A bit. Morgan's fascinating, but troubled. She worries a lot, too. Her attention to detail makes her a great assistant, but she never seems to wind down."

"She can get a prescription for something to help with that." Something that might, if taken in quantity, stupefy a man of Bryce's size.

"Oh, she has one," he said.

"You don't happen to know what, do you?"

He squinted. "Xanax, I think. She kept it by the bed. Why?"

"Bryce had been drugged, remember. Do you know if she still has the prescription?"

Troubled, he shook his head. "I have no idea. You think Morgan might have done it?"

It was looking like it more and more, I might have said. Morgan's desire to break her ironclad contract with Daphne gave her a motive, and she'd found Bryce only minutes after he'd died. She'd left the party for a walk, and she might have returned to the farmhouse not knowing that Daphne was still out. Now it turned out that Morgan had a supply of the drug found in Bryce's system. I remembered her pouring out the cocktail found in the farmhouse that night.

Yes, I did wonder if Morgan was the unwitting murderer. Instead, I replied, "There's a lot to figure out yet. I'd better get back to work. Good luck with your research, and let me know if you need anything else."

"Josie." Leo touched my arm for a split second and let his hand drop to the desk. "Would you like to go for a walk sometime? Maybe a hike? The countryside here looks amazing."

"That sounds nice." Maybe he'd have more information for me, I thought. That's why I said yes. It had nothing to do with those eyes.

CHAPTER TWENTY

I returned to Circulation, leaving Leo in Old Man Thurston's office to deepen his knowledge of folk magic. If only he knew he had a real live witch just across the atrium.

For a moment, I imagined being interviewed for his documentary, getting my moment of fame. People would travel from all over the globe to Wilfred to see me. They'd ask me to perform spells, thinking I could heal them or predict the future, and I'd suggest books instead. I could coordinate a dance number for novels with a live orchestra. *Hush,* I said silently as the treatise on logic snickered at my elbow.

Who was I kidding? My magic had to remain secret. I wouldn't end up the toast of the nation—I'd be tossed in the loony bin. And that would be after the library was plastered with hate graffiti by people thinking I was doing the devil's work. It wouldn't matter to them that I was by blood a truth teller.

All I wanted was to be a good librarian. That, and see justice done.

Ruth Littlewood, clipboard in hand, appeared in front of me. "That should do it for now."

"How's the work going up there?" I asked. Now that our books were catalogued online, I could have easily printed out a list of the birding books for Mrs. Littlewood, but she insisted on doing her own inventory, complete with notes on condition. To her credit, she'd discovered what looked like a dried raisin stuck to a photo of the spotted towhee, and someone had penciled a goatee on John Audubon's portrait. She'd generously funded their replacements.

"Fine, thank you." She handed me a stack of trifold brochures. "I've typed up some info sheets on the whippoorwill's territory and habits. Patrons need to understand that Roz has taken a grave fictional liberty."

I set the stack on the circulation desk. Roz would no doubt toss them in the recycling bin tonight. "Done. Thank you."

"One more thing. There's a pair of nesting Cooper's hawks I'd like you to see in the big fir tree in the cemetery." She pulled up a chair. "I'm convinced if you spent more time with birds, you'd be fascinated. It would be so good for the community to have our librarian appreciate the avian world."

"I'd love to," I lied, "but I'm working this afternoon."

"Surely Roz can keep an eye on things for an hour or so?" she countered.

"I really need to stay," I said. "But thank you."

As she left Circulation, Sam, in uniform, crossed paths with her. I'd tried to replicate Gibbous's hairdo this morning. Maybe he'd notice.

"Hi, Josie. Daphne said the head of her production team—"

"Leo."

"Leo is here. Do you know where I can find him?"

"He's in Old Man Thurston's office with a pile of books."

"The book club needs research?"

"He has an interest in local history. Why? Do you have a reason to suspect him?"

With a faint smile, he looked at me a second longer than usual. "We need to question everyone."

"What about Bianca?" I stood. I didn't like him looking down on me.

"We've released her. She claims Daphne invited her to the farmhouse for a cocktail, but when she arrived, no one was there to let her in. She waited in the garden for a few minutes, then returned to her campsite."

"So, you didn't have enough to hold her. Did she see anything?" I asked.

"Yes. She saw Roz."

"Oh, Sam. You know Roz was only—"

He turned up a palm to signal *stop*. "I've already heard Roz's story."

"Bianca doesn't have much of an alibi," I pointed out. "Can she prove it?"

"That's my job, Josie."

"I see. Is she camping again?"

"Just for another couple of days until her return flight home." He shifted feet. "There's some old camping gear in the attic at Big House. I gave it to her to use."

He was kind. Thoughtful. Plus, it gave him the chance to keep an eye on her. Poor Bianca—poor Bianca who could be a murderer, that is. Or Morgan. "Leo told me Morgan had a prescription for Xanax."

"I know all about that. And you might want to question what people tell you." Sam turned toward the atrium. "Thanks."

"Wait," I said. "What's that supposed to mean?"

"Just that not everything you hear is necessarily the truth. Be careful. That's all."

"You mean, about Leo?"

"Have a good day, Josie."

He wasn't going to tell me, the stinker. "Will you be around tonight? Maybe I can help you think through this. I have some ideas."

He hesitated just long enough to clue me in that something was up. Without looking at me, he said, "Not tonight. I have plans."

It could be he planned to stay home with Nicky and make a curry while he listened to *The Magic Flute*, but I had the sinking feeling that wasn't the case. "Daphne?"

He nodded. "She's not safe. She's bringing in security, but they don't arrive until tomorrow."

I pasted on a smile. "Well, I guess she's safe tonight, under police protection."

There was too much I didn't know about Morgan to give me confidence in Daphne's safety. Reluctantly, I had to admit she needed Sam around. For the moment, at least. "If you'll excuse me, I need to see Mrs. Littlewood about some nesting hawks."

* * *

"I'm so glad you changed your mind," Ruth Littlewood said. "Once you tune in to the world of birds, there's no going back. You'll see how Roz might have chosen any number of native birds for her book. The western meadowlark, for example."

We walked along the sunbaked highway, over the dozing Kirby River, and took a right into Wilfred's tiny residential neighborhood. Once I'd convinced her it was for her own good, Roz had left her protected spot in the basement's book repair room and seated herself at my desk in Circulation. No doubt she'd be fielding questions about Bryce's murder from curious Wilfredians—if any were foolish enough to ask her.

"Has Daphne Morris come into the library?" Mrs. Littlewood asked as we passed the farmhouse and began the climb to her house. "I saw the production manager. Now there's a nice boy. He really should get his glasses fixed, though."

"She came for a bath the other night, in fact." I was surprised Mrs. Littlewood hadn't known. I figured Wilfredians had charted the actress's doings hour by hour at their nightly gatherings in the front yard of the This-N-That after having trashed the library's kitchen during the day.

"Something's not right about her. She has an unhealthy interest in herself. Nature created something rare in her, like the peacock, and she's forgotten that other people have lives, too. I wouldn't be surprised if she's lonely."

I'd never heard Mrs. Littlewood wax introspective. She'd seen a lot in life, though, running a company and losing her husband, then her daughter. The bird world seemed to absorb any leftover emotion.

"Here we are," she said.

Mrs. Littlewood lived in one of Wilfred's few modern houses, built sometime in the 1950s. Her late husband had been an architecture buff and had modeled their home on a Frank Lloyd Wright photo, siting it on the hill at the southeast edge of town. Wide windows reflected the sun onto a terrace. We weren't going inside, though. We were going up to the bird-watching platform.

The platform was built in the crotch of a wide-armed oak tree that seemed to have spent a hundred years growing specifically for this job. A wooden ladder leaned against its trunk.

"Take these." Mrs. Littlewood handed me a pair of binoculars from a chest at the base of the tree. "You go up first."

I looped the binoculars around my neck and climbed the oak's gray-and-brown mottled trunk. *Thank you, old girl*, I said silently as I placed a hand on the tree's bark. The real source of my magic was books, but the earth's energy was so encompassing that even I could feel it radiate up from the ground to mingle with the rushing life force of trees and rivers. Anyone could, really, if they tried.

Mrs. Littlewood's bird-watching platform, like everything about Ruth Littlewood, was tidy and precise. Before she'd sold the canning operation in the valley that she'd inherited from her husband, her staff had quaked at her direction, and Littlewood Legumes had graced the shelves of grocery stores throughout the state, all delivered on time and at a fair price. General Patton could have learned something from her no-nonsense style.

Behind me, she climbed to the platform. "That cat didn't follow us, did he?"

Mrs. Littlewood and I had a long-running dispute

about Rodney's predator instincts. Rodney was not interested in birds and would never, ever attack one. I couldn't exactly explain how I knew this, but I'd bet every witchy bone in my body it was true. Just like I knew why Rodney had decided to stay home. He wasn't up for wearing another of Ruth's bell-spangled collars.

"Don't worry about him." I lay on my stomach and rested on my elbows, putting the binoculars to my eyes. "Now, where are those hawks?"

"In the fir at the cemetery's edge."

Through the grande dame of an oak's branches, Wilfred's few platted blocks lay like a toy world. To my right was the church with its wooden steeple and cemetery. Maybe someday the church would be used for more than funerals and christenings. Nowadays most worshippers drove to Forest Grove. Wilfred didn't offer enough business to support a full-time pastor.

To the left, the quiet two-lane highway—really more of a lazy main street than a real highway—lay like a blue-gray ribbon through town. Beyond that, the Magnolia Rolling Estates formed two short rows and the Kirby River, shrouded by cottonwoods, curved behind and around the green meadow buffering Wilfred proper from the millpond and old mill site.

"This is so nice," I said, the summer breeze ruffling the leaves and my hair.

"Isn't it?" Ruth said. "Buffy and Thor beg me every day to let them come up and take photos, but it isn't safe for kids."

"How do you keep them away?" I asked.

"I tell them it will cost them a dollar each."

Buffy and Thor. They'd taken photos the evening of the party. They couldn't have missed capturing parts of

Wilfred across the highway—the old café, the entrance to the trailer park, and further north. Plus, who knows what they might have documented by accident? I wished I'd remembered this sooner. When I finished here, I'd track them down.

For now, I had other work: get a feel for Morgan and Daphne's relationship when they were alone; and look for a pill bottle on Morgan's nightstand.

I pointed my lenses down the hill and tightened their focus on Daphne's farmhouse. Strolling up to the house's front porch was Sam. He hadn't spent much time with Leo. Daphne was already waiting to meet him. The sun seemed destined to throw golden light on her wherever she was.

"You'll notice the swallows nesting in the church tower," Ruth said. "Every once in a while, a hawk comes by, and they put on a real show."

What Sam wanted to do with his life was none of my business, I reminded myself. I was here to do a job. I trained my binoculars on the bedroom window I knew to be Morgan's. The window had been thrust open, probably in the vain hope of letting in a cooling breeze, and as far as I could tell, the room was empty. I tightened the lens. The nightstand was out of sight, but I could just make out a pill bottle on the dresser. Reading the label was impossible.

"An owl has made its nest in the Douglas fir out front of the Tohlers' bungalow," Ruth said. "You can't really see it now, but come dusk, he's active. I wouldn't want to be a mouse on that block."

"Hmm," I said, still focusing on the farmhouse. Now I saw Morgan. She was in the backyard, talking on her phone and waving her arms. She was angry, no doubt about that.

The coldness in her expression turned my blood to sleet. If looks could kill, dead shrubs would ring the garden.

A queer warbling came from Ruth's throat, followed by *chick-a-dee-dee-dee*.

I cocked my head. "Mrs. Littlewood?"

"Let them know you're a friend." She craned her neck. "This afternoon there are a few hawks over the valley, in fact. Look at that. A miracle of nature. Josie, I'm so glad you're showing interest in our bird life. It's a—" Her tap on my shoulder startled me. "You're not looking at the sky at all."

I swung my binoculars upward, but it was too late. Ruth was on to me. She pasted her binoculars to her eyes and aimed them straight at Daphne's farmhouse.

"Oh my," she said.

My binoculars tilted to the farmhouse's front window. Daphne was in Sam's arms, her head pressed against his chest. My vision clouded and buzzing filled my ears. A meteor seemed to explode in my heart.

A loud fizz set Ruth Littlewood back on her knees. She yanked her phone from her rear pocket. It was still smoking. "What the heck?"

CHAPTER TWENTY-ONE

In the front yard of Patty's This-N-That, in the shade of a refrigerator, Buffy and Thor had set up a card table and two chairs. Buffy was hunched over a pad of paper and Duke stood, electric drill at his side, like a Roman emperor.

"Stay still," Buffy said. "I can't draw you right if you move."

Thor, who had added an eye patch to his costume of shorts, T-shirt, and his ever-present cape, looked on. "Make sure you get that curl on his forehead."

"I am," Buffy said.

Duke's brilliantined hair had drooped in the heat and a wavy lock fell over one eye. "Kids, I have to move on. I've got a gate to fix."

"Just one second," Buffy said. "I'm almost done."

"That will be five dollars," Thor said.

Duke broke his pose. "I'm not paying for this. You

said you needed a model. You didn't say anything about highway robbery."

Buffy pulled her drawing pad closed. "Fine. We'll keep this one as an example."

"I'll see you kids later." He tipped an imaginary hat at me. "Josie."

After he left, I moved into the refrigerator's shade. "How did the party photos come out?"

"Would you like a portrait?" Buffy asked sweetly. Her smile showed a gap.

"You lost a tooth!" I said.

"Last night," Thor said. "The tooth fairy hasn't been around yet."

"I'm expecting a big payout," Buffy said. "I was working on that tooth for days."

True. It seemed like every time I'd seen her lately, she had a finger in her mouth.

"So, what can we do you for?" Thor asked.

"Where did you hear that?" I said, as fitting as Thor's statement was.

"Duke."

"I'd like to see your party photos. Who knows?" I added. "Maybe I'd like to buy one."

"Perhaps," Buffy countered, "you'd like to sit for a portrait while you look at the photos."

Both kids watched me with dollar signs in their eyes.

"Fine," I said.

"Hurray!" Thor ran into the This-N-That and emerged a moment later with a tablet. He dragged his chair next to mine and lifted his eye patch to better navigate the photo program. "Here's a beautiful picture of Sailor."

Lalena's terrier panted on the screen. "That's nice, but I'd like to see photos of the party, please."

"Why?" Thor said. "Looking for something to sell to the tabloids?"

"We were going to do that, too," Buffy said, "But Grandma won't let us."

I imagined the note Buffy might have penned to the *National Bloodhound* in pink felt-tip pen on paper festooned with kittens.

"No," I said. "Just looking."

Buffy drew back, the sun catching her white-gold hair. "It's the murderer, isn't it? You want to see the murderer."

"If we have a photo of the killer, we're keeping that," Thor said.

"I just want to look. Aren't you going to draw me?" I asked Buffy.

"Okay." Thor handed me the tablet and Buffy reluctantly returned to the other side of the table. She eyed me, then picked up an orange pencil, no doubt for my hair.

I scrolled through the photos, looking for anything unusual, especially involving Morgan or Bianca. Maybe I'd catch sight of Bianca in the background or someone spiking Chef Bryce's cocktail. Thor had been all over the party. Who knows what he'd photographed without having a clue? I imagined the flush of victory I'd feel if I could show Sam something concrete. The sooner the murderer was apprehended, the sooner Sam could leave Daphne alone.

Thor hadn't been wearing his eye patch the night of the party, but he might as well have. The photos were all over the place. The first several focused on Patty in her armchair, which made sense given she was their grandmother. He also seemed to have been fascinated with the inside of a pink oven. Lots of close-ups of the racks and hinges. I scrolled further.

"Stay still," Buffy said. Her orange pen swirled over the page as Thor looked over her shoulder. Curls.

Due to Thor's lack of height, most of the photos focused on torsos and legs. I recognized Duke's pants and Lalena's sundress. Morgan's pale arm stretched into one photo. I pulled the tablet closer. Was she near the table Bryce had set up? Yes, there was the edge of his spatula with shredded potato clinging to it. I clicked on the photo.

"What are you doing?" Thor asked.

"Texting myself a photo."

"That'll be one dollar."

I examined the next few photos carefully. Morgan moved closer to Bryce. Now there was another arm, a man's arm. In another photo, that arm held a Golden Cutie. Whose arm was it? The next photo showed part of a black T-shirt. Had to be Gibbous. But I thought he didn't drink. Could this be the cocktail at the house the night of the murder? The one Morgan had dumped in the potted plant?

I clicked on three photos.

"That's four more dollars," Thor said, watching me with an intensity Mrs. Littlewood's hawks would envy.

"Three," I corrected.

The photos abruptly changed focus. In the next one, Roz's hand had connected with Lyndon's face. Man, was she angry. They'd been standing at the edge of the yard and in the background, I saw the tiniest bit of candy-floss pink. Something in the distance. I enlarged the photo, but it was just a hint, nothing more.

A hint of Bianca's hair. And she was headed toward the farmhouse. I clicked on this one, too, and hit *send*. This was a stunner. I imagined Sam's surprise when I showed it to him.

"Is that the one where Roz hit Lyndon?" Thor asked. "The sheriff wanted that one, too."

"Done!" Buffy turned her pad toward me. Her portrait showed me as I felt: frazzled and surprised, with saucer-like eyes.

"Sam's already seen these?" I said.

"Uh-huh," Buffy replied. "Three-fifty's worth. We gave him a professional discount."

Thor adjusted his eye patch and stood. "For you, that will be ten dollars."

Tonight the Constitution Club met in the library's conservatory. In recent months, attendance had been slim. William Barzlee, the club's founder and a long-retired history teacher, had moved to a senior living home, and he didn't get out much anymore, let alone make the drive to Wilfred. Still, his daughter reserved the conservatory for the last Wednesday of every month and made an annual gift generous enough that the library's trustees kept the club going, attendees or not.

Tonight, there were plenty of attendees. However, they couldn't have been less interested in the founding fathers.

"My money's on the yoga fellow," Orson said. "It's not natural to wear that much black. Especially when you're supposed to be interested in beauty. Why put color on everyone but yourself?"

An interesting observation. I watched from my seat near the potted banana tree. At my feet, Rodney licked a paw. I'd been successful at keeping out the booze and peanuts, and Mrs. Garlington had contributed a chocolate sheet cake, although she couldn't make the meeting since she had a student upstairs in the music room. The coffee urn burbled in the corner in accompaniment to the musical scales drifting down through the atrium.

"He wouldn't have the stomach for it," Duke said. He leaned back in his chair so it teetered on its two rear legs. The chair groaned but didn't topple. "You get used to all that meditating, and doing something active—say, killing someone—just doesn't jibe with your personality. Plus, I can't see him being all that knowledgeable about electricity."

"I say it's the tall man, the one with the broken glasses," Mona said. She held a doll's bottle to a kitten wrapped in a blanket. The goat must be at home. "It's always the cute ones that are the criminals. They think they can get away with anything."

I thought I'd better step in. "He wasn't in town the night Bryce was killed. We're clearly not going to be discussing the Articles of Confederation tonight. Why don't we go through the suspects one by one? Maybe someone here saw or heard something helpful."

This was all Ruth Littlewood needed to take charge. "Josie, could you bring out the whiteboard?"

From a corner cupboard I pulled a whiteboard and easel. I set it up at the head of the room and handed a blue marker to Mrs. Littlewood.

"Suspects," she said. The marker squeaked as she wrote. "I think we can all agree that we're in the clear? Including Roz?"

Roz was noticeably absent, probably plotting how she'd interrupt her and Daphne's TV segment with a blackberry pie to the face.

"Definitely," I said. Heads nodded throughout the room.

"That leaves the makeup man—"

"—Gibbous Moon," I said.

Mrs. Littlewood suppressed a snicker. "Plus the production manager, Leo—such a nice man. He asked me about the northern flicker nesting near Big House. Then there's Morgan, personal assistant, and Bianca, the stranger in town."

"Don't forget Daphne," I said.

"Why would she want to kill herself? She has so much to live for," Lyndon said. He'd been quiet all night and if history held true wouldn't ask another question. He'd come in early in the evening to close the conservatory's ceiling vents and, uncharacteristically, he'd stayed. He must've been bored without Roz. I wished they'd make up and get it over with.

"We need to be complete, that's all," I said.

"Next we'll examine the facts," Mrs. Littlewood said. She'd converted the whiteboard into a table with suspects' names down the left and columns labeled *motives, means,* and *opportunity* across the top. "We started with the Moon fellow. What do we have for motive?"

"Seems to me that working for Daphne is a pretty good gig," Duke said. He leaned forward, chair now flat on the floor. "If we assume the chef's death was a foiled attempt on Daphne, it doesn't make sense he'd do it, unless they have a past we don't know about."

"He wants to start his own cosmetics company," I said. "His contract with Daphne has him locked in for a few years."

Rodney left my side and padded toward the chair where Mona and the kitten sat. The kitten had finished nursing and now snoozed in a box with a hot water bottle at her side.

Mrs. Littlewood jotted down my comment. "Means and opportunity?"

"Nearly anyone might have spiked the chef's drink," Orson said. Deprived of alcohol, he'd applied his appetite to Mrs. Garlington's sheet cake. A chocolate-stained paper plate sat at his side. "That's the advantage you have in a proper bar. The beverage stays away from customers until it's ready to serve. Not that I was a huge fan of the Golden Cutie, anyway. Could have benefited from a shot of rye, if you ask me."

In Thor's photo, I'd seen Gibbous holding a fresh cocktail, but he could have been giving it to anyone or drinking it himself, despite insisting he didn't drink alcohol. "Did anyone see him heading to the farmhouse before the party ended? We should establish a timetable."

"He left fairly early," Mona said. "I noticed, because I wanted to ask him if I should reshape my brows."

"Daphne's personal assistant wandered off toward the trailer park at one point," Orson said. "That's the opposite direction of the farmhouse. She asked me what was over there."

That squared with what Lalena had seen. "If she'd wanted to get to the farmhouse without being tracked, it was a smart move," I pointed out.

"What would be her motive? She has a cushy job, too," Mrs. Littlewood said as she took down our information.

Rodney now put a paw into the kitten's box and gently nudged her. He licked the kitten's face and back, and my heart swelled with pride. He might be a stinker sometimes, but he could be a real sweetheart, too.

"I heard her unloading about some acting job Daphne had squelched for her," Orson said. "Years of bartending have given me a special appreciation for a customer's state of mind."

"And hers was?" Mrs. Littlewood said.

"Hopping mad."

So far, this all tracked with what I'd already heard.

"They think the murderer was after Daphne Morris, right?" Derwin Garlington, Mrs. Garlington's son, said. He still wore his postal uniform, which had suffered from repeat performances over the week without a trip to the washing machine. I resisted the urge to dab at a spot of crusted ketchup from his collar. "This Leo probably had a fling with her. Now he's jealous because she has the hots for Sam."

I didn't want to know how Derwin had clued into this fact. All eyes shifted to me and I did my best to appear blasé.

"She does seem rather clingy," Mrs. Littlewood said, glancing at me. "Sam has his hands full with that one." I smiled blandly. "Sitting around and speculating won't get us very far. Why don't we do some real research? We're in a library, aren't we?"

"You mean, like criminology textbooks?" Orson asked.

"I'm sure the sheriff's office has already done the research," I said.

"Sure," Mona said. Rodney lay by my feet again, and she pulled the kitten's box into her lap. "They check arrest records, bank accounts, things like that. That doesn't mean they look for clues to human nature."

"Excellent point," Duke said.

"I bet they never checked the *National Bloodhound*, for instance," Derwin said. "They've had quite a few tasty articles about Daphne Morris's divorce."

"Reading our mail, are you, Derwin?" Orson said.

Now that I'd had the library wired for internet, we did have access to a few databases. I didn't know if the *National Bloodhound* was in one of them, but it I could check. It was a more reputable activity than what might otherwise be happening tonight, and—who knew?—we might actually learn something.

"Let me get my computer," I said.

I grabbed my laptop from my office, where I ignored the Indy 500 history revving its engines in a drawer. I double-checked that the drawer was firmly shut.

Back in the conservatory, I took a place at the table next to Mona and did a search for Daphne Morris. *"Diet tips from a golden star,"* I read from the browser.

"Turmeric lattes. Yuck," Orson said, reading over my shoulder.

"Movies, the book club. Oh," I said. "Here's some dirt on her divorce."

"Bring it on," Duke said. From upstairs, a long vibrato on the organ underlined Duke's request.

"Okay. *National Bloodhound*, May fifteenth," I said.

"Is the Golden Cutie seeing red? Could be. Word has it Daphne Morris walked in on hubby and country-western music star Kevin Atchley strumming the fandango with the couple's dog trainer. Our source, someone close to the actress, says the affair has been going on for quite a while.

"Readers will recall that Daphne Morris's prior husbands—numbers one, two, and three, not to mention a string of discarded lovers—were famously abandoned by her. We hear this turn of events has driven the actress underground."

"Poor Daphne," Duke said with seeming genuine concern.

"What kind of brute is Kevin Atchley? To make her suffer like that?" Orson said, perhaps believing that drinking turmeric lattes was suffering enough.

Lyndon didn't say a word, but his gaze was eloquent with shared pain.

The women in the room looked more skeptical.

"I'm beginning to think she did it," Mona said. "Faked her own murder attempt to garner sympathy."

"Or distract from the real murderer, who she's having an affair with," Ruth Littlewood said. "Like the killdeer." In response to the bewildered looks around the table, she added, "A bird who pretends to have a broken leg to draw attention away from its nest."

"Not a bad theory," Mona said.

While they talked, I searched Morgan Stanhope's name. Beyond the social media profiles were a few notices of roles in obscure plays, all in small towns, and all ending a few years ago, presumably when she took up work with Daphne.

I returned to the social media links and clicked through to her profile. Her icon was a studio photograph, undoubtedly the photo her agent sent out. It might have been an early Grace Kelly screenshot. Her posts showed summering at Martha's Vineyard, a few swanky dinner celebrations, and backstage photos with other actors.

"What are you looking up, Josie?" Orson asked.

"Morgan Stanhope. She's Daphne's personal assistant, but they're not exactly best friends."

"Anything interesting?" Derwin asked, picking at his ketchup stain himself.

"Not much. She's an actor, but not the Hollywood type like Daphne," I said as I scrolled through her posts. "She's into theater. Seems to come from a WASPy family in the Northeast. It's curious, really, that she even took the job with Daphne. Maybe she thought it would give her an in."

Photos of champagne celebrations, Morgan with a cocker spaniel, college roommates scrolled by.

Then I stopped at one particular image. It was Morgan on a roof garden somewhere in Manhattan. She held a pink cocktail in one hand and was laughing. Her other hand was wrapped around a man whose head was pressed against hers. They were clearly a couple. That man was Leo.

CHAPTER TWENTY-TWO

The next morning, I overslept. All night, I'd surfed an ocean of dreams: Duchess with blood on her fur sitting on Morgan's lap; a hardback of *Crime and Punishment*; the roses at Lalena's mailbox whipping in the night.

I had to hurry through the library, opening curtains and muttering quick greetings to the books. When I returned to the kitchen to start the coffee, three heads filled the window in the door.

"Josie, open up. It's visiting hours," one of the Finn brothers said. Neither Theo nor Matt Finn were regular library patrons. Bryce's murder and Daphne's presence were scaring out the most reclusive of Wilfredians.

"Just a sec." I unlocked the door. "Looking for a good read first thing this morning, are you? Maybe a nineteenth-century novelist or a Stoic philosopher—say, Epictetus?"

Theo looked at me blankly. "Patty went to town for a doctor's appointment. Nothing's doing at the This-N-That."

I might have guessed. He went straight to the cupboard below the coffeepot to find the filters.

"Please don't make a mess of the place. And no gambling," I warned.

"Hello, fellows," Duke said, pushing open the door. "Coffee on?"

I left them to their—hopefully—benign devices as I rushed to open the rest of the library. There'd be no book ballet this morning.

The book return box on the front porch held only one item, *An Actor Prepares* by Konstantin Stanislavsky. The book I'd lent Morgan. The cover showed an elderly gent wearing a pince-nez and a thoughtful expression. The pages were still stiff in their binding—Wilfred's theater-loving readers tended to go for Hollywood biographies and DVDs of musicals.

I sandwiched the book between my palms. Because it hadn't had many readers, its voice was quiet, just faraway Russian-inflected words intoning something about posture and muscle relaxation.

I was about to set it on the cart to be shelved, when I had an idea. The book didn't carry the energy of many readers. Could I, perhaps, draw Morgan's energy from it? Maybe I'd have some idea of what was going through her mind. She'd said the book was a comfort read for her. That could mean she'd turned to it when she was distressed. Would her thoughts still be imbedded in the text?

Except for occasional laughter and the sound of chairs on linoleum from the kitchen, the library was quiet. I opened the French doors to the garden to let in the morning breeze, and I took the drama book back to my desk. Anyone passing by would think I was reading.

I let my mind relax and slid a hand into the book's pages. Images rose, as if I were watching a flickering movie screen. I saw the farmhouse's backyard and smelled freshly-cut grass. Morgan must have been reading there. In the background, someone chanted. Undoubtedly Gibbous. I saw a ceiling, a nightstand. Then Morgan's feelings shimmered very faintly.

I drew a soft but deep breath through my mouth and focused. *Come on*, I urged the pages. *What do you have for me?*

Morgan was worried, I could feel that. And, I hesitated, angry. Yes. She was angry. Bits of a phone conversation came to me. It was about the role she was offered in New York. Small theater, influential director. An argument with Daphne about it the night of the party. This was nothing new.

The next image shocked me. I struggled to keep locked to the energy's flow. A shower curtain. A hand reaching for a blow-dryer. Something fell. What was it? A branch from a rosebush, just an inch or so, plucked of petals, twisted and worried from Morgan's fingers.

"Josie. Josie!"

I dropped the book and blinked back to the library around me.

"Sorry," Lyndon said. He stood glum and expressionless, as always, framed by the French door. He held an orange heavy-duty extension cord. "You mind if I plug this in?"

The sight of the electrical cord recalled Bryce's body in the bathtub. I barely heard Lyndon's words. I had to get to Sam.

"Sure."

"It's for the movies tonight."

Movies? Whatever. "Excuse me." I picked up my phone and dialed Sam's number. I needed to talk to him. Now.

I pressed the phone to my ear. One ring. Two. I was preparing to run to Big House or call the sheriff's office, if need be, when Sam answered.

"The night Chef Bryce was killed," I said without waiting for his greeting. "Did you find a tiny bit of flower stem on the floor behind the bathtub?"

"Hi Josie." Nicky was fussing in the background, probably slumped over Sam's shoulder now. "We did. Along with a few bobby pins and a massive dust bunny. Why?"

"The branch. It was green, right? Not an old one?"

"As I recall, it was. The lab figured it must have fallen from someone's clothing. Hold on a second while I put Nicky in his swing."

I tapped my foot until he returned.

"I'm back. Now what's this about?"

"Morgan. She's the one who tried to kill Daphne."

"How can you be so sure?"

"Has Daphne's bodyguard turned up yet?"

"No, she canceled him. Long story. Why?"

My birthmark tingled and I pressed a finger to it. "Look, Sam, I'm worried. Morgan is at the farmhouse with her now. How do we know she hasn't tried anything?"

Sam had been with Daphne yesterday, and Morgan wouldn't strike until she had someone to pin the murder on. She'd already proven that. Now Roz was home and Bianca was camping in the woods. Morgan would have her choice of scapegoats.

I paced the mansion's former drawing room. "We've got to look in on her."

"And say what? We're just dropping in for a wellness check?"

I heard the doorbell in the background, so I moved to the French windows to see who'd arrived. Nicky's babysitter, her bicycle leaning on the porch, was at Big House's front door. Sam opened it, one hand still pressing the phone against his cheek.

"It doesn't matter," I said. "If something's happened to Daphne, you'll never forgive yourself."

"You're in luck. Cherie just arrived and I have a message for Daphne, anyway. I guess I could tell her in person, if you insist. Just to calm you down."

It was a testament to my urgency that my fear surrounding Morgan overcame my irritation at the thought of Sam and Daphne spending more time together. I had my own suspicions of why Daphne had decided against hiring security. "Fine I'll get someone to watch the library and I'll be there in five minutes."

But, who? Roz wasn't due in until the afternoon and it was Dylan's day off. I couldn't leave the library in the hands of the kitchen crowd, or they'd open an off-premises betting parlor or a petting zoo or something.

Fate answered in the form of Ruth Littlewood, binoculars slung around her neck. "Josie. Just the person I came to see. I can't tell you how thrilled I am that you've discovered the universe of our feathered friends. I—"

"Ruth. I need you to watch the library for a little bit. Just make sure the crowd in the kitchen doesn't get too unruly. If anyone checks anything out, take a note of it here." I set a pen on a tablet of paper and pushed them over the desk. "Can you do that?"

She looked startled for only a second. Then, Ruth Littlewood, former CEO of Littlewood Legumes, took over. "Leave it to me." She plunked another stack of whippoorwill brochures on the desk. "Besides, I see you ran out of these."

I dashed across the lawn to Big House, where Sam was getting into his SUV with the sheriff's office seal emblazoned on the door. I jumped into the passenger seat.

"In a hurry, aren't you?" Sam said.

My mother had the gift of foresight, not me. Maybe my imagination was on overdrive, fueled by last night's dreams, or maybe the nearness of Sam and frustration at Daphne had hijacked my brain's wiring, but the worry inside me escalated.

"Come on," I urged. "Let's go." Before it's too late.

CHAPTER TWENTY-THREE

From the street, the farmhouse appeared calm. The morning sun cast a halo on its peaked roof and glinted off its windows. Chickadees twittered from the lilac bushes. There was no foreboding bass music here, no warning of danger. No sign that anything more egregious had been committed than a skipped breakfast.

As we'd passed the This-N-That, we'd seen Gibbous giving Buffy a makeover, with Thor looking on and Patty next in line. From somewhere in the distance came the hum of a lawn mower.

"Satisfied?" Sam said.

He was humoring me. Had anyone else insisted he barge in on Daphne Morris, he would have refused.

"We still don't know what's inside," I said, my voice wavering. In for a penny, in for a you-know-what.

"What's this about a piece of plant stem, anyway? How did you know we found it?"

"I guess I must have seen it that day. Subconsciously, you know." I glanced sideways at him, hoping he'd buy that. "I think it came from Lalena's yard."

He led the way up the stairs to the porch. "How do you know that and what does that have to do with Daphne's assistant?"

At that moment, the front door opened and Duchess dashed out, circling our feet, then bounding down the steps to the lawn.

"Sam," Daphne said, honey in her voice. She wore a peach silk bathrobe too loosely tied over her bust, and her un-Gibboused hair had a sexy tousle. "It's so nice to see you."

Sam shot me a look that said, *You want to know what's inside? That's what's inside.*

In relief, I let out a deep breath. Embarrassment chased the relief. I'd messed up again. Yet I'd been so sure Morgan was the culprit. My burning birthmark told me something still wasn't right.

Daphne didn't even look my way. I could have been a fence post for the interest she showed in me. Her suggestive smile was all for Sam.

"I have an important message for Morgan," I said in my most official voice. "She returned a book this morning, and I'm afraid it has marks in it."

A mild frown crossed Sam's face and Daphne laughed outright. "In Wilfred you bring the sheriff for library infractions?" She pulled Sam inside by the arm. "Fine. Come in." She turned her head toward the house's interior. "Morgan?"

No response from Daphne's personal assistant. The television upstairs switched to a commercial about feminine hygiene products.

"Morgan!" This time Daphne yelled with a voice that, had we been in a theater, would have reached the back of the balcony.

Nothing. Sam's expression was unreadable. Daphne's smile flatlined and I had the impression she wasn't used to not getting an immediate *yes?*

"She's supposed to be here," Daphne said. "It's time for my turmeric latte. She knows how important it is. Dr. Mette says women with my dosha require it."

I vaguely remembered Dr. Mette as a TV personality who was practically a factory of books on Eastern medicine. They called him *doctor* for his PhD in communications.

"Maybe she's in the backyard," Sam said.

Daphne strode toward the sliding glass door letting out to the garden from the farmhouse's kitchen. Her bathrobe swirled around her calves suggestively, but her mood was all anger at Morgan's deliberate disobedience. If Morgan hadn't wanted to kill Daphne before, she would once Daphne was through with her.

Before Daphne reached the door, she shrieked and grabbed the counter's edge. From my place in the living room, the kitchen floor was hidden by a block of cabinets. I hadn't time to inhale before Sam was next to her. I was close behind.

There, on the floor, lay Morgan Stanhope, lifeless. She'd never pull a turmeric latte again.

It took me a moment to process what I was seeing. My nerves tightened like violin strings as I took in the view: Morgan, on her side, her blond hair caught in a shallow puddle of water, one arm straightened above her head, the other crumpled below her on the old linoleum. But for her sneer, she might have been modeling for the cover of a pulp crime novel.

While I stared, willing my brain to process the scene, Sam crouched and lifted her wrist. After a few seconds, he placed it gently at her side. He stood. The message was clear. Morgan was dead.

Daphne shrieked and grabbed Sam's chest, clinging to him, while I backed to the counter.

Morgan hadn't been strangled or shot or stabbed or otherwise obviously murdered. Maybe she'd been poisoned, but that would be for the medical examiner to say. Then I saw the tumbled mug and open jar of turmeric on the counter near the espresso machine. She'd been electrocuted. Just like Chef Bryce.

I nodded toward the espresso machine, and Sam disengaged Daphne.

"I'm going to shut off the power to the kitchen," he said. "Don't move. Don't touch anything."

At that moment, Gibbous, carrying case in hand, came up the back steps. "Stay there," Sam signaled through the French door. Gibbous saw Morgan's body and his eyes widened. If he were faking his response, he was good.

Sam snapped on a pair of disposable gloves. He backtracked through the living room and left through the front door, no doubt to find his way to the basement fuse box.

"She was making my latte. I'd asked her to. She told me she couldn't do it right then, that she was busy, that I'd have to do it myself." Daphne dabbed her eyes. "But she must have changed her mind. She died for me. I should have never stayed in this stupid farmhouse with all its electrical problems."

"There have been other electrical problems?" I asked.

Daphne sighed a long, hitching breath. "Just now. I was upstairs watching the Heartbreak Haven Channel when the television cut out. I yelled for Morgan."

"What happened?"

"She didn't answer. I decided to take care of it myself. My ex, that's Kevin Atchley, you might have heard of him—"

I nodded.

"—says I can do a lot more than I think if I put my mind to it. So, I went downstairs and tightened the fuse, and the power came back on." Her earlier shock turned into smugness.

"It might have been an accident. Bad wiring," I said. From across the kitchen, I examined the espresso machine. Its thick cord showed a clean nick, exposing the wire, as if sliced with a sharp knife. Morgan's electrocution was not an accident. I steadied my breath. "What were you watching?" Sam might need this detail to check times.

"Oh, it was good. Not as good as *The Whippoorwill Cries Love*," she said. "But not bad at all. It had to do with this single mother. She'd been knocked up by her childhood love, but the story took place years later. You see—"

"When Morgan said she couldn't make your latte, were you planning to come downstairs and make it yourself? Maybe you told her so?" Gibbous might have overheard, or Bianca, if she were near. They might have cut the cord thinking Daphne would be the next person to flip the espresso machine's *on* switch.

Sam reappeared through the front door with Leo behind him. Leo wore shorts and running shoes.

"What happened?" Leo said.

"How long have you been gone?" Sam asked.

"I left for a run, oh, about half an hour ago."

"There's been an accident involving Morgan." Sam pointed Leo to the couch. "Have a seat. Backup is on the way."

"What do you mean, *accident*?" Leo said.

I remembered the photo of him, arm around Morgan. She'd meant something to him. I wondered if he'd own up to it with Sam.

"Ms. Stanhope is dead."

Daphne gazed at Sam, then back at Morgan's body. "Poor girl," she said, her voice warm honey. "My best personal assistant ever. So meticulous, so smart. A talented actor, too." Tears glinted in her eyes.

Duchess stood at the kitchen's edge, whimpering. Daphne pushed her dog aside to return to Sam's arms. I studied my sandals. Gibbous joined us, having come in through the front door. He wasn't even able to summon a Kundalini breath exercise.

"Roz," I said. "Where's Roz?"

"I called Duke just now, and he confirms Roz was in her trailer getting ready to go to the library," Sam said. "She's in the clear."

Relief. Whoever was responsible for this, it hadn't been her.

"Now what am I going to do?" Daphne asked. "Who's going to help me with the book club? I don't even know what to ask Roz. Morgan said she'd give me questions. And now—"

"I can help you with that," I said. For Roz's sake, I'd do what I could to give the interview a fighting chance. I forced myself to look at the movie star, cradled by Sam.

Her eyes had closed, and one tear made a path down a pale cheek.

"Someone wants to kill me," came her muffled voice. "Two people are dead now. Maybe I should leave. Lock myself up somewhere before others die on my behalf."

She was a good actress, Daphne was. Was she good enough to have murdered Bryce, then Morgan? Daphne's life force fed on adulation. Once word got out that a killer was stalking her, it would eclipse the bad publicity surrounding her divorce. She'd no longer be the discarded woman. She'd be the tantalizing victim. The news cycle would shift from the footage of her ex and the dog trainer to poor, beautiful Daphne, hunted by a murderer.

The problem wasn't to find a motive to kill Daphne. It was finding someone who didn't have one.

CHAPTER TWENTY-FOUR

That afternoon, the library's kitchen was humming as Wilfred's grapevine digested the new murder. When Roz took over the afternoon shift, I made sure liquor was nowhere in evidence and pushed through the crowd to shut myself in my office. I needed time to think.

Morgan Stanhope was dead. Murdered. I'd been so sure she was Chef Bryce's killer. All the pieces had lined up: She was furious at Daphne for halting her acting career. She was the first person to find Chef Bryce, whom she could have easily confused with Daphne and killed by mistake. Her book had even shown me the murder scene. Now I was back to square one.

I pushed open the casement window to relieve some of the room's stuffiness and Rodney appeared, balancing on the windowsill a moment before dropping to the desk. I needed his comfort more than ever.

"Come here, kitten," I told him. He stepped gracefully

over the month's circulation report and into my lap. I kissed him on his forehead and slid my fingers over the silky fur on his torn ear. "Another death, and it looks like someone is still out for Daphne. What do you think?"

Rodney rolled to his back, showing me his belly with the star-shaped birthmark. He fixed me with his whiskey-tinted gaze. I wasn't stupid enough to pet him on that tempting belly—at least, not now. When I worked magic, he was placid enough to let me kiss his warm tummy with its faint scent of grass or the rosemary bush outside my office window.

The noise in the kitchen reached a new height and I heard—could it be?—two goats bleating. Rodney flipped to sitting and raised his head. No doubt it was Mona with another foster charge. I wondered if I should shoo them to Patty's This-N-That.

"Can I come in?" Lalena said. She pushed the door open a few inches.

"Sure. Pull the door closed behind you."

Today Lalena wore an Edwardian nightgown with a tattered hem and rust stains where it had been folded for decades, but was fresh and airy as a stroll in June.

"Did you know there are two baby goats out there?"

No wonder Rodney was using my office window as his library entrance. "I don't know what to do about them. When do you think Darla will come back and reopen the café? This is getting dire."

"Are you asking for my opinion in my professional capacity?" Lalena settled into the armchair.

"You've heard about Morgan?" She nodded. "I'm asking because I'm at my wit's end. After Morgan's death—well, the town needs somewhere to process all of this."

"Business has picked up for me," she said. "In the form of a movie star."

I sat up straighter. "Is Daphne is coming to you for a reading."

"Uh-huh. She'll be over soon. Even though her assistant just died, ten-to-one she wants to mope about her ex. I'll give her the 'Don't Mash Her Hopes While Inspiring Her to Move On' package."

"Do you think—?"

"Do I think I could feel her out about the murders?" She folded her hands in her lap. "That's what you were going to ask, weren't you?"

I dropped a palm to Rodney's back and silently told him, *Listen up, buddy*.

"And you tell me you aren't really psychic. It's just that the one thing these two deaths have in common is Daphne. When Morgan died, Daphne was the only one in the house. Leo was on a run and Gibbous was giving Buffy a makeover at the This-N-That."

"You think she's murdering her crew one by one and pretending it's someone who wants to kill her?"

"When you put it that way, it does sound ridiculous."

"Besides, what about Bianca?" Lalena asked.

"Good point. That's an open question. Still, I have to wonder about Daphne. I can't decide if she's innocent or if she knows more than she's letting on. Sometimes she seems as uncalculating as a puppy. Other times—"

"Uh-huh." Lalena nodded. "That's why she's a movie star and we're a librarian and a trailer park psychic."

"How do you feel about the title 'Detective Psychic'?"

"I prefer *intuitive*, thank you. And I see myself as a shrink does. Anything my clients say to me is privileged information."

In my lap, Rodney purred. My hand continued to rest, palm wide, over his back. "Couldn't you ask her a few questions? I bet she brings it up, anyway. Murder's a big deal. A lot bigger deal than your ex caught in flagrante delicto with the dog nanny."

Lalena looked at me a moment without agreeing, but she didn't say no, either. She glanced past me at the clock on my desk and rose. "I'd better go. I don't want to keep the Golden Cutie waiting."

The moment she cleared the door, I pushed Rodney toward the open window. "It's time you earned your kibble. Follow her."

His black tail was the last thing I saw of him as he leaped over the sill.

As Rodney crept after Lalena, I shut my office door, cursing that I couldn't lock it. I didn't want anyone to catch me as I did magic. If they had any inkling that I could go into Rodney's body—well, I didn't want to think about that. Most Wilfredians respected my closed door, assuming I was doing something boring and complicated with ledgers. The rumble of conversation in the kitchen, punctuated with occasional laughter and a goat's bleating, told me they were busy for the moment.

Now it was time to see what Rodney saw. *Focus.* Eyes closed, I took a deep breath and held it, then released it slowly. Another deep breath. And another.

I was in Rodney's body now, low to the gravel lane entering the trailer park. Color grayed and motion danced as far as the meadow beyond the last of the mobile homes. A grasshopper jumped in my peripheral vision, but Rodney soldiered on, Lalena ten or twelve feet ahead, toward her trailer.

"Good kitty," I whispered.

Lalena stopped at her mailbox and pushed back a vine of climbing pink roses to check the box's contents. As Rodney, I stopped and licked a paw. Lalena continued up the steps to her trailer and went inside, leaving only the screen door closed. Perfect.

I was just about to edge the screen door open with a paw, when I sensed someone approaching. Not just someone, but Daphne—and her dog, thankfully on a leash.

I dropped to the ground and hid under the wooden steps. Duchess paused halfway up the steps, sniffing at the air.

"Come on, sweetiekins," Daphne said and pulled at the leash.

Lalena opened the screen door wide. "Welcome. Have a seat at the kitchen table. Would you like anything to drink? Iced tea, maybe?" In her professional capacity, Lalena dropped her voice to sound authoritative and slightly mysterious, nothing like the friend who drank boxed wine in my kitchen while giving herself a pedicure.

She let the door go and in one motion I, as Rodney, leaped to the stairs and slipped through the door as it closed. I went straight under the sofa, where I had a view of the kitchen. It was dusty under here and one of Sailor's chew toys, wedged near the sofa leg, gave off a meaty odor. Sailor himself was busy wagging and sniffing Duchess's hindquarters.

Having made a positive ID, Sailor bounded to the couch and sniffed toward me. I shot him a "play it cool" glance and, surprisingly, he seemed to get it. He settled next to the couch. I—as Rodney—tucked my front legs under my chest, focused on the kitchen, and kept my ears alert.

At that moment, someone let out a whoop in the library's kitchen, jolting me out of Rodney's body and back into my own. Roz's scolding quieted them.

I drew another breath and closed my eyes, and I was once again inside Rodney. Through his flattened vision, I saw Lalena and Daphne at the kitchen table. Lalena drew a fat deck of tarot cards from a silk pouch. A lit votive candle smelling of drugstore lilacs mingled with Daphne's peach and rose perfume.

"What would you like to ask the spirits about?" Lalena said.

I'd never seen Lalena give a reading. We'd spent many evenings together over the ten months I'd lived in Wilfred, but in all that time, she'd never so much as glanced at my life line or commented on my aura. In a way, it was a mark of respect. Sailor sighed on the ground next to me, while Duchess, still on her leash, stared at us, tail wagging.

"Maybe the attempts on your life?" Lalena suggested.

"Actually, I'd like to know about my love life," Daphne said, a little nervousness in her words. She was a believer. Lalena had a live one on her hands. The evening TV entertainment show would have shelled out big bucks to see this.

Smiling blandly, Lalena handed her the deck. "Shuffle these and let your mind play through your romantic life, as if you were watching a movie." She tapped one bare foot on the linoleum, then stopped. "I was so sorry to hear about Morgan."

Thank you, Lalena. As Rodney, I kept my gaze on the pair.

"It was horrible. Someone wants me dead, and I can't figure out why." Daphne fumbled with the oversized deck.

"You can mix them flat on the table, if you want," Lalena said. "I suppose your crew is pretty upset, too."

Daphne looked at her blankly. Clearly Morgan's death had slipped her mind, as she'd focused on romance. "Gibbous wants to leave. He says all this death is bad for his brand." At Lalena's raised eyebrow, she added, "His makeup brand. The one he's launching. Or will launch, once his contract is up."

Lalena nodded solemnly. Not bad for a sleuth pressed into last-minute service. "I don't suppose you've seen Bianca around? I worry about you."

"Hmm?" Daphne said, gathering the cards into a pile. "I saw her this morning, walking in front of the house, in fact. Before Morgan, you know—"

"You did?"

"Sure. She didn't come in or anything. Didn't even knock. I was watching TV upstairs, anyway."

"You don't think it's strange that she tracked you down all the way to Wilfred?"

Daphne shrugged. "Why wouldn't she? She's obsessed with me. She says I'm the reason she goes on living."

Duchess started to whine in the direction of the couch. I retreated as far as I could while keeping an eye on the kitchen table.

"Aren't you going to give me a reading?" Daphne said, pushing the deck toward Lalena.

From my new position, I could see their legs—Lalena's strong and tanned with bare feet, and Daphne's shapely with peach-tinted toenails and sandals too strappy to be practical in the country. The cards slapped gently on the table. Daphne's feet drew back as she leaned forward.

"Very interesting," Lalena said in a practiced voice.

"Does it say anything about Sam?" Daphne asked breathlessly.

"The king of cups. A loving man. One who likes to talk."

"That could be Kevin. My ex. Sam's not much of a talker. What else?"

"Five of wands. Some kind of struggle. It's in the near future position. It might—"

"Sam and Kevin fight! They're fighting over me!"

"Well, I don't—"

"Who wins?" The chair creaked as she leaned back. "Kevin's personal trainer is good. But Sam knows weapons." She sighed. "I hope he doesn't get hurt. I could see myself in Wilfred. Part-time, anyway. He'd like my place in Hollywood."

In the library, my stomach grumbled, threatening to expel the tuna sandwich I'd had for lunch. Under Lalena's couch, Rodney swallowed in sympathy.

Did Sam know that Daphne had seen Bianca? I had to assume she'd told him. Perhaps he was questioning Bianca at this very moment. By Daphne's attitude, though, maybe she hadn't thought it was important enough to report. I had to figure out a way to let him know—a way that didn't involve explaining that I had gone into my cat's body.

Daphne let the leash loosen and Duchess lunged toward the sofa. As Rodney, I backed toward the corner, and Duchess whined and sniffed around the sofa's edge.

"Duchess, get back here!" Daphne said.

"Don't worry. She seems to get along fine with Sailor.

I bet she smells one of his chews." Lalena's fingers felt around the trailer's tired carpet at the sofa's edge and pulled out the lint-covered chew. "There."

A rap on my office door slammed me back into my own body. I recovered my breath and opened my eyes. "Yes?"

"May I come in?" Lyndon said.

Still a little shaky, I rose and opened the door.

"Thought you'd better come out and have a look at the setup for movie night."

CHAPTER TWENTY-FIVE

That evening, I emerged from the library to find the lawn between the library and Big House carpeted with blankets and rugs. In the twilight, dozens of LED votives sparkled here and there, echoing the night sky's parade of stars to come. A movie screen cast a dull white glow at the end of the lawn. Families with hampers of food and kids in pajamas were already arriving.

"What do you think, Ms. Way?" Dylan asked. Tonight he wore his grandfather's old tuxedo pants and a crisp white shirt with a pink dahlia in the buttonhole. His cheeks were flushed with excitement.

"It looks—it looks magical," I said. I'd been so wrapped up in the deaths that I hadn't paid attention to Dylan's plans. He had a brilliant future as an events planner, if he wanted it.

"All done practically for free." He ticked off his accomplishments. "The movie screen and projector came from the high school. They don't need them until school starts, and my dad takes care of the iguana and guinea pigs over the summer, so they owed him one. Patty's lending us the votives. She got them at a warehouse sale. She says once she's done with appliances, the This-N-That will specialize in candles."

"How about the rugs and blankets?" I said.

"That was easy. I told people if they wanted to reserve a space, they had to lay out their blankets early."

While I'd been inside, taking care of library business, Dylan had masterminded the whole evening. Had I agreed to all this? I guess I must have. "It's amazing. What's the movie?"

"*His Girl Friday* with Cary Grant—"

"Of course."

"—And Rosalind Russell. Public domain, so that was free, too." He waved toward a family with twin toddlers. "Not too close to the flower beds. That's better." Then, to me, "Lyndon made me promise to guard the rosebushes."

Buffy and Thor had set up a card table near the projector. "Bubbly water," Thor shouted. "Fifty cents." His cape flapped around him and he'd kept the eye patch.

"With lemon or lime," Buffy added, her sequined tutu catching Big House's porch light. Crudely sliced chunks of citrus filled a bowl next to the cooler. Patty watched her grandchildren from a lawn chair nearby.

"It's dark enough to start now," Dylan said. "I'll get Mr. Wilfred to turn off the porch light." He halted and his jaw dropped. "It's her."

Daphne rounded the corner, suffused in her own golden light. Wilfredians gathered on the lawn seemed to inhale all at once. She stopped at Buffy and Thor's table, Duchess scampering around her feet.

"May I have a water with lemon?" she asked.

Thor, goggle-eyed, nodded, and Buffy hurriedly handed her a plastic cup. "That'll be fifty cents, please."

Thor elbowed his sister. "No charge for you."

"Over here," Dylan said, gesturing toward a frayed Persian carpet I recognized from the library's attic. "We hoped you'd make it."

"My. Thank you. You're so handsome tonight." Daphne sat as gracefully as Venus alighting on her half shell. She slipped off her sandals and tucked her feet under her diaphanous skirt of featherweight pink cotton. Duchess curled up next to her. It was like having a freaking Boucher painting in the garden. One slender arm rose. "Sam, over here."

I felt like I'd swallowed a handful of lug nuts from Duke's toolbox. Sam, in worn jeans and a gray T-shirt, crossed the garden, stepping among hampers and children with stuffed animals. He held Nicky over his shoulder. I couldn't read his expression.

"Sit next to me," she cooed.

Sam obeyed—what man didn't obey Daphne Morris? Buffy abandoned her post at the water table and skipped toward them to play with Nicky.

I wanted to vomit.

"Hey, Josie."

I ripped my gaze away from Daphne and Sam to find Leo smiling at my side.

"I thought I'd sit with you, if that's all right." He laid out a plaid wool throw blanket. "I found this at the farmhouse. There's plenty of room for two. I even packed us a dinner."

Still distracted by Daphne and Sam, I lowered myself next to him. We were at the crowd's edge, near the library. "You didn't have to do that."

"It's the least I can do to thank you for the research

you pulled together for me." Leo followed my gaze. "I can guess what you're thinking."

I was grateful it was dark enough now that he couldn't see me blush. "Really?"

"You're wondering how Daphne can be so crass as to be watching movies the day her assistant was murdered. That's Daphne for you." He opened a brown bag to roast chicken and vegetables from the PO Grocery. "It's not that she doesn't care. It's her version of courage. Give the audience what they came for."

"The show must go on," I added.

"Exactly. In fact, that's a good lead-in to what I wanted to talk to you about next," he said. "The book club."

"Daphne's not thinking of pulling out of the interview because of Morgan, is she?"

"She's still up for it, even though Roz is avoiding her. Daphne seems to have found plenty of comfort," he said, casting a glance toward where she and Sam sat. "No, it's Roz I'm worried about. Will she show up, do you think?"

I scanned the families ranged across the lawn for Roz's comfortable shape and brunette head. To my surprise, she was here, settled near the library's side door. Lyndon was nowhere to be seen. His truck was gone, too. Maybe tonight was the ikebana society's monthly meeting, or maybe he'd driven into Forest Grove for dinner while he flipped through gardening magazines. This was good. It cut the chance of a replay of the night of the party.

"Roz isn't dumb," I said. "She knows how big this is for her career. I even caught her jotting on the back of an envelope the jump in royalties she'd need to move out of the trailer."

"That's a relief."

"In any case, she hasn't said anything about not showing up. I'll talk with her, remind her it's in her own best interest."

"Thank you. I'd appreciate that. Without Morgan to help, I'm not sure we could find a replacement for the show this late. Now we just have to make sure Daphne stays alive for the next two days."

Not far from us, Gibbous sat alone on a towel, his legs twisted into the lotus position, moonlight reflecting on his shaved head. Patting her hair, Mrs. Garlington approached him, maybe to ask his opinion of the lavender rinse she used.

"At least Sam's here to protect her," I said and tried to sound indifferent.

He laughed. "He'd better watch out."

"He doesn't seem to find the work difficult."

"I don't know," Leo said. "Warding off Daphne's attention is no joke. Yesterday at the farmhouse, he had to—"

Dylan hushed the crowd and the movie started, throwing black-and-white images and screwball dialogue onto the screen, but I couldn't focus. Daphne leaned into Sam, and he didn't lean away. She laid a hand on his arm. My throat clenched and Leo glanced over at me. I forced my head to turn toward the screen and plastered an *I'm so relaxed* expression on my face.

The mewling of Nicky's fussing drifted toward me, and Sam leaned to lift Nicky. Bedtime. Before Sam could get to his feet, Daphne planted a kiss on his cheek. Moments later, he disappeared into Big House and lights appeared in an upstairs window.

My eyes widened and chest burned. Energy, fed by the library's romance section a stone's throw away, kindled in my body, and I strained to contain it. *Calm*, I urged myself. All at once, the energy in me surged like a fireball and the votives sprinkled across the lawn flashed. Cary Grant and Rosalind Russell's rat-a-tat dialogue slowed to silence, and the screen went dark.

"Weird," Dylan said. "Just a minute. I'll reset the projector."

I looked up to find Roz standing, hands on hips, next to me. "You!" she shouted at Daphne. "You kissed Sam, right here in front of everyone. What, Lyndon's not good enough for you? You just break his heart and move on?"

"Roz, honey," Daphne said as if playing the role of the knowing Southern belle. "Why the sour mood?"

In a few quick steps, Roz was at Buffy and Thor's beverage station. She ripped the bowl of lemon and lime chunks from Thor's arms and stormed to Daphne's side. "Here's sour for you." She upturned the bowl over the movie star's head.

Before the crowd even had the chance to gasp, Daphne was on her feet. She picked a wedge of lime from her hair. "You." She jabbed a finger at Roz. "Apologize."

"No." Roz dropped the empty bowl to the lawn. I knew this tone. No amount of threats or cajoling would change Roz's mind. Not now. Daphne might as well tell the Kirby River to stop flowing.

"Then you can kiss your interview goodbye." Daphne's stare continued one second, two seconds, and she turned on her heels and vanished into the firs marking the highway turnoff.

Slowly, conversation on the lawn resumed. A toddler whined from one blanket and Rodney padded toward me and crawled into my lap. I closed my eyes and forced my breathing to become regular.

At last, the projector started again and the screen filled with motion.

CHAPTER TWENTY-SIX

That night, I couldn't shake the vision of Daphne and Sam, together. Didn't he know what a bad idea this was? Daphne went through men like lipsticks. She tried them on and used them up. And then there was Roz's fight with Daphne. Unless Roz apologized to Daphne, the interview was off. Roz had been compared to Eeyore for her pessimism. Well, she was like a mule in more ways than one. She was stubborn.

Outside, the crowd had gone home. The library was empty, except for Roz, who lingered in the conservatory in a mood that drifted from tears to rage to woebegone stares. Ostensibly, she was working, but I knew better. Once I was sure the library's doors were locked and curtains drawn, I joined her.

"What a night, huh?" I said.

I reached behind the tile woodstove for the pole to close the conservatory's glass ceiling panels. Without the ventilation in the summer, the room would be too moist and warm to stand for more than a few minutes, although Lyndon's orchids loved it. Even with the cross-breeze, in high afternoon the room was borderline unusable. Roz didn't care. She said her hot flashes canceled out any competing heat.

"Leave those open a few more minutes, will you? It's just starting to cool down." She patted the chair next to hers. "And come sit."

The manuscript for Roz's latest romance, decorated with red strike-throughs and scrawled additions, emitted dreamy sighs.

"Why the long face?" she asked.

"I'm not in the mood for horse jokes," I replied. "Besides, it's not like you're in a great mood, either."

"Why should I be?" she said. She swept her papers into a pile, but not without a whispered "darling" and a giggle escaping from the pages first. "Lyndon doesn't stand a chance with her, but he can barely feed himself, he's so excited about Daphne. Then she goes and drapes herself over Sam. No wonder Lyndon wasn't there tonight. He couldn't bear the pain."

"Roz, you amaze me." As angry as she was with Lyndon, she cared enough about his happiness to put her future as an author on the line. "Daphne will be leaving soon. You just have to get through the interview." I hesitated, trying to choose which tack to take, and decided on straight honesty. "Which means you have to apologize to Daphne."

Roz's cheeks were red, maybe with a passing hot flash, but she didn't bother to pick up her fan. A lock of dark brown hair streaked with silver stuck to her forehead. "Forget it. She hurt Lyndon, and for that I'll never forgive her."

"You don't know he was hurt," I said. "Maybe Lyndon had something else to do tonight. Or maybe he was ashamed of his brief crush, and he couldn't face you. You know how he is. It takes him a while to sort out his feelings."

"Okay. I know she won't be here forever. As you keep reminding me, she'll leave, and when she does, Lyndon will come to his senses. But who's to say some other dishy woman won't turn up in town? I can't live through something like this again. It's over between us."

"Will you at least consider going through with the interview? Why let either Daphne or Lyndon mess with your career? This interview will send book sales through the roof."

Staring through the conservatory's glass walls to the darkened garden beyond, she waited so long to respond to my question that I was beginning to think she hadn't heard me. Finally, she whispered, "I can't. Can't do it."

"Roz," I said. "This interview. It's sales, it's your ticket to freedom. It's a house, travel, whatever you want. Don't let your pride ruin it for you."

"I wish I could whip up a love potion to serve to Lyndon, to clear the Golden Cutie out of his head for good. But that's impossible." She locked her manuscript into her desk and collected her purse.

"It wouldn't be right, anyway, to give him a love potion." I hesitated. "Would it? I mean, hypothetically."

"Why wouldn't it?"

"Well, don't you want Lyndon to love you for you and not because you drugged him into it?"

Roz shrugged. "I don't know. In a lot of ways, love is a choice. One person needs to see the other person as an option, then choose to open the romantic floodgates. The problem here is that Lyndon's forgotten about me. If I could somehow make him remember, I would."

I waved at her desk. "But what about all those books you write? They're all about everlasting love at first sight. They say love and fate are intertwined."

"Not all of them. In *Forster Forever*, it takes the milk-maid months before she sees the viscount as a romantic possibility, even after he saves her from the runaway horse."

"You know what I mean," I said. "Is it right to compel someone to love you?"

"Why not? If I had a love potion, you bet I'd use it," Roz said. "As they say, 'All is fair in love and war.'"

Although frequently attributed to authors as diverse as Shakespeare, Cervantes, and Lyly, this quote is of uncertain parentage, intoned a book in Reference. I kept a neutral expression.

"Will you at least reconsider the interview with Daphne?" I asked.

"No. And that's final," Roz said. "In the meantime, I have a plan. Didn't we just restock toilet paper?"

"Sure. Why?"

"While he's away, I'm going to TP Lyndon's cottage."

Gathering the ingredients for the love potion was easy. Stars crowded the midnight sky, giving me plenty of light in the garden between the library and Big House. Dylan had done a thorough job cleaning up after movie night, and aside from trampled lawn here and there, I'd never have known that earlier it had been the scene of picnic dinners, Cary Grant, and the pelting of a movie star with citrus. Crickets chirped from the brambles covering the bank sloping to the Kirby River, and flags of white toilet paper waved from Lyndon's cottage. He wasn't home yet, and I wanted to finish my task before his truck rumbled up the driveway.

I snipped five roses about to open—three dark pink and two red—and laid them over an arm. I knew Lyndon hadn't sprayed the roses with anything. Surprising most people, he was vegan and couldn't even bear to see insects suffer. He held strictly to organic gardening and saved coffee grounds and eggshells for the compost heap.

Upstairs, I set the roses on my bed and picked up the silver-framed photo on my nightstand. It had been taken at Christmas when I was still a schoolgirl, and it was of my family, with my grandmother settled into an armchair in the foreground. My sisters, one older, one younger, flanked me. We were in our pajamas. My father, a pipe in his mouth—it was always there, rarely lit—rested a protective arm around my mother, who wore an uncharacteristically frilly robe. A gift from my father, no doubt.

This was the beloved object required for the love potion. As I fiddled with the back of the frame, Rodney appeared from his nighttime patrol of the property and jumped on the bed. I passed a hand over his silky back, and he bumped his nose against my palm and purred thickly, the decibel level he saved for when I worked magic. I felt my energy kick up a few notches.

Now the photo was free of its frame. Oh, how I hated to destroy it. But I wasn't really destroying it, I reminded myself. I was transforming it. It would become part of what would enrich my life with love. I tore the photo across its middle.

Rodney rolled onto his back, purring furiously. Even from here, my bedroom, buffered from the rest of the library by the living room and a floor, I heard the books singing low.

My grandmother's recipe said I should mix the shredded photo and rose petals with wine. I took a measuring cup to the downstairs kitchen. Enough moonlight flooded the windows to see by, and I fell in a dream state that I didn't want to rattle with electric light. I opened the cupboards and found half a bottle of tequila and a couple of miniature liquor bottles. No wine here. The refrigerator held coffee creamer and the remains of someone's roast beef sandwich.

Then I remembered Lalena's box of wine in my apartment's kitchen. The wine wasn't fancy, but the grimoire didn't specify that it had to be a premier cru Bordeaux. I returned upstairs and squirted the spicket of boxed pinot gris into the measuring cup, then poured it into a mixing bowl. I tore the roses' velvety petals into the bowl and tossed the pieces of photograph on top.

The mess in front of me hardly looked like a convincing love potion. How would I ever get Sam to drink it?

Rodney bumped his head against my calf, reminding me that the potion was not yet finished. Yes, it contained a beloved object, but it didn't yet hold my energy. The next step was the most important.

There was only one place to finish the love potion. I put a pink taper candle and matches into my robe pocket and carried the bowl downstairs. In the warm night, the bowl smelled of roses and wine. I took it to Popular Fiction and set it on the side table near the romance novels. I nudged aside the curtains to let in moonlight. The birthmark on my shoulder burned.

The books already seemed to know my plans. Their voices swirled around me in a miasma of sighs and whispered confessions of love, interspersed, curiously, with the clomping of horse hooves and faraway orchestral waltzes. I moved the side table so that moonlight fell across the potion and I lit the candle. Then I placed my hands around the bowl and closed my eyes.

A jolt of power erupted from my palms and fingers. I gasped but held my hands steadily an inch from the bowl. Pink light shimmered between my palms and the bowl, and I couldn't breathe quickly enough to fill my lungs. Rodney rubbed against my calves to calm me.

When I'd first experienced the depth of my power last fall, I'd had no idea where it came from or how to manage it, and I'd nearly burned down the library. I'd learned a lot since then. If I centered my attention, the magic focused, too. It meant being in the moment, undistracted, and tightening my focus like I'd twist a telescope. I became a conduit for the energy of the authors and readers who'd invested in the novels around me. It was exhilarating—and terrifying.

I had no idea how long I spent with my hands around the bowl, hearing the books moan with emotion, the energy hot as lava from my hands, but at some point my attention snapped and I was back in the mansion's old drawing room. Rodney was running around the room with a major case of the zoomies. The candle sputtered and its fire died, beeswax-scented smoke curling into the dark.

"Okay, baby boy," I said to Rodney. The sound of my

own voice startled me in the library's enveloping quiet, and I realized the books had silenced. I pulled my hands away from the potion and curled my fingers into a fist and released them.

The bowl's contents had reduced to a boozy pink syrup smelling of honey and roses. I took a few deep breaths to ground me, then carried the bowl through the atrium, its floor splashed with red and blue light from the cupola's stained-glass, to the kitchen. The potion now made up less than a quarter cup of liquid. What should I do with it?

I knew. I emptied one of the airline bottles—this one filled with sambuca—and rinsed it thoroughly with hot water. Here, trees filtered the moonlight. I clicked on the lights and continued my work transferring the love potion into the tiny bottle. Grandma had written it was powerful, that it could make anyone fall in love with me. All I'd have to do was pour two scant teaspoons into Sam's post-dinner tea as we sat on his back porch. It wouldn't be difficult. He was always getting up to fetch a bottle for Nicky or adjust the music's volume.

A tickle of feeling made me hesitate. The books wanted me to know something. I closed my eyes and let the feeling grow. A title slid into my brain: *Gone With the Wind.* In it, Scarlett O'Hara spends so much time mooning over Ashley that she misses a great love affair with Rhett Butler. As *Gone With the Wind* faded, *Madame Bovary* took its place. Poor Charles Bovary could never hold his wife's heart, because she hadn't chosen him. Finally, the books sent me *Great Expectations*, and the image of Miss Havisham came to mind, complete with rotting wedding cake and shredded bridal gown. I refused to be any of these protagonists. I was so much better than that.

In the kitchen's harsh light, I knew what I was doing was wrong. My parents' marriage wasn't perfect, but its strength came from the decisions they made together and the support they gave each other. Maybe passion had driven them together years ago, but it was something stronger, something woven of ongoing commitment, which had built them the sort of partnership I wanted for myself.

Besides that, wasn't the number-one quality of any romantic prospect that he wanted you—you alone—for exactly who you were? I caught my reflection in the kitchen window. *Look at me*, I thought. I was smart, funny, and kind. I'd turned the library into Wilfred's beating heart, and I'd helped people do everything from research a trip to China to learn Russian to crochet pot holders. I had a way with bossy cats. And, dammit, I was magic. I was the amazing Josephine Way, named after the queen who'd snagged Napoleon. If Sam couldn't see what a catch I was, I had no use for him.

Roz had been wrong—and right. Maybe love was somewhat random at the beginning. Maybe two people had to see each other as possibilities, and Sam didn't see me as one. The potion might open Sam's eyes to me, but it couldn't make him give me the kind of relationship I wanted. He had to want to be with me because of who I am. If not, well, it was his loss. I'd find a man who would.

I pushed the tiny booze bottle to the back of the counter, and I went upstairs to text Leo.

CHAPTER TWENTY-SEVEN

The next morning was the sort that makes Oregon's summers famous. The sky was a banner of blue, a blue that artists struggle to paint but never get quite right. Their brushes can't portray the soft breeze and birdsong. Leaves rustled in the oak trees and the sun was warm enough to bathe in. And Lyndon's cottage was free of all remnants of toilet paper. He must have been up early.

This morning, Leo and I had a date.

"Are you ready?" Leo said. "I found these at the farmhouse." He held up a bucket and a pocketknife.

"Perfect." I'd brought a canvas day pack with a mushroom identification guide in one pocket and a couple of sandwiches in the other. The guide was thrilled to leave the library and chuckled with happiness. "We'll take the path along the river, but when we get to the woods, we cut to a trail going south. Duke says the rain a few weeks ago brought out the chanterelles."

"I'll follow you. Thanks for texting me about the hike.

I'd hoped you would, but I didn't want to be too pushy," Leo said.

"It'll be fun," I said. "Besides, I wanted to know how Daphne is feeling about her interview with Roz. Has she given up on it?"

Down the bluff, the river meandered, sparkling in the morning sun. Our steps fell into an easy rhythm. While we walked, the mushroom guide chattered about lichen.

"She'll do the interview, but only if Roz apologizes. She'll apologize, won't she?"

I remembered Roz's refusal, emphasized every time she rounded a corner of Lyndon's cottage, toilet paper roll in hand. "Sure. She's looking forward to it. Just a minute, I need to send out a quick text about something going on with the library." I leaned against and tree and withdrew my phone from my day pack to text Sam. *Any chance you could convince Roz to apologize to Daphne?* I typed. *Am hiking with Leo, or I'd try it myself.*

Then to Leo, quickly changing the subject, I said, "How was everything at the farmhouse last night?"

"The power stayed on and we all woke in the morning, alive. Daphne was especially alive. She has a thing for the sheriff in a big way."

I didn't want to hear about it. I focused on Leo. I'd been mistaken about his eyes. They were blue, not gray. "That's good. At least one peaceful night."

"However, Gibbous thinks he saw Bianca loitering out front when we got home."

"Uh-oh." I let a few steps pass before continuing. "I'd wondered if she was still hanging around."

"I didn't see anyone, but Gibbous is super-paranoid about her. He reported it to the sheriff. I wish Daphne would have followed through with hiring a bodyguard."

"Why didn't she?" I asked.

"Why should she, as long as she can have the sheriff at her beck and call?" He gestured toward my shoulder. "Can I carry that pack for you?"

It wasn't heavy, but I handed it to him, anyway. Roz would have approved my letting him be chivalrous. My knife was in the pack and for a split second I remembered Sam's warning about not really knowing Leo. I glanced at him. He looked carefree and happy to be in the forest. Boyish, even. Nothing deadly there.

"She's supposed to leave for home tomorrow. Bianca, that is. That should relieve some of the tension," he said.

"I can't believe they're letting her go." I pointed left at the ancient Douglas fir that marked the turnoff. "We take that trail."

"She violated her restraining order, but that's all they've got against her. Frankly, I'll be happy when she's gone. Daphne's tense, worrying that Bianca will blab to the tabloids and we'll have articles saying 'Deadly Daphne' on top of all the bad press she got about her divorce."

"Nothing has come up in the papers about the murders yet, has it?" This was something to consider.

"Not yet." Leo emphasized the *yet*.

The trail took us up an overgrown logging road thick with sword ferns that brushed our waists as we passed through them. The tree's canopy cut the sun to isolated dapples on the brambles around us. This afternoon would be hot in town, but here we'd be cool.

Talking with Leo was easy, as if we'd known each other for years. He was like the boys I'd befriended in grade school—the geeks and misfits; boys who later ran tech firms and became artists.

I took a moment during the climb to catch my breath. "So, who do you think killed Bryce and Morgan? Do you have any ideas?"

"I don't. I'm stumped. Gibbous is in the clear. He was giving the little girl—"

"Buffy," I said.

"—giving Buffy a new hairdo when Morgan died."

"There's the question of motive, too," I said. "Daphne is his ticket to fame. Without her, his new cosmetics line wouldn't get very far."

"He's already well-known, thanks to her. He might not need her anymore. Maybe he could even get good press by doing her up for her casket."

I'm ashamed to say the vision of Daphne in a casket gave me a moment of pleasure, even if she'd probably still be gorgeous in death, with peach-colored roses ringing her head. "He does have a contract with her, though, same as you and Morgan. That will slow him down."

"Sure, but his comes up for renegotiation next year. He's been working for Daphne longer than we have."

This wasn't the impression Gibbous had given me. I turned this over in my mind as we walked.

"It's strange," Leo continued, "But I suspected Morgan for a day or two. That's out."

"I did, too," I admitted. "She was there when Bryce was found, and she'd been so angry with Daphne. We have to count Roz out, too, despite her fan and the electrocutions in her novel. She was on her way to the library when Morgan was killed."

"Which leaves Bianca and Daphne herself," Leo said.

"Do you think—do you think Daphne could be setting herself up as the victim?"

"By killing two of her staff?" He shook his head. "I don't see it. Not that she doesn't enjoy people fussing over her. Basically, she's too lazy." He stopped suddenly. "Look."

Through the trees was a grassy clearing maybe twenty

feet across. The sun turned the tiny meadow as freshly green as the new needle tips on the fir trees. Buttercups waved in the grass.

"A witch's circle," he said. "Come on, let's check it out. Maybe if we stand in it, we'll feel witchy energy."

I laughed and followed him to the clearing's center, where sun surrounded us. "Tell me. What would a witch do here?"

"First," he said with a comically officious voice, "she would cast a circle by asking each of the four directions—wind, earth, fire, and water—to protect her."

Ever since I'd recognized I was a witch, I'd studied up on contemporary witchcraft and learned that casting circles was a fundamental ritual among Wiccans. My grandmother's lessons had never mentioned it, although before performing a spell she recommended cloaking myself in a burst of energy to "clear the pipes," as she put it. Our magical tradition came from deep in our family tree, not from Wicca.

"Or him, I presume?"

He nodded. "Although hereditary witches seem to follow the mother's family line."

"I see," I said. "What next?"

"She'd do some sort of spell. Bless the crops or hex a neighbor or banish an illness. Get the cow producing milk again."

"Seems sort of risky, casting spells in public."

"It was. Especially during certain holidays or phases of the moon when zealots would be looking for her."

I didn't observe any holidays that other Wilfredians didn't share, but I was intensely aware of the moon's phases. Right now, the moon was waxing in its third quarter. Before I went to bed, I liked to open my curtains and let the moonlight wash over the room. On clear nights, the glow was bright enough to cast shadows. Being a witch far from family and anyone who knew my power was lonely for me sometimes. It was as if the moon and wind understood this. And Rodney, of course.

"Do you really believe in this?" I asked. "In witches?"

He shrugged. "Why not? The witches I've researched certainly believed in themselves. You could be a witch, you know. Do you have any unusual birthmarks?"

"You're hilarious," I said. "You think I could be a witch?"

"Let's see," he said. "You have red hair and a freckle in your eye. Traditional witch trappings."

"Lots of people are redheads. Lucille Ball. Bozo the Clown," I countered.

"People say you have an almost magical way with book recommendations, and the library feels like a different place since you arrived."

People said that? I smiled. "I do love books. That hardly makes me a witch."

"Then there's your black cat. Classic. I have to wonder, what would you do if I gave you a broom?"

I stepped back, toward the trail. "Wouldn't you like to know. Come on, those chanterelles aren't going to pick themselves." Although they might, I thought, if I asked them nicely.

We reached the top of the hill, and the trail—if you could call an overgrown track a "trail"—joined the brush-covered loop that circled the summit. Saplings sprang from fallen mossy logs, and the air felt cooler, moister. Here, where long-ago logging had disturbed the topsoil, chanterelles took root in loamy corners.

"I came up here last spring with Duke, and we gathered enough mushrooms to supply the café's omelets for a week. We're looking for mushrooms with orange-yellow tops. Sometimes they're barely popping out of the earth," I said.

"Wavy at maturity," the book droned. "Attention to the spore-bearing surface, which is perfectly smooth. Fibrous stalk."

One thing was sure. The mushroom identification guide would never be confused with a manual on seduction.

"Got it," Leo replied.

I glanced back at the entrance to the old logging road. Thanks to the thick ferns and brambles, it would be too easy to overlook it if we didn't mark it. I wasn't sure I could make my way home without finding the trail. If we wandered down the wrong side of the mountain, we could be lost in the wilderness of the coastal range for days.

"Hand me my day pack, please." I pulled a purple cotton napkin from under a sandwich and tied it to the branch of a salmonberry bush. "This will mark where we turn off to go home."

"I'll follow your lead."

"Check under the fir trees. Sometimes you can just see a bit of the mushroom's cap," I said.

"Usually free of maggots," the guide added helpfully.

Leo wandered ahead. He knelt and lifted a pale orange mushroom. "Like this?"

"Positive identification," the mushroom guide said.

"Yes," I said. "That's it."

"There's another one."

We spent the next few hours wandering the brush-choked rim road and gathering chanterelles. I thought of the heat rising over Wilfred and was grateful for the forest's shade and dappled shadows. While we scanned the ground and raked our fingers over the loamy soil, we were usually less than ten feet apart, and we talked about everything from the WPA writers' project to favorite high school bands. The mushroom guide only rejected one of our finds, a sulfur tuft, as poisonous.

"Are you getting hungry?" I asked. "There's a fallen log over there. We could sit for a minute and eat."

"Sounds good." Leo stretched his back. "What are we going to do with all these mushrooms? Bryce would have loved them. He was always up for a cooking challenge. Once Gibbous brought in five pounds of shelled pecans. Bryce made pie, rolls, nut-crusted chicken, and I-can't-even-remember-what-else from them."

I hoisted my bag to the log. "Tomorrow's the interview. Maybe we could have chanterelles and toast at the This-N-That to celebrate." Patty would love making a party of it, and Roz might enjoy the limelight, too—as long as Sam was able to convince her to take part.

I laid our remaining napkin as a makeshift tablecloth over a stump and set out the sandwiches. I was thinking of Chef Bryce. Maybe Leo was, too. Or of Morgan.

"Leo?"

"Hmm," he replied, reaching for a sandwich.

"How well did you know Morgan?"

For a moment, his hand hung in midair. He returned the sandwich to the napkin. "Why do you ask?" Understanding passed over his features. "Oh, I get it. We discussed each of the possible murderers, except for me. Maybe we had some sort of troubled past. That's what you wondered, right?"

I remembered the glint of his pocketknife as he'd sliced a mushroom from its base. "I'm sure the sheriff questioned you about her."

"He didn't, actually." This time, Leo did take a bite from his sandwich. "Remember, I was out of town when Bryce was killed. I couldn't have done it."

"In Portland, right?" I asked.

He hesitated. "Right."

I tried to keep my tone light, but for the first time, I wondered if I'd made a mistake coming out here with him. "Great, but that still doesn't answer the question."

He looked at me a second longer than he might have. "You're worried, aren't you?"

I didn't respond. Denying it would only make me sound more worried.

He drew a breath. "Well, to answer your question, I knew Morgan before I took a job with Golden Cutie Productions. I knew her from drama school, actually."

"You studied acting?" I could see it. He had an easy charm and could have easily been cast as the best friend.

He nodded. "But it wasn't for me. I didn't like the competition and performing wasn't enough of a reward. Plus, I was too curious. I wanted to learn. I used my drama background to get into production work, then turned that into the chance to research things that fascinate me."

"You and Morgan were friends." The memory of the photo of his arm wrapped possessively around Morgan's shoulders was impossible to forget.

"She got me the job."

"Just friends," I emphasized. This was Leo's chance to come clean.

I barely breathed as I waited for his response. We were alone in the woods. Except for the occasional call of a bird and wind through the tips of the conifers, it was quiet. Then something crackled in the underbrush. We both turned toward the noise. Then, silence.

"A squirrel, maybe," Leo said.

"It sounded too big to be a squirrel."

"A bear?"

"Maybe. There are black bears around here. If one heard us, he'd run away."

After a moment of listening with no further suspicious sounds, we relaxed. A bird *woot-woot*ed in the distance, as if to calm us. "So. Morgan," I said.

"We dated," he admitted finally.

"No kidding?" A relationship gone wrong wasn't a sure motive for murder, but I wanted to know more.

He tossed the remains of his sandwich on the stump. "I like you, Josie. I want to tell you the truth."

"Okay."

"Morgan and I were engaged. Our families are a big deal where we come from, and I've known her since we were kids. I suppose on some level we always thought we were supposed to be together. We dated, and we got engaged."

"Why didn't you say this right away?"

He rewrapped the rest of his sandwich and returned it to my day pack. "Daphne's contract. It forbids relationships between her staff. I guess I've gotten into the habit of playing it down."

"You and Morgan hadn't broken up by then?"

"We had. When I came to work for Daphne, we hadn't been together for years. But you don't understand Daphne. She would have always been suspicious if she'd known. We never mentioned it to her."

I took a moment to digest all of this. Morgan, Bryce, Gibbous, and Leo were all tied to Daphne because they needed something from her. Bryce was her childhood friend and traveled the world and met interesting people thanks to her celebrity. Gibbous needed the exposure that came with Daphne to attract investors to Lunar Looks and boost his profile. Morgan had needed Daphne for contacts in the acting world. Leo needed Daphne for the experience and income to make his documentaries—as long as she didn't find out.

In return, Daphne exacted her payment. She insisted on complete loyalty and devotion, and she got it in writing, in their contracts. The rub was that this demand stood between her and what these people wanted, in some cases wanted passionately. I'd certainly heard worse motives for murder.

"You know, maybe it's time we headed back." I rose from the log. "You probably need to prep for tomorrow."

"You understand, don't you, Josie?"

"I understand, all right."

He stood, too. "It was over a long time ago."

"I get it." I brushed my jeans. "I really do." I felt the strong urge to return to the library and its routine and comfort. "Come on. Let's go."

I pulled our things together and returned to the trail crowning the mountaintop, leaving Leo to follow me.

"I'm sorry I didn't say anything sooner," he said. "I know it looks funny. I'm being completely open with you now."

"That's fine." I kept my gaze straight ahead. The sooner we were among other people, the better.

"Polypores," the mushroom guide said. "Off-center stalk and bracket-like growth."

"Shut up," I told it.

"What?" Leo asked.

"Nothing."

He hurried a few steps to catch up with me. "You can't think I killed Morgan, can you?"

I searched the brush for the purple napkin I'd tied to mark our path.

"Josie. Look at me. Do you think I had anything to do with her death?"

We'd spent most of the afternoon wandering the forest, but we'd stuck to the old logging road and surely by now we'd circled the mountaintop. The trail marker should be somewhere here. We'd hadn't passed it earlier, I was sure of it.

"Where's our marker?" I said.

Summer had carpeted the forest floor with dry fir needles, making footprints impossible to track. Everywhere I turned, the forest looked the same: dim masses of sword ferns, mossy piles of fallen branches, leafy brambles.

I pulled out my phone. I'd text Duke or Orson and get help finding the path back. I tapped in my code. No signal. But I did have a reply to my text to Sam that must have come in when we were still in cell phone range. *Watch it with Leo. He was not in Portland when Bryce was killed. Still checking alibi.*

I glanced up from my phone. At any point, Leo could have hidden the marker, trapping me with him. He'd told me he was "completely open" with me. He knew I wanted to find the murderer. We'd talked it through. I might have stumbled across something he wanted hidden.

"What's wrong?" he said.

As I said the words, I couldn't believe them. "We're"— I searched the forest one more time—"We're lost." Then I ran.

CHAPTER TWENTY-EIGHT

I hadn't made it more than a few yards before Leo grabbed me by the waist. I spun to face him.

"What's wrong?" he asked.

I yanked myself away. I could make a break for it again, but I'd be tearing up brambles as I ran—and running where? Wilfred was down the mountain, but down which side?

I flipped open my pocketknife and pointed it at him. "Stay away."

He stepped back and held up his palms. "You can't think I'd hurt you."

"Sam says you lied to him about where you were when Bryce was killed. Now someone has stolen the trail marker." I glanced at the light filtering through the forest canopy. How many hours did we have until nightfall?

"Look." Leo tossed his wallet and pocketknife to the ground and turned his pockets inside out. They were empty. He handed over his bag of mushrooms and I felt around its edges. No napkin there. "See?" he said. "It wasn't me." He kicked the knife my way. "Take it."

"You lied to the sheriff's office. You weren't in Portland when Bryce was killed."

He retreated further. "You're right. I did lie. But I swear I wasn't anywhere near Wilfred that night. I was at the coast, following up on a story about folk medicine."

"Prove it," I said. "What town were you in?"

"Florence. Right on the ocean," he replied promptly.

"What did you do?"

"Went to the courthouse to look up a few deeds. Visited a farmhouse at the edge of town. Stayed in a noisy hotel called the Seaside Hideaway."

I knew that hotel. He could have looked it up earlier, though. "I bet you went to Molly's Famous Seafood Buffet. Everyone goes there. It's right on the boardwalk."

He wrinkled his brow. "Molly's, you say?"

I nodded.

"I didn't see a place called Molly's. I must have missed it."

He passed the test. There was no Molly's Buffet. "All right, I believe you. Why didn't you tell Sam where you really were?"

"I couldn't," he said. "I didn't want Daphne to know I was working on my documentary, so I told her I was going to Portland. I figured if I said I was visiting a friend, she wouldn't get suspicious."

Could I believe him? I held his knife and he didn't have any other weapons. He could overpower me, but why? He had no reason to kill me.

He pushed his glasses back up his nose and waited.

"All right," I said. "When we get home, you're going

to have to come clean with Sam." Was it darker already, or was it my imagination? "We've got to get out of here while it's still light. Can you get a signal on your phone?"

"No. Nothing."

"That tells us one thing, at least."

"What's that?" Leo asked.

"The smart mushroom gatherer always brings a compass and a whistle," the mushroom guide said officiously. I zipped it shut in the day pack's pocket.

"That we're on the opposite side of the mountain from Wilfred." Wilfred was on the edge of the valley. The mountain range was sparsely populated. If we were on the side of the mountain opposite the valley, the lack of a cell phone signal wouldn't surprise me.

"The problem is to know when we're facing town. Everything looks the same up here to me."

"We can circle the rim road again and keep checking our phones. How much power do you have?" I was at 25 percent.

"Not much. Not enough if we have to use them as flashlights."

Flashlights, yes. But at that moment we had more serious concerns. Someone had stolen our trail marker, and I hadn't forgotten the noises we'd heard in the forest as we ate.

"Someone wants us trapped on the mountain," I said. "Why?"

"It can't be anything we know," Leo said. "Maybe he wants us out of the way for a while."

"To get at Daphne," I said.

I found a thick branch the size of a baseball bat, but it was light with rot. I tossed it aside and looked for another. Leo followed my example. A club wasn't much help against someone with a gun, but it was better than nothing.

"Come on," I said. "Let's walk. We'll check our phones as we go."

We set off along the overgrown logging road, this time not looking for mushrooms but listening for sounds of another person in the woods around us. The trees' canopy was too thick to admit much sky, but light slanted at an increasingly sharp angle through the trees. Every once in a while, we checked our phones. Aside from birds and wind, the woods were still. We seemed to be alone. This was both the good and the bad news.

Finally, half an hour later, Leo got a signal. I checked my phone. I had a signal, too, although weak.

"Only one bar. Let's keep on," I said, "And check again in a few minutes."

Soon, both of our phones had stronger signals. We were facing the valley. There was no sign of a trail, but at least we knew we were headed in the right direction.

"We're going to have to make our own path," I said. "Too bad we don't have one of your witches with us. Maybe she could wave her wand and send up flares." I was too far from books to harness their magic. The mushroom guide would be terrific for keeping us from eating anything poisonous, but it couldn't get us home.

"Or she could beam us straight to the library," Leo said.

"Or to the yard in front of the This-N-That where someone might be grilling burgers." Lunch seemed like a long time ago.

We used our sticks to push aside brambles and Leo thoughtfully held back branches to keep them from smacking me in the face. Despite that, I knew I'd have scratches along my arms, not to mention blisters on my feet.

"Wait." Leo stopped as we passed through a cluster of sword ferns. "Isn't that the witch's circle we saw this morning?"

Beyond us was a clearing, its buttercups now dull in the waning light. "Could be. We're at a different angle. If it is, the path should be somewhere along here." For the first time since we'd lost our way, I felt hope. "Maybe if we walk its edges."

"My idea exactly." Leo seemed to have lightened up, too. We were going to make it.

At that moment, motion in the brush caught our attention. This time, it wasn't rustling, but a full-on trample. Whoever was coming wasn't afraid we'd hear him and was headed straight for us. And then the person yelled.

"No!" A blur of black and pink burst into the clearing. It was Bianca, and she had a knife.

Leo lunged at her, bringing her down at her knees. Her head thumped as it hit the forest floor and Leo pinned down the hand with the knife. I wrenched it from her grip. She stopped struggling and lay limp. Her face was taut with red-rimmed scratches.

"Let me go!" she said, tears in her voice.

"No," Leo said.

"It's you," I said. "You're trying to kill Daphne. You wanted us out of the way so you could get to her."

"No." Bianca let her head sag against the dried fir needles. "No, I swear. Someone's trying to kill me."

CHAPTER TWENTY-NINE

We propped Bianca against a fir tree, both of us ready to grab her should she try to escape.

"What do you mean, someone's trying to kill you?" I asked.

"I was at my campsite." She nodded to her left, her eyes wide with panic. "Over there. And someone came up behind me. I grabbed my knife and ran as fast as I could. I think you scared him away."

Of course, this is what she'd say if she wanted to draw suspicion away from herself. Wilfred was too full of actors these days to believe anyone's story. At the same time, she seemed genuinely freaked out. Her gaze darted beyond us and her breathing came in uneven spurts. And she really needed a shower.

"We're going to have to take you into town," I said and swapped glances with Leo. Presumably she knew where the trail was. We didn't need her to draw us deeper into the woods where she could make a run for it—or worse.

"I'm going to hold your hands behind you, and you'll lead the way down the trail," he said, as if we knew exactly where we were headed. "We'll send the sheriff back for your things."

"No," she said. "I'm not safe there."

"Bianca," I said. "We're not giving you a choice. You're coming with us. Besides, it's not like you're safe here, either."

She sniffed back a tear and stood. I kept a hand clenched on the knife.

"Okay," she said. "All right."

A rustling in the underbrush caught my attention. "Leo," I said in shock. "Look. He found us."

Rodney padded into the clearing as if we'd simply been hanging out in the library's garden. He ignored Bianca and trotted toward me, mewing. He head-butted my leg. I put my arms through the day pack so it faced front and slipped Rodney inside, where he gratefully curled up and purred. His warm presence was more comforting than he could have known.

"Let's go that way." I pointed toward the edge of the clearing where Rodney had emerged. Sure enough, it was the trail.

Docile now, Bianca stumbled with us along the path. I patted Rodney's purring weight against my chest and smiled grimly at Leo.

We were going to make it.

What a day, I thought as I cleaned my plate of the tuna noodle casserole Mrs. Littlewood had brought over. I had been lost in the woods with a geekily attractive man who, I'd thought, may have been a murderer. We'd stumbled over another potential murderer, who—surprise of surprises— claimed someone had tried to kill her. My cat turned out to be a seasoned mountain climber. Tonight I deserved peace and quiet, and I was going to get it.

When we'd arrived back in Wilfred, Sam had reassured us that Daphne was fine and had taken Bianca away to question her. He then deposited her at Helen Garlington's house for a good dinner, warm bath, and bed. She had a deputy on speed dial. Sam had no need to hold Bianca, but he wanted her close.

As I toyed with the idea of searching the freezer for ice cream, Sam appeared at my door with a happy frown at seeing me. "How are you? We haven't had the chance to talk since you came home."

That frown warmed my heart. "I'm fine. That is, I am now. I didn't get your text message about Leo until we were already on the mountain." I explained to Sam where Leo had really been the night Bryce died and left it for the sheriff's office to confirm.

"It might have been Bianca who took the trail marker," he said.

"It's possible, but I'm not convinced. When we found her, she was terrified."

"There are still lots of open questions," Sam said.

"True." I pulled my napkin off my lap and leaned back. "I'm simply happy to have a peaceful evening." A hot bath and a vintage crime novel would perfect it. "Did you make any headway with Roz on the interview?"

"No. She refuses to apologize to Daphne, and Daphne refuses to interview her unless she does. It's a stalemate."

I considered appealing to Roz myself, but not tonight.

I needed a drama-free evening. I'd try her first thing in the morning.

We both turned at a banging on the kitchen door. Daphne, face flushed and breathing heavily, pushed her way in.

"Are you all right?" I asked.

As she caught her breath, she thrust a note at Sam. "This was in my the screen door."

The note was written in black ink on white printer paper in small, neat block letters. *Tomorrow you die*, it read. No salutation, no signature. The note was all business.

Sam glanced at it, then at her. "When did you find it?"

"Just now. I ran all the way here."

He held the note at its edges to preserve any fingerprints it might have. "Does it look like the first note you received?"

"I don't know. Who cares? Oh, Sam, someone wants to kill me! Why did I ever come to this town?" Daphne snaked her arms around Sam and sobbed. She'd been nonchalant about her first death threat, but this one really seemed to frighten her. "The stupid book interview isn't going to happen. People are trying to kill me." She gazed at Sam. "You're the only reason I'm glad I'm here."

"Can I give you tea or a glass of water? Or something stronger?" Sam offered.

Bianca was back in Wilfred. Could she have left the note? Mrs. Garlington would know if she'd left the house. Seeing Daphne in Sam's arms was all the convincing I needed to leave the sleuthing to him.

"I'll be in my apartment if you need me," I said and headed for the service staircase.

Upstairs, I paced my living room, Rodney watching from the empty kindling box, where he'd been sleeping off his hike up the mountain.

I was all too aware of Sam and Daphne downstairs. I lifted my bedroom window to let in the cooler evening air. The horizon was pink tinged with orange. As beautiful as nature was, I was so grateful to be home with the mantel clock's comforting tick and the fistful of daisies in a vase on my dresser. Rodney crawled out from the kindling box and milled around my calves, closing his eyes and purring.

Downstairs, the kitchen door slammed. Good. Maybe Daphne was leaving. I went to the window to be sure, but instead saw Roz's rounded form hurling itself toward Lyndon's cottage. I hadn't even known Roz had been in the library. Had Daphne slipped out of Sam's arms long enough to say something about Lyndon and infuriate Roz? She pounded on the caretaker cottage door, it opened, and she disappeared inside.

I was determined to ignore the drama around me and have a serene evening. I had just one task left to do: lock up the library for the night. Hoping that Daphne and Sam would move on, I lingered over refastening my hair and changing into clean jeans and a fresh T-shirt. Eventually, taking the service staircase from my apartment, I reluctantly returned downstairs. Sam and Daphne were still there—their voices rose in the atrium. Hers was soft but carried perfectly, an asset as an actress.

"I'm so scared, Sam," she said. "Will you stay close tonight?"

I couldn't make out his reply.

I marched through the atrium, making as much racket

as I could so I wouldn't interrupt anything I'd rather not see. "Hello, you two," I said before I actually made it to the kitchen.

I found Daphne and Sam standing near the stove, the gloaming illuminating the space in a way that was all too romantic. I clicked on the light switches and starchy white light filled the room. They stood closer than I would have liked. Sam backed up a step. Daphne shot me an irritated glance. Duchess was helping herself to Rodney's kibble.

"Just here to make sure things are clean and to close up the library down for the day." I squirted dish soap on two mugs in the sink. Sam and Daphne must have made tea.

"Josie," Daphne said, "I'm glad you're here. I have something to ask you."

What, to be a bridesmaid? I thought. "How can I help you?" I asked with as much nonchalance as I could muster.

"I really admire what you've done with the library, and people keep saying how good you are at making book recommendations. It's a pleasure to spend time here."

"Thank you," I said. Scratch the bridesmaid idea, she wanted to book the library for the wedding.

"Now that Morgan is . . . gone, I need a new book club coordinator. You'd be perfect."

"I—"

"Now, hear me through. You'd get to choose our monthly book and hundreds of thousands of people would read it. You'd travel with me to the author interviews, no matter where they were. I'd pay you a good salary." She named a figure that made my current salary look like coffee money. "The only thing is, you'd have to do a lot of reading."

I was so stunned, I couldn't reply. "If I chose a book whose author lived in Paris?"

"We'd travel to Paris." Daphne tilted her head a micro-degree. "And so would Leo."

Visions of foreign landscapes, author chats, and stacks of novels filled my head. "I don't know what to say."

"How about yes? I realize this is coming out of the blue, so I'll give you a day to think it over." Her expression softened and she turned to Sam. "Hey," she said in what a romance novel would have called *dulcet tones*. "Will you walk me home?"

"Good night, Josie," Sam said.

Sore, I mumbled a "good night" to the closing door. I felt rather than heard a book slip from its shelf and fly up the atrium, probably to my nightstand. Ten-to-one it was a self-help book on letting go. Or maybe a career manual.

Whatever. I had a lot to think about, but I'd mull it over later. Tonight I was determined to clear my mind and take it easy.

A motion to my left caught my attention. "Rodney, you're not supposed to be on the counter." I don't know why I bothered to tell him so, since he went wherever he pleased.

Rodney was nosing a capless miniature booze bottle. He licked its neck. Before I could grab him, he backed away, then shot through the cat door. What was up with him?

I went to toss the bottle into the trash and froze. This wasn't just any mini–liquor bottle. This was the sambuca bottle with the love potion, and it was empty. I glanced at the mugs in the sink, then back to the bottle, and I groaned.

CHAPTER THIRTY

Two empty mugs, one empty bottle of love potion. There was enough potion in that bottle to send both Sam and Daphne into a week of romance that all of Dylan's Cary Grant movies combined couldn't match.

I imagined the scene. "How about some tea?" Sam might have said, thinking it would calm Daphne.

"With perhaps a shot of something extra?" Daphne would have replied, seeing the liquor bottles on the counter.

Ugh. I closed my living room window facing Big House and shut the curtains. If anything romantic was happening, I didn't want to see it. One glance would amp my emotion enough to fritz every light bulb in Wilfred. Sure, Sam had said he'd hired a babysitter for the evening, but maybe he and Daphne couldn't make it as far as the farmhouse before falling into each other's arms. And it would all be the fault of my stupid love potion.

The cat flap creaked at the top of the stairs. Rodney wandered in, looking dazed. He jumped to the arm of my chair, then to the bookshelf, where he gracefully angled past a vase of dahlias and a photo of my sisters. He stared up at me and if a cat could sigh, he sighed. Added to that was a low, longing-filled purr.

"What's wrong, Rodney?" I said.

He blinked slowly at me, and his purring amped a few decibels.

"What's up with you? Where have you been?"

The last I'd seen him was in the kitchen downstairs. Then I remembered: the love potion. He'd licked the bottle's neck. I pressed my nose into the silky fur on the back of his neck and smelled peaches and roses. Daphne's scent—and her dog's.

"You got into the potion, didn't you?"

He closed his eyes and lifted a paw to let me scratch his belly. Rodney was in love with Duchess.

"You dummy," I told him. "She's not even your species." His purr ramped up in response, and he nuzzled my hand. "You didn't get enough of a dose to charm you for long. Good thing, too, since Daphne will be leaving soon. If she's still alive, that is."

My thoughts turned to the afternoon's events. Someone had untied the napkin marking the return trail. Someone had wanted to keep Leo and me out of Wilfred. Now I was convinced that it wasn't to attack us, but to get us out of the way so he could make an attempt on Daphne's life. Then there was Bianca's story. Was she telling the truth or was it a cover-up?

Daphne was safe as long as Sam was with her, but he couldn't be with her every minute—even if he wanted to, thanks to my potion.

I lowered myself into the armchair turned toward the fireplace, empty and cold this summer's night. I'd messed up everything. I'd demolished my chances, thin as they were, of attracting Sam's attention. I'd been so sure Morgan had mistakenly killed Bryce in an effort to get at Daphne, and I'd also been wrong there. As wrong as you could get. Now Daphne and Roz's interview was squelched, too. My plans for a peaceful evening went out the window.

I could take a hot bath and cry. I could ravage a box of cookies while I read *Jane Eyre*. Or I could find the real murderer. But how?

A book's glow at my elbow caught my attention. It was a mapback copy of Helen McCloy's *She Walks Alone* from 1948. I loved her series with the psychiatrist-sleuth Basil Willing. What did the book want me to do? Surely it didn't want me to walk anywhere alone. Not with a murderer out there.

Bibliomancy could be frustratingly cryptic, but I'd give it a try. I opened the paperback to a random page. On it, the chief of police reviewed his suspects. *He knew it was time to get help*, the text read.

I knew it was time to get help, too, but from where? From Dr. Basil Willing? Why him? The shelves downstairs held scores of detectives, each with their own skills and specialties.

Then I understood. Basil Willing was only an example. The books wanted me to consult with a fictional detective. I'd never done anything like this before. Besides bibliomancy, I'd asked books directly for information. But I'd never interacted magically with a character. Could it work?

There was one way to find out.

I went to the hall overlooking the atrium, now dark. I felt rather than heard the summer night air rustling the leaves of the oaks around us in the moonlight.

What should I ask the books? If I asked all the library's fictional detectives to report to Old Man Thurston's office, the office would be too full to squeeze into. No, I needed a sorting mechanism.

I calmed myself and focused my energy. Rodney, perkier now that he sensed magic, rubbed against my calves. I pressed my finger to my tingling birthmark.

I drew three long breaths, holding each one a few seconds before releasing it. I opened my eyes again, and the lamps throughout the library glowed with the force of my magic.

"No," I whispered. "Back into the books."

The lights flickered and the library was dark once again. Then books shimmered like fireflies from their rooms. For a moment I closed my eyes and let the energy cycle through my body as warm as sun at the beach. From his amped purring, I knew Rodney felt it, too.

It was time. "Books," I said.

A cycle of cries and "yeses" whooshed through the library in different voices, some murmuring bass, others high; some with accents, others nearly singing.

"We're going to try something new. I want to speak with your characters. Can you do that?"

My body thrummed with energy as the books said *yes, yes, yes*.

"First, I want the hard-boiled detectives to meet in Old Man Thurston's office and make yourself as one character." On second thought, I added, "Sober, please."

Would it work? I bit my lip as the bookshelves groaned below me—Popular Fiction—and streaks of green energy pulsed like jellyfish to Old Man Thurston's office. In their trail whisked a few trench coats and fedoras. Yes! I focused again and kept my energy calm, authoritative.

"Next, we'll have girl detectives. Nancy, Trixie, Cherry, that means you."

A roadster and a magnifying glass accompanied by giggles streamed pink across the atrium into the office. Rodney, all the way from the third-floor hall, batted a paw at it.

One more. This one would be the trickiest and might result in the most infighting. I'd have to be careful. "Finally, we'll have British detectives from Sherlock to the Golden Age. Become as one."

A meerschaum pipe and a deerstalker cap glimmered silver among a monocle, mustache comb, and cocktail shaker, followed by a butler. Toddling behind them with a bag of knitting was an elderly lady. Oh, boy. This could get interesting.

I took the stairs down to the atrium, my body electric with energy. I wasn't used to drumming up so much magic, and it rattled my muscles and fizzed through my blood. The doorway to Old Man Thurston's office shimmered, and I entered to find three small characters on the broad mahogany desk. They glowed like Barbie-sized holograms.

The hard-boiled detective was easy to identify. He sat in a worn leather club chair the size of a grapefruit and he wore his fedora pulled forward. He smoked a cigarette. True to the novel, he had Sam Spade's devilish face rather than Humphrey Bogart's basset hound expression, and his trench coat could have belonged to Philip Marlowe, William Crane, or any of a dozen other fictional gumshoes.

The girl detective edged away from the cigarette smoke and looked at me eagerly from a freckle-smattered face. She wore a poodle skirt and an angora sweater. Titian-hued waves bounced at her shoulders.

I caught the hard-boiled detective checking her out. "Don't get any ideas," I warned him.

Hard-boiled and Girl Detective had turned out all right, but a glance told me I'd blown it with Golden Age.

The Golden Age detective was a Mr. Potato Head of diffcrent sleuth's features. He—I think it was a he—wore a plum silk smoking jacket and a monocle, like Lord Peter Wimsey might have. However, he was smoking Sherlock Holmes's pipe, and a deerstalker cap was on his head, on top of what looked like Miss Marple's—or maybe Maud Silver's?—gray curls and Hercule Poirot's mani-cured mustache. He was bulky and he leaned on a walk-ing stick. I had the sense of a butler waiting in the ether. The detective advanced a step and a deep Gothic-style chair appeared behind him. With a sigh, he settled in.

Oh boy.

I rounded the desk and sat, putting on my best "don't mess with me" librarian face. "Thank you for coming here."

They stared at me, silent. What if my magic hadn't ex-tended them the ability to talk? That could be a good thing where Golden Age was concerned.

"I have a murderer to find and I need your help."

Golden Age nodded and Girl Detective said, "Gee." Hard-boiled stared impassively, the smoke curling up from his cigarette and vanishing while the cigarette's ash never tumbled.

At least they could speak. "We had two murders in Wilfred. One was a chef and the other was Morgan Stanhope, assistant to a Hollywood star named Daphne Morris. The killer left a note saying he would kill the actress tomorrow."

"Details, please," Hard-boiled said and pushed back the brim of his hat.

"Yes. We need more to go on," Golden Age said with a high-pitched British accent. As he leaned forward, I caught a glimpse of calico under the smoking jacket.

"The actress and her people, which had included the now-dead chef, are staying together at a farmhouse in town. The first victim was found dead in a bathtub. Although the medical examiner said he'd died by electrocution, a large quantity of an anxiety medication was found in his bloodstream. Plus alcohol."

"Was the gentleman prone to nervousness?" Golden Age asked.

"No. That's just it. The medication likely belonged to Morgan Stanhope, the second victim."

"Gee. What was he doing that day?" Girl Detective said.

"He'd been making cocktails at a party for the town." I looked at the trio. "How much do you know about Wilfred?"

"We know quite a bit about the library patrons, Miss Way," Girl Detective said. "I've met many of the town's young women. When we're in their houses, we see what happens there, too. Why, I have a working knowledge of heartthrobs from Bobby Sherman on up."

"Let's return to the case, shall we?" Golden Age said.

"All right," I said, "At some point, probably feeling the effects of the pills, the chef returned to the farmhouse and decided to take a bath."

"Where some gunsel—what, fried his tripes?" Hard-boiled said.

"Dropped a plugged-in blow-dryer in the water," I replied.

"Gee," Girl Detective repeated. "Who were his chums?"

"Well, Bryce was the childhood friend and now the personal chef for the movie star, Daphne Morris. We think Bryce's death was an accident and that the killer intended to kill Daphne. Normally at that hour, she'd be the one in the bathtub."

"Surely one could discern between a burly chef and a lady of the stage?" Golden Age said in a tone that skipped from regal to elderly soprano.

"The shower curtain was drawn."

Girl Detective leaned her forearms on the back of Hard-boiled's chair. "Other chums?"

"Next is Gibbous Moon. He's Daphne's stylist. The silent, monkish type."

Hard-boiled snorted. "What does this mug want?"

"He's starting his own cosmetics line, and he's using his association with Daphne to bring him publicity and maybe even start-up money."

"Not a motive," Golden Age said. "Perhaps even a reason not to kill the movie star."

"If she was really the intended victim," Girl Detective pointed out.

"Daphne's death would bring him more publicity. It would also release him from an ironclad contract to work for her," I said.

The moon had risen and its light through the office window made the trio of sleuths more luminous and sheer.

"Who else?" Hard-boiled asked.

"Then there's Leo, head of the film crew. He works with Daphne when she needs someone to tape her interviews for television. He's innocent, though," I said.

Golden Age steepled his fingers. "We'll move the gentleman to the top of the list of suspects."

"What's his deal?" Hard-boiled said.

"He doesn't seem to admire Daphne much personally, but he doesn't have a reason to kill her. Besides, he was with me on the mountain when someone stole our trail marker so we'd be lost in the woods and couldn't interfere."

"This jasper is tall, dark, and handsome, I take it?" Hard-boiled said.

"Well." My face heated up. "Not exactly, and yet . . ."

"Sounds dreamy," Girl Detective said.

"Might be having an affair with the actress. Does he have a contract with her, too? Money is always a motive," Hard-boiled offered.

"Does he stand to inherit a title?" Golden Age said.

"No titles involved here. We're in rural Oregon, remember? But, yes, he's caught in a similar contract with no easy way out," I said. "Okay, two more suspects. Daphne has a fan who's been stalking her. The fan—her name is Bianca—seems desperate to spend time with Daphne, but she'd sold information to a tabloid about Daphne's recent divorce, so Daphne has a restraining order against her."

"Gee. If she likes the movie star so much, why'd she sell her out?" Girl Detective stood now. "Girlfriends don't betray each other like that."

The saddle shoes and bobby socks look was actually kind of nice. Maybe I'd try it around the library some time. "The last suspect was Morgan Stanhope. She's the one I was sure was the murderer. She's an actor, too, and she had a chance at a role off Broadway she really wanted. Daphne put an end to that."

"Contract again, no doubt," Hard-boiled said.

"Bingo," I said and drew back. Hard-boiled's language was getting to me.

"And your deductions, given these clues?" Golden Age said.

"Well, as I said, I was sure Morgan was the murderer. She had a motive and a half-filled bottle of the anxiety medication that had drugged the chef. Plus, she'd left an energy impression on one of the books she'd been reading that showed her at the murder scene. Then she ended up dead, too."

"You forget the most obvious suspect of all," Golden Age said.

"Who?" Girl Detective, Hard-boiled, and I answered at once.

"Daphne Morris herself." Golden Age settled back. He plucked a teacup from the air and sipped from it.

Daphne did love attention, and a trail of bodies meant that Sam would be near her as long as she stayed in Wilfred. She'd been at the party when Bryce had been murdered, but she might have had an accomplice. Still, why now? Why in Wilfred?

"You've got some questions to consider here," Hard-boiled said, waving his eternally smoking cigarette.

"Think of facts, not what you want to believe," Girl Detective said. "It's too easy to treat assumptions as facts. For instance, you assume someone wanted to kill the movie star."

"She's received death threats," I said.

"Says her," Hard-boiled put in.

"And, sadly, people have died," Golden Age said. "That doesn't mean they were murdered. In my village, there was a farmer whose sheep kept vanishing. He insisted they were stolen. In fact, they'd died of natural causes and he'd buried their bodies. The town raised money for him to rebuild his flock."

"Sheep, *shmeep*," Hard-boiled said. "You don't know motive for sure, and opportunity is muddled. You want answers? Shove your iron up the perp's schnoz and demand them."

"The facts," Girl Detective said. "Isolate the facts and drop the assumptions. Examine whatever theories arise that the facts support, as crazy as they seem. In the meantime, memorize Morse code for *help* and make sure your roadster always has a full tank of gas."

If Girl Detective ever grew up, which I knew she never would, she'd make a fine physicist or logician.

Meanwhile, Golden Age morphed from Miss Marple to Poirot. His mustache extended a few millimeters, and his British voice acquired a French accent. "Once you have laid out these immutable facts, I feel certain the answer, no matter how surprising, will come to you."

"Doesn't mean the answer will be convincing to the local cops," Hard-boiled said.

Golden Age nodded. "*Oui, mon ami.* You may have to encourage the killer to incriminate himself. Create a situation where he will be forced to reveal his hand."

Girl Detective nodded with enthusiasm. "Get your chums involved."

"*Ix-nay* on the *ums-chay*, but pack a heater," Hard-boiled said. "My opinion."

"Leave no one out," Golden Age said.

Girl Detective waved an index finger. "Or ones."

"No matter how innocent they seem." Golden Age's mustache shrank and a monocle appeared on one eye. "Now, if you'll excuse me, I'd like to get out of this horrid wig."

"Nice talking with you, babe." Hard-boiled gave me a two-fingered salute.

Girl Detective's face burst into a sunny smile. "Bye for now!"

Each figure contracted into a point of light so bright I closed my eyes. When I reopened them, the detectives had vanished.

CHAPTER THIRTY-ONE

Here it was at last: the morning of Roz and Daphne's big interview. Only there was to be no interview. Daphne had refused to be in the same room with Roz unless she apologized, and Roz would rather eat gravel than crow.

My talk with the fictional detectives had sparked an idea. I'd been up a good part of the night examining the facts and laying them out, just as the fictional sleuths had suggested. Now it was time to put that planning to work. Fingers crossed, it would pay off. The fact that the interview had been called off and the library would be empty was an advantage.

When I returned to the library after setting the plan in motion, I stopped short at seeing Leo at the front door, Dylan in tow. Tripods and silver suitcases of camera gear surrounded them.

"No one told you there's not going to be an interview?" I said.

"It's back on," Leo said. "We're going ahead."

"You're kidding. As of yesterday, it was a bust." For Roz's sake, I was glad for the interview, but this was going to put a major crimp in my plans.

"That's what I'd thought, too," Leo said. "Roz dropped by this morning and talked with Daphne privately. Next thing I know, we're prepping for the interview."

His hair had a bit of wave this morning. I bet it was like the hair of Letty, my toddler niece, which tightened when humidity rose. His mother must have adored it as much as my sister adored my niece's curls. He wore his usual jeans, but also a light vest fitted with pockets. Pliers stuck out of one pocket, and a roll of blue tape filled another.

Dylan gazed at Leo with adoration. Uncharacteristically, Dylan wore jeans, too, but he'd topped it with a short-sleeved Western-cut shirt and bolo tie and had slicked back his hair.

"Well," I said, still stupefied at Roz's change of heart. "Come in."

"This way," Dylan, playing the host, said to Leo. "I'll show you where the electrical outlets are."

Leo and I had long ago scoped out the outlets. Leo smiled at me and indulgently followed Dylan.

In the library's kitchen, Roz was sliding a tray of sandwiches from the PO Grocery into the refrigerator.

"Hi, Roz. You decided to go through with the interview."

"Beautiful morning, isn't it?" she said with a dreamy smile.

I raised an eyebrow. "It's the day you're to be filmed on TV, remember?"

"What a wonderful opportunity," she said. Her round cheeks were rosy, and with her slight overbite she looked like an adorable chipmunk. "I couldn't let it pass. I took a bouquet of roses to Daphne first thing this morning and apologized. She was gracious enough to accept."

"Who are you and what did you do with Roz?" I asked.

She giggled and eased into a chair. "I must be the luckiest woman in the world."

"Yes?"

She sighed languorously. "I'm going to be on national TV. Sales of *The Whippoorwill Cries Love* will shoot through the roof. And . . ." A smile that could have lit Manhattan illuminated her face.

"And what?"

"Lyndon asked me to marry him."

"Oh, Roz, I'm so happy for you!" I rushed to hug her and she laughed with joy. "When?"

"No details yet. Well, except for planning on the floral end. Lyndon was up half the night sketching ikebana centerpieces. Could we use the library for the ceremony?"

"Of course," I said, wiping away a tear despite myself. "That's such wonderful news." As I released her, my gaze swept the airline booze bottles at the back of the counter. "How did it happen? You swore you wouldn't forgive him for his crush on Daphne."

"It's the craziest thing. Last night, here at the library, all at once I felt a wave of love wash over me. I couldn't believe I'd been so petty. What Lyndon and I have is priceless. No movie star, gorgeous as she may be, can ruin that. Lyndon and I are destined to be together. Our bond is impossible to break."

"And in the grand scheme, Daphne is unimportant," I added.

"Lyndon told me Daphne is like a rare orchid that requires just the right light and humidity and is a devil to get to repeat bloom. He said I'm like a rugosa rose that blossoms year after year for everyone to enjoy. He even said I was own-root, not grafted."

Something in her expression reminded me of Rodney's goofy stare last night. "Roz. Yesterday. Did you . . ."

She followed my gaze to the mini–liquor bottles. "Sure, I downed a bracer. You don't mind, do you? I was so frustrated with Lyndon and then there was Daphne, spreading her love-goddess vibe everywhere. I couldn't take it."

"It was the sambuca, wasn't it?"

"That's what the label said. It tasted kind of funny to me."

I remembered Roz dashing out the side door like a rabid cougar was on her tail. "Then you went to see Lyndon."

"It was so strange. I was standing there, feeling so sad and alone, and as that sambuca hit my stomach I thought, Why am I letting her come between me and the most wonderful man in the world? Suddenly, it's like I was all the heroines combined in the *Lord Love a Duke* books and the *Bazillions of Billionaire Brides* series."

Whoa. That potion was even more powerful than Grandma had warned.

"Daphne simply didn't matter anymore. Whatever stupid crush he had on Daphne, it was nothing compared to what we have. Last night, reason prevailed. And now I'm the happiest person alive."

"Did I hear my name?" Daphne stood at the doorway, Sam right behind her. Duchess, panting, pushed her way in, no doubt on a search for Rodney.

"It's so nice to see you this morning, Daphne," Roz said. "I hope this dress will be all right on camera. Of course, no one will be looking at me with your beauty in the room."

Daphne looked as surprised as I'd first been when Roz finished her affectionate outburst. "How's Lyndon?" she asked warily.

"He's wonderful," Roz said. "We're getting married."

Sam watched the exchange with curiosity. "Congratulations. He's a lucky man."

Was it my imagination, or did Daphne shoot a knowing look at Sam?

Then it occurred to me. Roz had drunk the love potion, not Sam. Sam was not bound to Daphne by magic. No, it was a hundred times worse. His bond was for real.

A few hours later, it was showtime—in more ways than one. In this show, I planned to trap a murderer.

When I'd charted my plan last night, I'd expected the library to be empty. With a television crew and the interview, the plan would be more risky, but I decided to go ahead anyway. Tomorrow, Daphne and her crew would be gone. Besides, the note specified today as when Daphne would die. Sam would be keeping a close watch on her. If luck was with me, we'd be safe.

The library's atrium had been transformed into a television studio, with lights on tripods, a screen blocking the staircase, and cords taped to the parquet. Two Victorian chairs angled toward each other, interview style, flanking the table holding Lyndon's vase of roses and a propped copy of *The Whippoorwill Cries Love*. Ferns the size of ottomans with the label of a rental company stuck to their pots marked the edge of the interview area. In a few weeks, Roz—or Eliza Chatterley Windsor, that is— would be a household name.

Sam and I surveyed the scene from outside the music room upstairs. I glanced at Sam, in uniform and definitely on duty. He'd already scouted the library's front, side, and kitchen doors and made sure windows were locked, despite the warm day. From here, we had a clear view of the ad hoc TV studio. What Sam didn't appreciate about our position, but I counted on, was that by moving a bit to the left, I could see into the second-story bathroom, converted into a makeup room for the day. The memory of Daphne's death threat—*tomorrow you die*—played in my brain on repeat.

Below us, Leo put on a headset. Daphne and Roz settled into their chairs. Daphne was, of course, radiant. Instead of her usual flowing sundress, she wore a smart-looking linen suit with a peach-colored silk shirt unbuttoned lower than what corporate etiquette books might recommend. Not that she could ever look like an insurance adjustor, no matter how many pearls were slung around her neck.

Roz also looked beautiful in her rounded, Snow White's aunt sort of way. She also wore linen, but instead of a suit, which would have been too rigid for her curves, she had on a violet tunic and green skirt. Her beauty didn't come from her clothing, though, but from her glow, which for once didn't stem from hot flashes. I knew Lyndon watched with pride, out of sight in Circulation below us.

"All right. Ready?" Leo said. "Roll."

Daphne's face lit up as if she'd flipped a switch. "Welcome to the Daphne Morris Star Reads book club. Today I'm thrilled to bring you Eliza Chatterley Windsor, pen name of Roslyn Grover and author of the captivating *The Whippoorwill Cries Love*. I have to tell you, Roz, I couldn't put this story down."

I think she was actually telling the truth. I turned to Sam, who was completely absorbed by the scene. He wore a faint frown. In other words, he was happy. Nauseating.

He glanced my way, then did a double take. "What's with you?" he whispered.

"Nothing," I replied tartly.

After a peek toward the bathroom-slash-makeup room, I redirected my attention to Roz and Daphne. The interview was planned to last an hour and a half, giving plenty of material to edit down to fifty minutes. I didn't know if my nerves could take Sam's mooning that long.

I lowered myself to the floor, getting cozy on the oriental runner that rimmed the hall. The view through the banister was clear. Sam sat next to me.

Daphne's voice rose through the atrium. "I felt you really understood a woman's soul. Especially heartbreak, which, you may have heard, is something I'm all too familiar with. Who inspired the lead character, Marjorie Bloomingheart?"

Roz smiled, her adorable overbite giving her the look of a teenager. "All of my characters have a bit of me in them—especially the heroines. I think every author does this. We're always gathering material from the people in our lives."

"Then you've known great heartbreak," Daphne said.

Roz lowered her voice as if she were sharing a secret. "For years and years I loved a man who barely knew I existed. I tried to shake him—I really did. I just couldn't stop thinking about him. It was torture. A sweet torture."

"Torture," Daphne confirmed. "Marjorie Blooming-heart faced the same thing, until the fateful accident in the potting shed."

Roz nodded sagely.

"I don't want to reveal any spoilers, but surely you can tell us about how your own unrequited love worked out."

Roz's face broke into an ear-to-ear grin. "I'm engaged. It happened last night."

I snuck a look at Sam. His concentration on Daphne never wavered. He was in full ghost mode now: tight focus, inscrutable expression. He was protecting Daphne. Or he simply couldn't take his eyes off her.

"You don't have to stare like that," I whispered. I couldn't resist.

Without taking his eyes from Daphne, he said, "Look who's talking."

"What do you mean?"

"A certain cameraman seems to be getting a lot of attention."

I snorted. "Says Mr. 'Wait, I'll walk you home.'" I might have heightened my tone in a bad imitation of Daphne. Leo glanced up at us. I lowered my voice and returned my gaze to the interview. "I bet you're sorry she's leaving."

I didn't think Sam would respond. Finally, he whispered, "I'm just doing my job." His eyes crinkled as he frowned. "I think you're jealous."

"As if!" This was really bad. "I'm sure she'll hire you a good nanny for Nicky, and you can move into her house in LA with the view and the swimming pool."

"What's it to you, anyway?" he said.

"I just hate to see you churn through the mill of Daphne-digested men. You guys should form a union. Demand better tabloid coverage."

He narrowed his eyes and returned his gaze to the atrium floor. "I have a job to do. If you can't be quiet, you'll have to move." Sam's voice was low but firm.

I opened my mouth to deliver a smart response, then shut it again. As it was, I'd already be burning with shame for weeks. I moved away a few inches.

"I wish everyone could feel the joy of having a soul mate," Roz said, beaming, from the atrium below.

"Indeed," Daphne enthused.

Gag me.

Motion from my right caught my attention. Bianca emerged from the servants' staircase and crept around the opposite side of the atrium. Sam rose to stop her, but I whispered, "No."

He hesitated, then slowly nodded. Going after Bianca would mean interrupting the interview. He'd decided to trust me.

"Thank you," I mouthed.

So far, so good. Bianca slipped into the bathroom.

While below us Daphne and Roz waxed dreamy about love, I backed to the wall. Creeping quietly, I edged toward the corner, where I had an unimpeded view of the bathroom. The copy of *Crime and Punishment* I'd stashed under the towels murmured without concern.

Bianca settled into the chair where Daphne and Roz had undergone their makeovers an hour earlier. Gibbous lifted Bianca's hair and looked into the mirror, just out of view. I stood in shadows. I'd deliberately worn dark jeans and a black blouse, but my skin would make me easy to see if Bianca turned in my direction. For now, she seemed absorbed in her reflection.

I hadn't told Sam about my plan. Part was perversity, and part was that I wasn't sure my theory was correct. This was the only way to know for sure.

Daphne and Roz's words drifted up from the atrium.

"What inspired the secret baby?" Daphne asked. "Surely, that part isn't from real life, too?"

Roz's laughter was genuine. Joy had transformed Eeyore to Pollyanna. "You have to give me credit for some imagination."

Upstairs, Gibbous brushed Bianca's hair back into an approximation of Daphne's. He set down the hairbrush and uncapped a lipstick. I didn't need to see it to know it was Daphne's signature caramel-peach shade. Bianca pursed her lips.

"Let me share something important," Roz said. "I would like the audience to know that the whippoorwill is not native to the Pacific Northwest."

"It's fiction, right?" Daphne said. "Besides, who cares about the birds? Readers will love this story for the romance."

Bianca was shorter than Daphne, true, and few people were blessed with Daphne's figure. But right now, she might have been the movie star's twin. Golden hair, golden-peachy makeup, sculpted cheekbones. I studied her with an intensity that Sam even in his ghosting days couldn't have matched. I looked down at the real thing under the television lights, then back to her double in the bathroom straight ahead. Eerie.

Bianca watched Gibbous with unwavering focus. Her right shoulder dipped. She was reaching for something in the bag next to her chair.

My panic ignited an energy that spread through the books like wildfire, unleashing shrieks and groans from the shelves. The bathroom door shut with a firm *click*.

"Sam," I whispered urgently.

"Danger! It's a gun," *Crime and Punishment* told me with a Russian accent.

"Sam!" This time I yelled.

It wasn't Bianca I was warning him about. It was Gibbous.

CHAPTER THIRTY-TWO

Startled by my cry, Gibbous flung open the bathroom door. He pivoted from Bianca and aimed the gun toward me. I dropped to the ground. A shot cracked, splintering the molding above me.

Sam rounded the other side of the hall, but not in time to reach Gibbous, who'd slipped down the main staircase at the back of the house. His steps pounded toward the atrium and Sam took off after him.

In seconds, I was at the bathroom, where Bianca, looking so strangely like Daphne, stood, wide-eyed. I pushed her in and shut the door. "Lock it, and don't come out until I say so."

From downstairs, the sound of Roz and Daphne's screams mingled with the intense humming of the books. I imagined a steel band encapsulating my energy so it wouldn't explode out of control. I circled the hall and locked the servants' staircase from the inside. This would keep Gibbous from coming up this way, but there was no way to block the main staircase. I just had to hope Sam could keep him on the ground floor.

Another shot ricocheted through the atrium, raising more screaming. It sounded like it had come from the library's foyer. I raced down the main staircase, intending to herd Roz and Daphne into my office, but found Sam had already taken care of it. Duchess's yap sounded from the other side of my office door. I sensed that Rodney was there as well, huddled under the desk.

For a split second, I considered joining them, but I couldn't. This whole situation was my fault and I had to do what I could to help. Had I told Sam what I'd planned, he never would have exposed Daphne and Roz to the risk of a shoot-out. It didn't matter that the interview was an unexpected complication. I bore responsibility for this.

"Gibbous!" Sam yelled from deeper in the library. "Drop the gun."

Where was he? Not in the conservatory. He had to be in Fiction or in Old Man Thurston's office. I hid in the arch connecting the kitchen to the atrium, my pulse pounding in my ears. The screen surrounding the interview area had tumbled. I edged behind it for a view of both the atrium entrance to Fiction and the entrance to Old Man Thurston's office.

Where were Leo and Dylan? I didn't know, couldn't tell. I hoped they'd made it safely outside.

A flash of khaki showed Sam flat outside the door to his great-great-grandfather's office, weapon drawn. Movement to my right caught my attention. It was Lyndon, armed with an edging tool. He crept toward Fiction, wielding the tool, its long handle out, like a lance.

"Back off," Gibbous yelled from the library's recesses.

Sam stepped back. I knew his thoughts as clearly as if they were my own. He was calculating the safest next steps. Should he pursue Gibbous, or let him run free, knowing Daphne and the rest of us were safer that way, and that sheriff's deputies were on their way?

I closed my eyes. The energy inside me boiled. Sam and Lyndon's lives were so much more important than arresting Gibbous. *Books*, I said silently. *Protect them.*

As I directed my magic, I felt a release like the hiss of the valve of a pressure cooker. The books contained my energy now, and they had a purpose. If necessary, they could box Gibbous into a corner or trip him up.

"All right," Sam said. "I'm retreating. The front door is open. Take it." Sam stepped backward, hands up. "Lyndon. Follow me." I couldn't see Lyndon, but I heard both him and Sam moving away. As he backed away from Gibbous, I slipped behind the tumbled white screens to the conservatory. Sam's and Lyndon's steps slowly led to the kitchen, out of sight.

"Books," I said silently, "We're going to do a special ballet. Right now. This one is called 'immobilize Gibbous.'" I sucked air into my lungs and quietly hummed the first few bars of "Maple Leaf Rag."

From where I stood in the conservatory, I couldn't see the library's stacks, but in my bones I knew books were flying to the atrium. I edged to the doorway and saw a set of green encyclopedias spin like a tornado around Gibbous. Two volumes of poetry flew to the chair where Roz had draped her scarf and snatched it between their pages, like a dog carrying a newspaper. Within the space of a breath, they'd wrapped it around his head, blinding him.

Gibbous batted at the air, a handgun still clasped in his fingers. "What's going on?" he said as his head twisted in mauve silk.

*Crime and Punishmen*t sailed down from the bathroom, over the banister, and knocked the gun from his hand. It hit the wooden floor with a thud and skittered beneath the table holding Roz's novel.

A few dozen books from Arts and Leisure were doing some sort of cancan near the foyer. I closed my eyes and focused my thoughts. *This isn't for fun*, I told them silently. "Get him!" I shouted aloud.

The books hung in the air for the duration of a wink, then chopped at Gibbous from every angle—behind his knees, at his waist, at the side of his skull—taking him down in seconds.

I ran to leap on the stylist to keep him in place. "Sam! Come here. It's Gibbous. He fell."

Sam was beside me before I could even clamp Gibbous's hands to the parquet. Books lay scattered around us, but Sam didn't seem to notice them. He nudged me aside and clamped handcuffs on Gibbous's wrists.

I went limp with relief. It was over.

From the doorway, Leo stared, mouth open in disbelief. He'd seen it all.

CHAPTER THIRTY-THREE

While we waited for Sam's backup to arrive, we took seats around the kitchen table. I'd sent Dylan home, but Leo lingered, giving me an odd look. I ignored him. Whatever he'd seen, he'd been in shock, I'd remind him eventually. It was all that reading on witches he'd done that had encouraged his ridiculous vision, I'd tell him. Things like he'd seen simply didn't happen in real life.

Handcuffed, Gibbous sat at the head of the table, in front of my office door. Sam stood just behind him, to his right. Daphne sat to his left, clutching Duchess. Roz and Lyndon huddled at the table's opposite end, and Bianca stood nearby and stared at Daphne.

"Gibbous," Daphne said with a shuddering sob. "I can't believe you're a murderer."

"He's not," I said.

"I told you," Gibbous said, his voice rising. "You have the wrong person. Bianca's right here."

Bianca shrank against the counter. Sam raised an eyebrow but made no move to remove Gibbous's handcuffs.

"Gibbous is not a murderer," I said, "But if we'd waited another minute, he would have been."

"I don't understand," Daphne said. Mascara streaked her cheeks and even then, damn it, she was beautiful. Duchess whined and tried to wiggle from her lap, probably to get at Rodney, but she held him tight. "Two people are dead and you've arrested Gibbous. But he's not the murderer?"

"Maybe you'd better explain," Sam said.

This was my moment. I drew a breath and prepared for the sort of scene that would make Golden Age proud. My audience was as prepped as any audience could be. I cleared my throat.

"All along, I'd suspected that Morgan had killed Chef Bryce. When I dragged Sam over to question her, we found her dead. That's where I went off track. I'd originally assumed whoever had killed Bryce had also killed Morgan. Now that Morgan was dead, I thought I'd deduced wrong. In fact, I'd been right all along. Morgan had killed Bryce and tried to pin it on Roz."

"I don't get it," Roz said. "What did she have against Bryce?"

My gaze touched everyone in the room: Sam, watchful; Daphne, a mass of damp tissues in her hand; Roz and Lyndon, frankly curious; and Bianca, looking tense, as if she'd only heard one shoe drop and the second was sure to be a doozy.

"Nothing," I said. "As far as I could tell, she liked him.

But she was hell-bent on punishing Daphne for ruining her chances of taking an acting part in New York."

"That director was a nobody," Daphne said. "And a harasser. She wouldn't have lasted a minute with him."

"I guess she thought that was her decision to make."

"Not with the contract we had," Daphne said, tears now replaced with a firm conviction that she was the real victim here.

"Back to the story," Sam said. "Morgan killed Bryce."

"Yes," I said. "Morgan came home to lay out Daphne's bath. She was furiously angry at Daphne. She planned to make her pay, one way or another. She found Bryce in the bathtub and to all appearances, he was dead."

"He was only passed out," Roz said, horror in her voice.

"She didn't know that. She filled the tub with water and tossed in the plugged-in blow-dryer to frame Roz." I nodded in her direction. "I don't think she was a fan of *The Whippoorwill Cries Love*."

"Snob," Roz said.

"It doesn't track," Daphne said. "How does framing Roz for Bryce's death get at me?"

Sam simply listened. We'd played this game many times on his kitchen porch, gazing down at Wilfred, although the stakes had been much lower.

"It was a setup for when she did kill you. When she killed you, she'd plant more evidence against Roz. She'd seen you flirting with Lyndon and she knew Roz was angry. Maybe angry enough to kill. All of us saw Roz threaten you at the party, a few hours before Bryce died."

"Sweet pea." Lyndon pulled back and looked at his fiancée. I'd never heard Lyndon's pet name for Roz. I filed it away for future use.

"Beat her up, maybe. Break that famous nose," Roz said. "But I'm no murderer."

Daphne dumped Duchess on the floor and the dog rushed to Rodney, who turned his back on her. She wagged harder and panted. The love potion had worn off.

"I can't help it if men find me attractive," Daphne said, directing a sultry smile toward Sam.

Sam ignored her. "Okay. Morgan killed Bryce. Who killed Morgan?"

"Daphne did." Maria Callas couldn't have been more proud of a standing ovation than I was to see the shock on everyone's faces.

Daphne bolted to her feet. "I did not! I was upstairs when she died. I had nothing to do with it."

"You killed her by accident. Morgan's plan was to electrocute you. She knew you'd come downstairs for your turmeric latte, so she took a knife to the espresso machine's electrical cord. First, though, she had to un-screw the fuse. When she cut the power to the espresso machine, she also unknowingly cut the power to your TV upstairs."

"Oh," Sam said. He got it.

"You went out the front door to get to the outside base-ment door to find the fuse box, right?"

Daphne nodded.

"Morgan was in the backyard, having just unscrewed the fuse, on her way in through the kitchen."

"So when she nicked the cord, the power was on," Lyndon said.

"Electrocuting her," I finished. "Daphne had essen-tially killed her own would-be murderer."

Daphne stared first at me, then at Sam. Finally, she settled her gaze on Gibbous, who seemed to be in his own world. "What does this have to do with Gibbous?"

Gibbous had retreated into monk mode. Hands behind his back, his gaze drifted somewhere toward the defunct set of service bells lined up near the ceiling.

"Gibbous drugged Bryce with Morgan's anxiety medication. It was another accident. He'd intended the Golden Cutie for someone else, but Bryce downed it, no doubt planning to shake up another one to replace it. He'd already had a few. The combination of that much alcohol with as many as five Xanax made Bryce too drowsy to think straight. He wandered back to the farmhouse and probably thought he'd take a shower to get himself straight. Instead, he fell asleep in the bathtub."

Gibbous's indifferent expression broke and he laughed. "What a story. Accident after accident. You're really stretching it."

"Listen," Sam said. "She's not finished."

How I adored that man. Too bad for him that he'd never know how fine I was. "All along, Gibbous intended to kill Bianca."

"Bianca?" Daphne and Roz said at the same time.

Bianca dropped to a chair.

"What about the notes threatening Daphne?" Lyndon asked.

"Daphne can enlighten us about the first one," I said.

"What?" Her blank expression once again proved what a terrific actress she was.

"Do you want me to tell them?" I said.

"All right." She snuck a glance at Sam. "I wrote it. I knew I needed . . . uh, personal protection from law enforcement, so I wrote it."

A muscle tensed in Sam's jaw and he wore the bare smile that spelled irritation. "Noted. What about Gibbous?"

"Well, what did he want more than anything else in the world?"

"Enlightenment?" Roz guessed.

"His own cosmetics company, Lunar Looks. He needed capital to start it. He had one asset to sell, and that was his insider knowledge of Daphne's divorce."

"It's true," Bianca said, speaking for the first time. "I overheard him on the phone with the *National Bloodhound*. I tried to warn Daphne, but she'd taken a restraining order out against me."

"At Gibbous's insistence," Sam said.

"Exactly," I said.

"You sold my secrets?" Daphne's voice wavered. "I trusted you."

Gibbous gave her one of his blank zen gazes.

"He knew he had to shut up Bianca before Daphne found out the truth. So he texted Bianca and spoofed the number to look like Daphne's. He invited her for a Golden Cutie cocktail and a conciliatory chat at the farmhouse during the party. His plan was probably to drug her, then kill her. Maybe take her body to the woods."

The shock on everyone's faces was palpable. Only Duchess was oblivious, wagging her tail and panting.

"Gibbous turned Bryce and then Morgan's deaths to his favor by running with the assumption that someone was out to kill Daphne. He wrote the second death threat against Daphne, the one she received yesterday, to focus attention on her while he went after Bianca."

"Then he lured Bianca here today, the last chance he'd have in relative obscurity," Sam said.

"Actually, I lured her," I said. "I thought the interview had been canceled. I told Gibbous I thought it was time he and Bianca reconciled, and that they would have the library to themselves to make up."

"Got some woodwork to repair now," Lyndon said. "I'll be patching bullet holes most of tomorrow."

Sam said nothing, but he gave me a look that promised I'd have more explaining to do later. The kitchen felt a little too warm. Where were the other officers from the sheriff's department?

"Gibbous tried to kill Bianca yesterday in the woods, but she escaped," I said. "Today was to be his final try."

"Third time's a charm," Roz muttered.

English idiom of uncertain origins, a manual in Reference stated drily.

At last, sirens sounded up the highway. In seconds, the gravel would crunch with the tires of the sheriff's department's SUVs. It was almost over.

And then it wasn't.

"Stand back!" Gibbous yelled. A bent bobby pin clattered to the linoleum.

I froze and gasps went up around the table.

For the second time that morning, Gibbous held a weapon. This time it was a carving knife and this time, Daphne was in his other arm.

While I'd jabbered on about the murders, Gibbous had picked the locks of his handcuffs and leaped to the block of knives on the kitchen counter. Now he stood in front of my office door with a handcuff dangling from one wrist and a blade against Daphne's throat. I didn't remember this ever happening to Poirot.

Sam stood, legs apart, pointing his service weapon at Gibbous. It was a standoff, and it was not going to end well.

Blood roared in my ears. Already I heard the thunk of SUV doors closing outside, but what could they do? The knife's honed tip pressed against Daphne's jugular.

This was my fault. If I hadn't been so pigheaded about Daphne and Sam, if I hadn't been mesmerized by my trio of fictional consulting detectives, I would have explained the whole situation to Sam. He could have questioned Gibbous.

And learned what? came the voice of Golden Age.

The gunsel wouldn't have told them a thing, Hard-boiled added. *Zilch*.

A girl detective has to be, above all things, brave, Girl Detective said.

"Help," Daphne squeaked. "Sam?"

"Shut up," Gibbous said in a decidedly un-zen tone. "Everyone. Step aside. Move!"

He tightened his grip on Daphne and edged toward the door. He planned to slip out the kitchen door while the sheriff's office stormed the front. As to what he'd do with Daphne, I couldn't say.

We all glanced to Sam for guidance. He lowered his gun and followed Gibbous's instructions, leaving a clear path to the door.

Meanwhile, an explosive mix of fear and regret ignited my magic. I was in my library, the locus of my power, but I could do nothing. My skin sizzled with the energy my emotion had drawn from the thousands of volumes around us. I couldn't access it, though. Unlike earlier, I had an audience.

"Open up! Washington County Sheriff's Department!" Instead of taking the front door, as expected, they were at the kitchen door.

"Move!" Gibbous shouted, and Daphne yelped.

"Do what he says," Sam said calmly.

Preparing to dash through the atrium, Gibbous retreated a few feet, bumping open my office door.

Just then came the familiar sound of engines revving and brakes shrieking, and it wasn't more sheriff's deputies pulling up outside. Exploding from my office as if from the starting line at a track came *The Indy 500: America's Race for the Ages*, knocking straight into Gibbous's arm holding the knife. Before I was completely aware of what had happened, Sam had Gibbous pinned against the counter. A hand to her throat, Daphne stumbled toward the opposite wall.

Meanwhile, undoubtedly to prevent the door from being battered to kindling, Lyndon opened it for the deputies.

For the first time in too long, I was able to draw a full breath. Sam released Gibbous to two burly colleagues.

"Sam," Daphne said and raised her arms to him.

He didn't even give her a glance. "Josie," he said. "Are you okay?"

I looked up at him and managed a faint smile. I would be okay now.

CHAPTER THIRTY-FOUR

"**I**s everyone ready?" Dylan said.

In a reprise of movie night, a patchwork of blankets carpeted the lawn between the library and Big House. Most of Wilfred had turned out to watch the replay of Roz's interview with Daphne Morris. Nearly a month had passed since the movie star and her crew had left town. Days were still warm, but nights were lengthening and cooling, and the chirping of crickets and the fresh, damp smell of mornings hinted that autumn was just around the corner.

Buffy and Thor had started leading a sanitized tour of the farmhouse, now empty, for a dollar. Thor pointed out where Daphne's bedroom was and Duchess's food bowl sat, and Buffy offered refreshments for an additional fee. A wave of journalists had come and gone, and the kids' schemes for new sources of income would be put on hold when they went back to school.

As I'd expected, Sam had found a dummied-up suicide note in Gibbous's makeup case. The note had been intended to be from Bianca and had explained, falsely, how she had killed both Bryce and Morgan in revenge for Daphne's having alienated her. Gibbous's phone records showed he was talking with the *National Bloodhound* again and ready to sell the whole story as an anonymous informant. He'd be in prison for a very long time.

Meanwhile, Bianca had replaced Morgan as Daphne's assistant. It seemed to suit both of them well. Daphne wanted worshipping and Bianca wanted to worship. This news came from Leo. We'd kept up a semi-regular correspondence and I'd pointed him toward the Library of Congress and some oral histories of witches for his documentary. He was able to come clean about it to Daphne. After the experience with Gibbous, she directed her attorney to renegotiate the contracts with her staff, giving them the opportunity to pursue other projects, as long as they didn't mar the Golden Cutie brand. Leo occasionally teased me about being a witch after what he'd glimpsed with the books, and I laughed it off as his hyperactive imagination.

Of course, I'd remained in Wilfred. Returning to the East Coast to manage Daphne's book club would have meant running away from something rather than toward it. Sometimes I dreamed of what life might have been like to be a permanent part of Daphne's circle—traveling, reading all day, meeting authors—but all I'd have to do was look down from my apartment in the library to the books below, or greet Roz in the kitchen, or wave at the folks hanging out at the This-N-That to know I'd made the right decision by staying.

Sam and I had fallen back into our routine of post-dinner

talks on his kitchen porch, but they were different now. I enjoyed his company, but I didn't need it. It might have been my imagination, but as my feelings toward him shifted, his attitude toward me seemed to subtly transform, too. He sought me out, lending me a Margaret Millar mystery he'd found at Big House and once even leaving a bouquet of tiger lilies at my door because they'd reminded him of me. Whatever happened, I wouldn't rush it. I reminded myself that it hadn't even been a year since his wife had died.

"Would you like to say a few words before the interview, Ms. Grover?" Dylan asked Roz.

"No," Roz said. "Just roll it."

"I can't wait to see this," Darla said. Yes, Darla. At last she'd returned from her tour of the South, and she'd brought home a gentleman from Georgia who was as fascinated by Pacific Northwest cuisine as she was by Southern food. To the town's relief, they were already rebuilding the café. Good thing, too, since Patty had decided to feature birdcages and candles at the This-N-That. The vintage appliances had disappeared and evening cookouts in the store's front yard were over.

"Before we start, I have something to say." Lyndon stood, tall and gawky, Ichabod Crane without the pumpkin head.

A public announcement was astonishingly rare for him. Talking to more than two people at a time—well, talking at all—was a feat. Making a general announcement was practically unheard of. What could it be? The town was already up to date on his and Roz's engagement.

"*The Whippoorwill Cries Love* is officially a *New York Times* bestseller." He proudly waved a newspaper.

Roz batted a fan and, I swear, actually giggled. "It's going to be a movie," she said. "You'll never guess who stars in it."

Nicky grabbed my knee and hoisted himself to standing before falling on Sam. Rodney yawned and crawled into the empty picnic basket.

I reached out and scratched his ears. "I sure love a happy ending. Don't you?"

From somewhere inside the library, a book rumbled like thunder.

Visit us online at
KensingtonBooks.com
to read more from your favorite authors,
see books by series, view reading
group guides, and more!

BOOK CLUB
BETWEEN THE CHAPTERS

Visit us online for sneak peeks, exclusive
giveaways, special discounts, author content,
and engaging discussions with your fellow readers.

Betweenthechapters.net

Sign up for our newsletters and be the first
to get exciting news and announcements about
your favorite authors!
Kensingtonbooks.com/newsletter